TURNED ON

TURNED ON

ANGEL M. HUNTER

URBAN
Renaissance

www.urbanbooks.net

Urban Books, LLC
78 East Industry Court
Deer Park, NY 11729

Turned On Copyright © 2009 Angel M. Hunter

ISBN 13: 978-1-60162-296-9
ISBN 10: 1-60162-296-1

First Mass Market Printing April 2011
First Trade Paperback Printing August 2009
Printed in the United States of America

10   9   8   7   6   5   4   3   2   1

Distributed by Kensington Publishing Corp.
Submit Wholesale Orders to:
Kensington Publishing Corp.
C/O Penguin Group (USA) Inc.
Attention: Order Processing
405 Murray Hill Parkway
East Rutherford, NJ 07073-2316
Phone: 1-800-526-0275
Fax: 1-800-227-9604

Dear Friends:

Here we go again, on another wonderful journey of words, adventure, sexual revolution, and finding out more about who you are and what you want to represent.

I thank you for continuing to read my work, it's so appreciated. I enjoy every email I receive, every thought and every emotion. I enjoy what I do, and that's move you, the readers, emotionally, physically, and mentally.

I enjoy taking you out of your world and putting you into someone else's world or opening a door that you didn't know you had cracked opened and peeped through.

I enjoy giving you words of wisdom, words of hope, and words to think about. And this time around I'm giving you these words.

Do not allow another person to take you outside of yourself.

What does that mean? It means don't let others control your thoughts or your actions. Don't let others define you and don't let others determine your reaction to a circumstance.

Very often we get into relationships/friendships and allow others to convince us, to trick us, to push, provoke and have us doing things we normally wouldn't do and/or reacting in ways that leave us asking ourselves "what the hell?"

You have to stay true to you, even if it means hurting someone or making someone unhappy. You have to stay true to you and *trust in your-*

self that you are doing the right thing or doing what you want to do. You have to stay true to you because your future is created by your choices and your decisions. So decide to *be true to yourself*.

I hope you read this novel and enjoy every moment. This time around the focus is on Alexis. Some of you may remember her from the first *Turned Out*. She's Champagne's best friend. If you want to know more about Champagne and you haven't had a chance to pick up the first *Turned Out*, you really should. These girls are a trip and will take you for a ride emotionally.

I chose to end this book with a cliff-hanger and what I'd like is for you, the reader, to contact me and tell me what you would like to see in my next novel.

I'd love to hear from you and if I use your suggestion you will be mentioned in the book. Email me at *msangelhunter@aol.com* and/or *www.myspace.com/angel mhunter*.

I hope after reading these books, you allow yourself to look in the mirror and ask yourself am I being pleased sexually. Am I allowing every pleasure point in and on my body to be touched, tasted, and explored? Have I allowed my lover to give me mediocre sex and what kind of lover am I? Am I open to new things, to new positions, and to new ideas sexually? How far am I willing to go? How far is my partner willing to go and what can we do to make our sex life the best it's been without sacrificing one another or our dignity? Ask your partner what turns them on, don't just assume to know.

Also, be with someone that offers words of encouragement and shows their love through their actions, where it counts the most. We all know that relationships are not easy or perfect. They require work. It's like a full-time job and you have to have the energy and stamina to sustain it. You have to be willing to compromise, experiment, and allow each other to "be themselves."

The last thing I want to say on this subject (for now) is to be bold and step outside of your comfort zone sexually (and other ways of course) and most important while you're doing this *practice safe sex*.

Peace and Love
Friends-In-Spirit
Angel M. Hunter–Irby
www.angelmhunter.com
msangelhunter@aol.com   www.myspace.com/angelmhun ter

Coming soon . . . "Faking It Again", "Sister Girl 3" (what would you like to see in it?), "Lovin' the Skin You're In" (self motivational book) and more. Don't forget to pick up my other books *Sister Girl 2, Sister Girl, Turned Out, Faking It, Around the Way Girl, and A Dollar and a Dream.*

TURNED ON

Chapter 1

People Only Do What You Allow Them To

As Alexis Oliviá walked through West North National Airport to her car, so many thoughts were running through her head. How could she not have known Khalil was married? When she really thought about it, the signs that he wasn't all he pretended to be were there. She should have seen them because they were what every television show, every book, and every woman that's probably been burned say to look out for.

There were times when he didn't answer the phone or call her back until hours later with half-ass excuses about what he was doing. There was the smell of a lady's perfume in his car, which she ignored. There was him coming to her house all the time and her never going to his. All these signs and more she ignored because when they were together he made her feel like a queen. He made her feel like she was all that mattered. He made her feel safe and he made her feel desired in a way that no other man had.

"Alexis . . . Alexis, wait!" Thomas yelled.

Alexis kept walking; she didn't want to wait. She was embarrassed because she felt like she had been played yet again and one would think that after receiving a master's degree in Psychology and being a therapist at West Park High, she would know better. She thought about her college days and how she was in love with Brother. She thought he was the best thing since sliced bread. He was saved, studying to be a minister, and even had her turning her back against her friends because they weren't Christian enough. Only to find out he was cheating on her with a woman from the church; a woman who counseled her and had Bible study with her. She thought about her high school sweetheart John and how he cheated, and now here she was in her early thirties and being made a fool of by another man. She'd already made up her mind that this would be the last time it happened and if there was anything she meant, anything she was going to keep her word on—this was it.

No one would ever use her again. No one would ever make her feel like she didn't matter. She would not be treated with disregard ever again, meaning she wouldn't accept not being a priority. She would not accept the excuses when a phone call wasn't returned or a date was canceled at the last minute. She would not be made to feel like she's "the one" when what she really represented was one of many, or maybe even unbeknownst to her, "the chick on the side." Oh, hell no, not again.

Alexis would not give her soul, spirit, love, or body to another living being without getting something in return.

At this point, and with the way she was feeling, the something she wanted would have to be material and substantial. If she became dubbed as a gold digger and as a user, she could care less. Alexis was going to be a woman on a mission. A one woman man; was there such a thing? She wanted there to be because she'd always been a one man woman.

If people considered her new plan as one that would make her a whore, she didn't care about that either. There was a time when that's all she cared about, her reputation and what people thought of her. Well, no more.

The only thing she cared about from this point on was getting what was hers and what she felt was owed by all the men out there that had wronged a sister, namely her. How did that Destiny's Child song go? "No more, no more, no more." Alexis was not taking the bullshit anymore. She would accept nothing less than the best. She was going to start looking out for number one; herself.

It was time for her to become someone else. No more Miss Goody Two Shoes, as she was known from middle school, high school, and college. During this time she lived for the Lord. She tried her best to live according to the Bible. Alexis wasn't perfect. No man or woman was, but she tried and that was all she could do. She tried her best not to stray, not to fornicate, although sometimes she fell short. She didn't swear, she rarely drank and she tried her best to submit when it came to her relationships. Her motto was, "I'll do whatever it takes to please my man." Well, change had come and it was time for her man, or should she say men, because she planned on having more than one, to do whatever it took to please her.

"Alexis, wait up," Thomas yelled.

Alexis turned to see him jogging toward her. All she wanted to do was get to her car. She turned back around and sped up. She wondered if everyone in the airport was looking her way. Did they know that she'd been bombarded by people she cared about? Her best friend, Champagne, Champagne's husband, Zyair, and his best friend who she knew had been lusting after her for years, Thomas Hughes. Did they know that they had destroyed her reality?

All she wanted to do was return from Cancun with her man and get on with their life together. They were supposed to be gone for four days and ended up extending their vacation to six days and seven nights because they were so into each other. When they arrived at the airport, the last thing she expected to see was Thomas and Champagne standing there.

Initially, Alexis was irritated that they were in the airport waiting on her like she was a child and aggravated when Champagne told her they needed to talk. When Alexis asked her if it could wait and she said no, Alexis told her to go ahead and say whatever it was she had to say in front of Khalil. She thought about the pleasure in Champagne's voice when she revealed that Khalil was a pimp. Why would her best friend take pleasure in hurting her? It's a good thing that he'd told her about his past life, and her response when he told her was she didn't care because they didn't even know one another existed at the time.

After Alexis revealed to Champagne that she already knew the deal, Zyair appeared out of nowhere with a white woman on his arm claiming she was Khalil's wife. Initially she didn't believe him, but when Alexis looked at him and saw the look on his face she knew it was true. She really knew it was true when she asked Khalil what was Zyair talking about and his reply was "what is there to say?" Not only did she know it was true but she knew it was over, because adultery she would not commit.

To keep from breaking down, Alexis walked away, leaving Khalil, who Thomas punched in the face; Khalil's so-called wife cursing him out; Champagne, who looked smug and Zyair who looked like he was wondering what he got himself into.

"Please Alexis, wait up," she heard Thomas say again.

Alexis decided that she would stop and see what he could possibly have to say to her. "What, Thomas? What do you want?" She knew she sounded like a bitch, but you would sound like one too, if you'd just found out the man you just got engaged to already had a wife. Again, Alexis wondered how was it that she allowed Khalil to play her.

Thomas stopped a few inches from Alexis. He was standing so close to her that she could almost reach out and touch him. She could see that he wanted to by the way he was rubbing his hands together. But the look on her face must have said, keep your distance because he just stood there and said, "I just wanted to make sure you were okay."

Alexis started laughing and it wasn't a laugh where one found something funny. It was a laugh of a person who had been through it, a laugh of someone that was mentally drained and a laugh of someone who was almost to the point of not giving a damn anymore.

"Do I look okay to you, Thomas?"

Before he could respond, Alexis placed her palm on the side of his face, looked him straight in the eyes and caressed his cheek. "I know you're concerned about me, but I just need to be alone right now. Can you respect that?" She dropped her hand and started to walk away but something stopped her. Perhaps it was the new person she'd decided to be. The more aggressive person. *Maybe I'll start the new me right now.*

"If you need—"

Before Thomas could finish what he wanted to say, Alexis turned back around and stepped to him. She placed her lips on his. She kept her eyes open so she could see what his response would be, which was to part his lips and let her do whatever she wanted to.

Alexis let her tongue slide into his mouth. She ran her tongue around his slowly, then pulled his tongue into her mouth and slowly sucked on it as though it were a flavor. She put her body a little closer to his and could feel Thomas' dick getting hard. She wanted with every fiber in her being for him to pull her close. She wondered what she was doing to him, what she was making him feel on the inside and not just on the outside physically. She moved her body even closer and pressed into him, to the point where they could have been one. She gave him a look that said, *don't hold back*. She could tell that he got the message because he grabbed her ass and pressed his dick into her and moved his hips slightly.

Alexis couldn't believe she was letting Thomas rub up against her in plain view of people. This was so out of character but she couldn't help herself. She was hoping Khalil was watching because she wanted him to be as hurt as she was. Maybe he'd even wonder if something was going on with Thomas the whole time they were together. That thought alone made Alexis wrap her arms around Thomas' neck. She continued to dip her tongue in and out his mouth. She kissed him with such passion she wasn't giving Thomas a chance to think about or comprehend what it meant, if anything.

This is not me Alexis said to herself. She

knew she should pull away because here she was playing with this man's attraction to her.

"Wow," Thomas said when she stepped back.

Alexis looked down at his dick and could still see the imprint. He followed her eyes and told her, "I apologize. I just got carried away by the kiss."

Alexis shut him up and placed two fingers on his lips. "Don't apologize. I'm the one that initiated it."

Thomas started to say something else, but Alexis shushed him. "I have to go. I need to be alone."

Thomas grabbed her hands and asked her not to leave.

Alexis finally looked around and noticed that people were looking their way. She didn't see Khalil but she did see Champagne and Zyair staring at them with a look of bewilderment.

"Am I supposed to stand here in the airport?" she asked him.

"How are you going to get home?"

"My car is in long-term parking."

Still holding onto her hand Thomas said, "Alexis, I'm really sorry it came out like this. It's just that—"

Alexis pulled her hand away and told him, "Don't say another word. I need time and space." And on that note, she turned and walked away. She knew he was watching her walk, so she not only added a sway to her hips, but she turned and told him, "Call me."

* * *

Standing not too far behind, watching the whole episode, was Champagne who felt a little guilty about what transpired. She knew she could have and should have addressed it in another way but she couldn't help it because she didn't like Khalil the second she laid eyes on him. Call it instinct, call it woman's intuition, call it whatever you want, but whatever it was ended up being correct.

Next to her stood her fiancé, Zyair. He looked at her. "What the hell was that about?"

Champagne knew he was talking about the kiss. She was wondering the same thing, so all she had to offer by way of explanation was a shrug of her shoulders and a "your guess is as good as mine but believe me, I will find out."

Zyair couldn't let it go at that. "I thought she couldn't stand Thomas." He'd heard Alexis say it numerous times. She had called Thomas every possible adjective that could describe a male whore.

"Well, maybe she changed her mind."

Zyair didn't say a word. He just watched Thomas watch Alexis and hoped some shit wasn't about to go down. His gut instinct told him it was and he wondered if there was anything he would be able to do about it. From the look on Thomas' face, he doubted it very seriously. He knew Khalil's type. He wasn't about to let this go without repercussions. They all would have to watch their backs.

*   *   *

That evening alone in her bedroom Alexis lay in her bed and stared at the walls. She looked at the paintings she'd collected that depicted black love. A painting of a man and woman embracing; a painting of the man carrying the woman in what looked like a garden; and her favorite, the one of man, woman and child being embraced by a black Jesus. Normally when she glanced at them, she would feel warmth. This time she felt disgusted, with herself that is. Was she really that desperate to have love in her life that she hung paintings up in her bedroom? She knew she would be taking those down tomorrow. Her eyes then fell on the picture of Khalil that was on her dresser, in a frame no less. She got up out the bed, walked over to the dresser, snatched the picture off it, walked into the adjoining bathroom, took the picture out of the frame, ripped it up and threw it in the small waste basket that was under the sink. She placed the frame on the sink, looked in the mirror and wondered why she couldn't bring herself to tears. *Maybe once I cry I'll feel better.*

She so desperately wanted to cry, to have some sort of release. She was confused in her emotions. A part of her wanted to call Khalil and ask him how he could do this to her, how could he declare his love and be married. *I should have known better, we were only together for a couple of months.* But Alexis wanted to believe in him. She wanted to believe that someone could fall for her so quickly, someone who appeared to have it all together, someone that said they wanted a monogamous relationship. *What a joke; all he wanted was my pussy.*

She walked back into her bedroom and opened her armoire. Inside were movies that she liked to watch over and over. Since the tears she wanted to fall never did, she pulled out one of her old-time favorite films, *She's Gotta Have It*, written, directed and produced by Spike Lee. She hoped that the movie would give her some insight about men and relationships that she hadn't caught before. She put in the DVD, grabbed her remote, laid back on the bed and pressed play.

After the movie was over, Alexis felt so empowered she declared out loud, "Fuck it, I'm going to be like Nola Darling. Men will be for my pleasure only and any type of relationship I have with them will be on my terms."

Later that night Alexis lay in her bed with her eyes closed. For a moment her thoughts kept drifting to Khalil and all the promises he made to her. What he would do for her and what they would mean to each other. She thought about the way he made her body feel so alive. She thought about the first time they met at the Laundromat. She thought it must be fate that her dryer stopped working that day. She recalled how when he walked in, she couldn't help but notice how strong he looked. His muscular physique was evident in the T-shirt and jeans he wore. He was definitely her physical type.

That day Alexis did something that was out of character for her. She approached him and asked him was he from the area. He told her he was new in town and that his name was Khalil Simmons. It wasn't until they went out to dinner that she learned he was in construction. Well, that's what he told her but by then she was smitten. Heck, he even claimed to be a Christian. How could she not have known the truth? Alexis opened her eyes and tried to get him out of her head.

Think of something else, think of someone else, she told herself. Her thoughts started drifting to Thomas. *Imagine him making love to you . . . let your body take over your mind.*

Alexis, not one to really masturbate, decided to do just that.

She closed her eyes and imagined Thomas' tongue circling around her clitoris, stroking it and dipping inside. From the thought alone she could feel a warmth travel up through her thighs. She squeezed them together and tried to suppress the pleasure but then decided to go with the feeling, to allow the emotions that were going to come. She had on a thin nightgown and placed both palms over each nipple as she ran her palms over her nipples in circles and started pinching them.

Damn, that feels good.

Alexis allowed her hands to go lower as she pushed her hips up off the bed and pulled her gown up over her waist. She stroked her pussy through her panties gently at first, but wanting to feel the pressure from her own hand she pressed harder using mostly the bottom of her palm.

Realizing the pleasure she could give herself,

she pushed her panties to the side and ran the fingers of her right hand between her pussy lips. She didn't want to put them inside just yet. She was enjoying teasing herself more than she thought she would and she wanted to make this moment last. With her left hand she played with both nipples.

At this point, Alexis wasn't pretending or trying to imagine that it was Thomas or any other person trying to please her. She was pleasing herself and thinking, *shit, this can become a habit. I don't need a man. All I need are my two hands.* Masturbation wasn't something she participated in but she'd heard women say all they needed were their fingers and she was about to find out how true it was.

She then took one of her fingers and dipped it into her pussy. She dipped it in and out, pumping her hips up and down, loving every moment of it. She'd keep her fingers deep inside her for a couple of seconds and move them in circles.

Alexis could feel her heart beating and her breath coming quicker and quicker. So she pulled her fingers out to catch her breath and start all over again. This time, she used both hands, one to move the skin from around her clitoris and the other to touch it. The first touch caused her to jump.

Relax, Alexis, relax.

She relaxed her body and tried it again. She thought about how Khalil would touch her there with his tongue, moving it in circles, so she copied the movement with her finger. She wondered if that's why she fell so hard so fast. Was it because of his oral skills? When he made love to her, she experienced her first real orgasm; the kind that made her body shake, quiver and jerk—the kind that made her call out. She couldn't believe that she'd missed out on that. Heck, she'd been having sex since her last year of high school. Just thinking about it made her feel a rush in her stomach and that caused her to moved her hand away. She took another deep breath.

Just go with it.

She tried it again but first she put her finger in her mouth to make it moist and put it back on her clitoris. Whenever she felt her clitoris becoming dry she'd put her finger back in her mouth, wet it and back on her clitoris. She was ready to come. She was ready to feel the explosion that would take over her body and leave her exhausted.

Her heart was racing, her nipples were stinging and she could feel an energy building up from her feet to her thighs, to her back and finally to her pussy.

Alexis surprised herself by screaming out loud as she arched her body and put two fingers inside her to feel the moistness that was dripping from deep inside. She felt her body relax and sink into the bed as she left her hand cupping her pussy. She closed her eyes and sighed. *Oh my god, I can't believe this. I can't believe I actually made myself come. I'll never judge another person that says they masturbate. This*

*may have been my first time doing so but it won't
be my last.*

Alexis felt the need to call someone up and tell
them about this experience. The orgasm made
her feel as though a weight had been lifted,
even if it was temporary. Guilt? Did she feel
any? Not at all. *Damn, does that mean I'm going
against God?* She hoped not and if it did, she
knew that He would forgive her.

When Alexis moved her hand the tears finally
fell, and with the tears came feelings of hope-
lessness. She wondered if she would ever get it
right with men. What was she doing that was
wrong? Why couldn't a man stay faithful to
her? Was she not good enough? Did she wear a
sign on her forehead that read, I'm a fool, you
can take advantage of me?

Alexis shook her head and tried to erase
these thoughts. "I will not go there, I will not go
there, I will not go there," she repeated over
and over until she fell asleep.

Chapter 2

Change Is Challenging, Yet Necessary

The second Alexis entered The Red Oak, which was the new hot spot in town, she saw that it was crowded. Normally she wasn't into crowds but since this was the new her, she'd have to deal with it, accept it and make the most out of it. As she excused her way through the crowd she took in the cream and gold decorum. The tables were set with what appeared to be satin material, candles and a slim vase with one lily, which gave the appearance of an upscale club. The lighting was dim and the music was old-school R&B, which suited the twenty-five and over crowd just fine.

Alexis glanced around and was relieved when she spotted Champagne who already had two Martini glasses in front of her.

"What's up girl?" Alexis greeted as she bent over to give Champagne a kiss on the cheek.

"Nothing. I ordered us each a Watermelon Martini."

"Thanks," Alexis said as she sat down.

Champagne was glad to see Alexis and surprised to see her in a form-fitting dress, when normally she dressed conservatively. They hadn't talked in over two weeks and after what took place at the airport, she had started wondering if it was because Alexis was through with her. She wondered if she had crossed the line.

Champagne tried calling Alexis numerous times and either Alexis didn't answer the phone or when she did she told her she was busy. Champagne knew that meant to back off. She was going to give Alexis one more week and then she was going to knock on her door and make her converse.

Not one to beat around the bush, Champagne asked as she sipped her Martini, "So, what was up with that kiss you gave Thomas at the airport?"

Of course she was concerned about her friend's well-being but ever since the kiss, Champagne had wanted to ask her that question. She surely couldn't leave it on the answering machine. After all, she knew Alexis was going through it emotionally. Who could blame her? She was obviously hurt and needed time to process the damage done to her heart. The pain was noticeable because of her behavior and her not reaching out.

By not calling Champagne or really taking her calls it was understandable that Alexis was feeling dejected, despondent, and distant. Who wouldn't want to be left alone at a time like this? Being best friends and not communicating like they normally do left Champagne concerned about their friendship and Alexis' state of mind. But instead of hounding Alexis like she wanted to, she chose to let Alexis work through it.

Not that she had any choice because Alexis wasn't ready to open up and after hearing Alexis tell her when she was ready to discuss it with her, she would, Champagne decided to leave well enough alone. So, Champagne let it go and moved on. She made the decision to just be there the best way she could for Alexis, in spirit. The way she figured it, when Alexis was ready for her support, an ear or a shoulder, she would be just a phone call away.

So when Alexis finally called her, Champagne was pleased. She missed her friend and wanted to talk about what transpired and when Alexis suggested they meet for drinks, Champagne was surprised. She asked Alexis was she sure she wanted to meet for drinks or should they meet for dinner.

"What? A sister can't go out for a drink?" Alexis asked her.

It wasn't that a sister couldn't go out for a drink. It's just that Alexis wasn't one to drink unless it was a special occasion.

So Champagne told her yes and they agreed to meet at The Red Oak.

Seeing Alexis sit across from her, Champagne realized just how much she missed her and

how worried she was. She wanted to find out
what the hell was going on with her friend and
she wanted to catch her up on her and Zyair.
They had finally set an "almost" date for the
wedding.

"So," Champagne asked, "what's up with you
not returning a sister's phone call, cutting me
short when you did and making me stress out?
I was worried about your ass and again what
was up with that kiss you gave Thomas?"

Alexis didn't answer right away. She continued to sip on her drink and glance around the
room. After surveying their surroundings, she
told Champagne, "Girl, I don't know what came
over me. I think I temporarily lost my mind."

Champagne didn't get it. "So, you tongue
someone down because you're losing your
mind?"

Alexis didn't like her tone. "Are you judging
me? Is that what I'm hearing?"

"No, no. I'm not judging you. You know that's
not my style. Shit, we all have our stuff with
us." Champagne still hadn't told Alexis about
her bisexuality. Yep, that's what she had labeled
herself and the reason she hadn't told her was
because like Alexis, she didn't want to be
judged. The episode she had with a stranger
when she and Zyair went to Hedonism, plus the
encounters with her ex-employee Candy and
friend Sharon meant more to her than she at
one time was willing to admit. To go by without
revealing this to anyone for three months,
much less her best friend, was killing her.

Of course, she couldn't express her mind-set

to Zyair because he thought that "phase" as he liked to call it was over. It's funny because adding a third party to their relationship was his idea, although going to Hedonism was hers. It just ended up being more than he could handle.

"I'm just surprised that's all," Champagne told her.

Alexis didn't respond right away because her attention was elsewhere.

"Oh girl, look at all the men up in here," Alexis said, "especially that one over there."

Champagne looked around and was not impressed with the abundance of men. Just like Alexis, she wasn't a club attendee because being in her thirties she felt like she was too old. She felt that people went to clubs to pick up potential bed mates and that was not something she was interested in. After all, she had the pick of the litter when it came to men. Not only was Zyair handsome, strong mentally and physically, but he was also supportive. The added benefit and one she didn't take for granted or abuse in anyway was that he came with what most women desired in a relationship; security.

He also loved her regardless and unconditionally. Her man was one that excused her when she messed up and overlooked many of her flaws. He actually found some of them amusing.

Champagne turned around to see what or who had Alexis' attention and noticed him right away. Even she had to admit, the man Alexis was staring at was a looker. He was well over six feet and cocoa complexioned, with the most immaculate goatee Champagne had ever seen. You could tell beneath what appeared to be a shirt made for his physique that he went to the gym on the regular and when he laughed, which he was doing wholeheartedly, his dimples showed across the room.

Now a man that fine has to have a whole bunch of issues with him. There has to be some kind of drama in his life.

"He's definitely fine," Champagne remarked.

The next thing Champagne knew was Alexis had placed her glass on the table and stood up.

"Where are you going?"

"I'm going to introduce myself. Where do you think I'm going?"

Champagne sat stunned as she watched Alexis head toward Mr. Handsome.

I can't believe she's doing this. It's so unlike her to be so aggressive. Champagne watched as Alexis approached him and tapped him on his shoulder. Then again, maybe she shouldn't have been surprised because Alexis told her that when she first met Khalil, she went up to him.

Oh my god, she's actually interrupting his conversation. Alexis is really showing her ass tonight. Please do not let this man disrespect her. I really don't feel like dealing with any bullshit tonight. Please do not let him disrespect her.

Champagne continued to watch to see how it would all play out. She saw him turn around and watched as they exchanged a few words. She noticed Alexis laughing.

Okay, good, he must like her.

A few seconds later, Alexis came walking back in Champagne's direction.

Before Alexis even had a chance to sit down, Champagne said, "Girl, I can't believe you did that."

"Did what?" Alexis asked with a sly look on her face. "All I did was introduce myself."

"Yeah, that's what I'm talking about. When did you become so bold?"

Alexis laughed. "Girl, this is a new me. I've made the decision not to allow men to lead me. It's time for me to be the leader, to take the first step, it's time for . . ."

Alexis stopped mid-sentence and was looking over Champagne's shoulder. The frown on her face made Champagne turn around. Alexis was staring at Khalil, who was dressed in a casual but tailored suit that looked expensive, even from a distance. Champagne looked around to see if his wife was in the vicinity. She didn't spot her. He was actually standing by himself with a drink in his hand perusing the area. Although Champagne could see why Alexis was attracted to him, she still couldn't stand him. It was obvious he hadn't noticed them yet, because if he had, she was sure he'd come over and Champagne did not want that to happen.

"It's time to go," Champagne said. The look on Alexis' face told a tale of a woman scorned and she didn't want a scene.

Alexis shook her head, breaking her trance. "We don't have to leave. I came out to have a good time and a good time I will have."

"Are you sure?"

"As sure as ever. I refuse to let him ruin my night. Plus, we're about to have company." Alexis nodded her head to the right.

Champagne turned again to see who she was talking about. Heading toward their table, making their way through the crowd was Mr. Handsome and a friend.

Alexis couldn't help but to sneak another glance Khalil's way. She wanted to confront him but knew she wouldn't. So, it was a relief that company was heading their way, although unpleasant and unexpected.

"I invited them to sit with us," Alexis told Champagne.

This invitation threw Champagne for a loop. "You know you're wrong for this. You should have asked me first. I thought this was our night out together." She couldn't care less if they heard her or not.

What Champagne wanted to do was walk away but she wouldn't do that to her girl. One, she wouldn't want it done to her and two, with the way Alexis was acting, she didn't think it would be a good idea.

"Hey ladies," Alexis' new friend greeted.

Champagne looked at him and his friend, who was just as handsome. She did have to admit to herself that if she were on the market, he definitely would have been her physical type.

"I'm Shamel and this is my boy True." He was looking at Champagne when he said it.

Alexis moved closer to Shamel staking her claim.

"What's up, sexy?" True asked Champagne as he swallowed her with his eyes.

Champagne decided to play nice, make conversation but not lead him on. She was here with Alexis and she might as well make the most of it. There was no sense in adding to the myth that black women are bitches.

"Come on," Shamel said, "let's go upstairs to the VIP room."

Upstairs was where the people with clout went. VIP wasn't something Champagne had not experienced before; it wasn't anything new. She didn't take it for granted but she did expect it and that's because of Zyair. She was used to getting special treatment. Whenever she and Zyair went out, they were treated not only with respect but like royalty. Zyair was to the restaurant business what Jay-Z was to hip hop and she was Zyair's Beyonce. Although she wasn't a singer, she was independent, and ran her own public relations and personal assistant company for the wealthy. She made sure she had a life of her own, and didn't depend on her man to bring her contentment or happiness.

Shamel led the way, followed by Alexis, Champagne and then True. Champagne could feel True staring at her ass the whole way up. She thanked God that she wore pants. She hoped that this man did not become disrespectful because she would have no problem putting him in his place. However, her intuition, sixth sense or her third eye as she sometimes called it, was telling her, she was going to have to let him know that this was not that kind of party.

When they reached the top of the steps, the bouncer gave Shamel daps and let them right in.

When they walked in Champagne glanced around. She appreciated the color scheme which was purple and gold; royalty colors. There were plush loveseats scattered throughout the room, a couple of loungers, couches and oversized comfy chairs. Tables were in the corners for privacy and the bar went around the room. The stools at the bar were full.

Champagne noticed quite a few celebrities scattered about. Amongst the celebrities were the pop singers Whitney Snow and Tina Carey, the actor from the new reality show on BET, Benjamin Washington, and several sports figures, Michael Lee and Carm Pippin, just to name a few. She looked at the crowd which was mixed; Black, White, Hispanic and even a few Asians mingling with one another.

Shamel led them to a table and pulled out a chair for Alexis as True pulled out a chair for Champagne.

Once everyone was seated, Shamel asked, "So what are you ladies doing after you leave here tonight?"

"What are you doing?" Alexis asked, with a seductive undertone.

What the hell? Champagne looked at Alexis, who purposely would not look her way. Champagne knew Alexis could feel her staring at her. The old Alexis would never have behaved this way, walking up to a strange man, inviting them over to their table and basically throwing herself at him.

"Maybe you ladies would like to join us?" True suggested, getting straight to the point.

"I have to get home to my man," Champagne said, hoping to squash any ideas he may have had about them getting together. "I do have a man, you know."

Alexis gave Champagne a *why you gotta blow up the spot* look.

She looked like she wanted to go off on her but instead she told Champagne, "Damn, girl, loosen up. We're just trying to kick it."

"That's right sexy," True said. "You've got a man and I've got a woman. What's the big deal?"

Before anyone could say another word, Champagne heard a familiar voice asking, "So? What do we have here?"

It was Thomas and not too far behind him staring in their direction was Khalil. She hoped they had not spotted one another.

Chapter 3

Think About What You Really Want Before You Go Making Demands

When Thomas entered the VIP room, it seemed like the first person he spotted was Champagne. She was with two men and if his eyes weren't deceiving him, there was Alexis, who was wearing a dress that hugged every curve on her body even with her sitting down. She appeared to be laughing and touching on the man that sat next to her.

"What the fuck?" Thomas swore. This was the last thing he needed to see especially after learning that Louis Johnson, one of Rutgers University's top basketball players had decided to sign with another sports agent. He'd been trying to win him over for months with dinners and the promise of more money than he could spend, only to have his rival James Giovanni sign him.

"What? What's wrong?" the young lady he came upstairs with asked.

Playing it off he said, "What the hell is my boy's lady doing sitting with those knuckleheads?"

Although his initial reaction was because of Alexis touching a man that was not him, he was also curious why Champagne was out and sitting with these two men.

Where the hell was Zyair? Was he in Atlanta? Did he know that while he was in Atlanta checking on his restaurant that Champagne was out with another man? This shit was not cool and Thomas was going to let them all know it. He was definitely going to inform them of his presence.

Thomas looked at Alexis and wondered if this was why she hadn't returned any of his phone calls? Was it because she'd found someone to replace Khalil so soon. What happened to her heartache over Khalil? Not that he wanted her to be heartbroken over what another man did or how another man treated her. He didn't want that at all. What he did want, he had to admit even to himself, is to be her knight in shining armor, the one who came to her rescue.

"I'll be right back," he told the young lady he was with. He tried to remember her name and couldn't for the life of him. He thought she'd told him it was Precious, Luscious, something like that.

"Where are you going?" she asked.

He looked in Champagne and Alexis' direction. "Over there."

Of course the young lady he was with didn't like it one bit, but she really didn't have much of a choice.

"For what?"

"They're good friends of mine and I want to make sure everything is okay."

She looked in Champagne and Alexis' direction and told Thomas, "They look fine to me."

Not wanting to disrespect her because Thomas was trying to change his ways, he told her, "Well, looks can be deceiving. I'll be right back."

"Why don't I go with you?" She was persistent. Thomas had to give her that.

"Listen . . ." he couldn't say her name because he couldn't think of it and he hoped she didn't catch it but she did.

"My name is Luscious," she told him with her hands on her hips, pissed that he would even forget.

"Listen Luscious, why don't you wait for me by the bar and I'll be right back. Get whatever you want."

Luscious was pissed. She placed her hands on her hips again and told him, "Well, don't think I'm going to wait too long."

Thomas, who wasn't in the mood for attitude, especially after seeing who he hoped would one day be his future wife up in another man's face, told her, "Do what you have to, we're not a couple," and walked away.

He thought about the day after the airport incident when he told Zyair that he was going to end up marrying Alexis. He had laughed and asked him didn't he think he was jumping to conclusions. He told him he was being prophetic.

The second Thomas was up on the table, he asked, "So, what do we have here?"

When Champagne heard his voice, she jumped out of her seat so fast that it appeared as if she'd either been busted or was waiting on him to come over.

"Thomas, hey." She hugged him and whispered in his ear, "I am not having a good time. Alexis has lost all her mind. Get me out of here."

Not knowing if it was because she was caught in the company of another man or if these, what he assumed to be knuckleheads were bothering her, he told her, "Your man just called me," loud enough for all to hear.

On that note Alexis stood up, "Excuse me, fellas." She looked at Champagne and asked, "Do you mind if I steal Thomas for a second?"

Champagne moved to the side as Alexis grabbed Thomas' arm and pulled him a short distance away.

"What are you doing?" Alexis asked him with much attitude and with her hands on her hips and neck snapping.

Thomas started laughing.

"What the hell is so funny?"

"You," Thomas told her.

"What's so funny about me?"

Thomas, who was a bit amused, asked her,

"What's up with the street attitude? You know damn well that's not you."

"What do you mean it's not me? You don't know me." Alexis knew she was just acting out.

"I know enough about you to know that you're not street and that you're a lady. I also know enough to know that you might have had one too many drinks."

Alexis rolled her eyes.

Thomas started laughing again.

This time Alexis stomped her right foot. "Why are you still laughing?"

Thomas didn't bother responding. He looked over toward Champagne who looked bored by whatever the two men were talking about. "I think your girl is ready to leave."

"No, she's not." Alexis looked at Champagne and saw her unease. "We're having a good time."

"Maybe you are, but she's not and I think you should let her leave. As a matter-of-fact I think you both should leave."

Alexis looked at Thomas like *how dare you*.

"And I think you should leave with me."

Alexis looked in Thomas' face, only to see that he was dead serious. "First you come and interrupt my good time and now you're trying to steal me away."

"Exactly." Thomas wasn't beating around the bush. "Come home with me."

"For what? Sex? I'm not fucking you."

Thomas was surprised that Alexis used the word fucking. He had never heard her use profanity before and it must have shown on his face.

"That's right, I'm not fucking you."

Before Thomas could respond, Luscious was up on them. "So, who's your friend?"

Thomas turned around and said, "I thought I asked you to wait by the bar."

"You did and I told you I wasn't going to wait forever." She was eyeing Alexis the whole time.

Alexis stepped back and told Thomas, "I see you have your hands full. I'll leave you two alone."

When she turned to walk back toward Shamel, Thomas took her arm and told her, "No, you stay right here."

"Oh," Luscious said, "you're just going to disrespect me like that."

Thomas let go of Alexis and told her, "You know what. We didn't come here together, so there's really no need to act like we did. You're up here in VIP where you wanted to be, so go do your thing."

"You know you are so right. I just used you to get in here anyway. There are other men that have it going on in more ways than you."

Thomas didn't bother responding. He wasn't with that ghetto shit.

Luscious looked around and recognized several ball players and celebrities. The same ones Champagne noticed when she walked into VIP and the few new ones that had arrived. She faced Thomas, "Shit, there are better looking men in here than you, with more money anyway," and walked off.

Alexis was still standing there when Thomas faced her.

"So that's your type?"

"No, you're my type," he told her as he wondered how he was going to get her to spend the rest of the evening with him.

Chapter 4

Watch Your Back and Your Front; You Never Know Who's Eyeing You

Off to the side, Khalil was watching everything and he could feel his pressure rising. What he wanted to do was go and knock Thomas the fuck out for ruining what he had with Alexis. He knew that he handled the situation at the airport wrong. He was thrown off guard. He would have never thought that Alexis' crew would dig into his past and pull out his wife. Yes, he was married but he was also in the process of leaving her. He regretted not telling Alexis but he knew that she had morals and beliefs and one of those was married men were off limits. He knew this because she told him that during one of their conversations. He wasn't playing with her mind. He'd fallen in love with her, with her innocence, with her vulnerability, and with her sense of right and wrong. It was something he missed in women. It was something he missed in his wife. He wanted an opportunity to speak with Alexis to explain his side. To apologize.

Khalil looked over at their table and every fiber in his being wanted to knock Thomas the fuck out. However, he knew that wouldn't do anything but soothe his ego and piss Alexis off. Now was not the time, it would have to wait. He also knew from the first time he met Thomas over Champagne and Zyair's house that this Thomas character was feeling Alexis. It was all in the way he looked at her and sneered at him.

Khalil needed to come up with something that would destroy Thomas, but he knew that would take some time and time was all he had.

Khalil had spotted Alexis and Champagne the second they walked through the door. He chose not to approach them just yet because he wasn't sure what he wanted to say. He watched them as they headed upstairs to the VIP section and made the decision to follow them. His boy who was working the entryway let him in.

His first thought when he looked at Alexis was *she is looking fine as hell.* His second was why the hell did she have on that tight ass outfit? He knew Alexis, hell, he loved Alexis, and when they were together tight clothes were not her style. He wondered if she was looking for trouble and his third thought was *would she want me back if she knew I was physically separated from my wife?*

Yes, he never told her he was married and yes, he kept most of his past from her. He would have eventually changed that, all he needed was time and because of Thomas, his time had run out.

He watched Alexis approach Shamel. He watched Shamel and his friend take them up to VIP and he followed them. He stayed just a few people behind.

The plan was to approach Alexis the second he had a chance. Like all women did, he knew that eventually she would have to go to the ladies room and that's when he would make his move. The thing of it was, it appeared like it was never going to happen. Right when he'd just about made up his mind to just walk over there, who approached her but Thomas.

I'm a man just like he's a man. I'm stepping up. Khalil made the decision to approach the both of them, Alexis and Thomas. Whatever the hell went down was just going to go down.

"No, you're my type." Khalil heard Thomas say.

"Alexis," Khalil said.

Alexis looked past Thomas, who turned around with swiftness.

"Oh, hell no! You need to step the fuck back!" Thomas said as Khalil stepped up. He was two seconds away from punching him in the face once again, but Alexis placed her hand on his arm.

Khalil ignored Thomas and looked directly at Alexis. "Can I talk to you?"

Alexis was in shock. Her heart was pounding and she felt like she was about to start hyperventilating. *This can not be happening . . . This can not be happening.*

At the exact same time, Champagne just happened to look in their direction. When she saw what was taking place she stood and headed over in their direction to protect her girl.

Shamel and True also stood. Shamel was wondering what was going on and if he should intercept.

"Please, I just want to apologize. I want to explain."

Thomas, who was two seconds off Khalil's ass told him, "I'm going to say it one more time—step . . . the . . . fuck . . . back."

By this time Shamel, True, and Champagne were up on them. "Is everything okay Alexis?" Shamel asked.

Alexis placed her hand on Thomas' shoulder. "It's okay."

Thomas didn't think it was okay and he didn't want to let it go.

"Is there a problem?" Shamel asked Thomas.

"I don't know. Is there?" Thomas had not taken his eyes off Khalil.

"All right y'all, this shit is getting out of hand. Khalil, you need to leave," Champagne said.

"Please, will everyone let me speak?" Alexis asked.

No one said a word, they just looked at her.

"Khalil, there is absolutely nothing you can say to me to justify what you did or how you hurt me, so please just leave, please."

The tone in her voice sounded wounded and Khalil could hear it.

"Please," she begged. "Please just go, I don't want any trouble."

Khalil took a step toward her, but Shamel and Thomas took a step toward him.

Khalil looked at Shamel, "Who the hell are you supposed to be?"

"A friend," Shamel answered.

Thomas looked at Shamel as well. "Man, I got this."

Shamel didn't move. He stood his ground. "I'll step off when Alexis tells me to step off."

"Khalil, please just go," Alexis said.

Khalil looked at them and knew to leave well enough alone *for now*. He didn't say a word; he just turned around and walked away. It would be the one and only time he'd ever done that or planned on doing it.

Alexis then turned to Shamel, "Shamel, it was a pleasure meeting you—"

Shamel cut her off, "Are you dismissing me? I thought we were going to get to know one another."

"I'm not dismissing you or telling you I don't want to get to know you. I'm just letting you know that this night is over for me and I'll call you."

"Damn, man. She ain't worth it," True said.

"Man, shut up," Shamel told him and looked over at Thomas, who looked familiar. Shamel had never had this happen to him before. He'd never been dismissed and he contemplated making a scene but what would be the point. It was evident Alexis didn't like drama. He'd just look like an ass. Plus, he and Alexis had just met. So he told her, "You make sure you do that," and walked away with True behind him talking shit.

"Come on girl, let's go." Champagne took Alexis' hand and tried to pull her along.

"No. I'm going to stay here and talk to Thomas."

"Huh?" Thomas and Champagne said at the same time.

Alexis looked at Thomas, "We'll be back."

Alexis started walking away with Champagne following behind her. They were headed toward the ladies room.

"What's up?" Champagne asked the second they walked through the door.

Alexis looked at Champagne, she opened her mouth to speak but the next thing she knew, she was crying.

Champagne knew there was no reason to ask why she was crying, it was obviously because of all the drama that just took place. The only thing she could think of to do was pull her friend close to her and tell her "let it all out, it's all right, that's what I'm here for."

A short while later Alexis pulled away. "I'm sorry, it's just that seeing Khalil made me realize there was never any closure and maybe I should talk to him. Maybe I need to find out why he wasn't honest with me."

"What! Are you crazy? You need to leave well enough alone, you need to just let his ass go and move on."

"It's not that easy Champagne. I was in love with him."

"I understand all that but what I don't understand is why you're staying here with Thomas."

"Maybe it's to spite Khalil. Maybe it's because Thomas obviously cares for me and I feel like I owe him an explanation for the kiss. Maybe it's because you've been ready to leave for quite some time and I'm not."

Champagne didn't say a word. She realized there was nothing she could say. This was Alexis' moment and she was going to let her have it, even if it meant biting her tongue.

"I'll be all right. I'm with Thomas. I'm sure he won't let anything happen to me."

Champagne gave Alexis a tight hug. "I'm sure he won't. Just be careful. I love you and I know you lost someone you cared about because of our actions and I apologize. I'm sorry if I'm being insensitive. It's just that I want what's best for you. That's why I did what I did; searched his background and shit. Please forgive me."

Alexis hugged her back but she couldn't forgive her just yet. She still felt it could have been handled better. "I love you too sweetie."

They stepped away from one another. Champagne wanted to know, "So, are you ready to leave?"

Alexis laughed. "I told you, I'm going to stay here and hang out with Thomas for a little while."

"Are you sure?"

"Yes, I'm sure. I never got a chance to thank

him for trying to be there for me." Alexis couldn't help but notice the worried look on Champagne's face. "I'll be all right. I'm a big girl."

"Well, I just want you and him to know that if he does anything stupid, I will kick his ass."

Alexis laughed. "I'm sure you will."

Chapter 5

Sometimes You Want What You Think You Can't Have (but the reality is you probably could if you just asked nicely).

As Champagne was leaving the bar, she felt her phone vibrating. *Who the hell? I'll look at it when I get to my car.*

Champagne waited in front of the club for the valet to bring her car around. She decided to check and see if maybe it was Zyair. She opened her purse, pulled out her phone and noticed that there was a text message. It was from Candy, her old employee and lover.

"Hey beautiful. I was just wondering how you were. I'm going to be in town next week and would love to get together. Let me know what's up."

Champagne was about to text her back but decided to wait and think about if she really wanted to do that because it'd been over a month since she last saw Candy and that was in a motel room and it wasn't just for a visit. Champagne thought back to that moment. A few weeks prior to their last sexual encounter, Candy informed Champagne that she was giving her a few weeks notice. This surprised Champagne because she thought they had a good working relationship. She hired Candy when she first started the Agency. She was thinking of training her to be a publicist when she gave her notice.

"What? You don't like working here anymore? You have a new job?" Champagne asked her.

"Oh no, it's nothing like that. It's just that I'm going to support a friend. He has AIDS and well, he needs me."

What could Champagne possibly say about that? If it were her she'd probably be doing the same thing.

"Are you sure you don't just want to take a leave of absence? I can hire a temp and hold your position for you."

"I don't want to tell you yes because I don't know how long I'll be away or even how I'm going to feel after this is over with."

Champagne could hear Candy getting choked up. She reached out and tenderly took Candy's hands in hers. "You do know if there is anything and I mean anything you need, I'm there for you."

"All I want is you," Candy told her, "but I know that's not possible because of your man."

"This is true," Champagne pointed out.

"And I know that what happened on our business trip to DC was supposed to be a one time thing. But I would love to make love to you again Champagne as a way of saying good-bye."

Pretending that she didn't hear what Candy said, Champagne looked toward the filing cabinet and started moving in that direction.

"If you can get someone in here right away, it would give me the opportunity to train them," Candy told her knowing Champagne wasn't going to respond to what she just said.

Business was business and Champagne had hers to run so she got on it. She appreciated the fact that Candy gave her so much notice in the first place.

Champagne went through the resumes that flowed in consistently from experienced people to students who wanted to intern. She was seriously considering going the intern route because it would save her money.

Within a week's time she and Candy interviewed over fifteen people. It was exhausting but they finally hired Shana. She was an intern who appeared to be doing a great job for little pay. Not only could she type over 65 words per minute, but her phone etiquette was professional and she was ambitious. She already let Champagne know that she wanted to be more than an administrative assistant. Eventually

she wanted to be a publicist or personnel assistant as well. Shana was a quick learner and
eager to please. Candy had done an excellent
job training her.

On the weekends prior to Candy's leaving,
she would travel to DC to be with her friend. He
seemed to be having moments when he was
ready to just move on with the afterlife and moments when he wanted to live. He kept saying
he'd do anything to make that happen, whatever it took, even if it meant experimental
drugs. By the time Candy returned to the office
on Mondays she was mentally drained.

Candy's last week of employment had finally
arrived. Champagne asked her if she wanted to
spend Friday together, since she wasn't leaving
until Sunday.

"Friday after work?" Candy asked.

"I've decided to close the office Friday. I don't
have any appointments and since you're leaving, I was thinking we could spend the day together, go to a spa and have lunch."

Champagne knew Candy wasn't a spa type
girl but since she was leaving soon and because
Champagne was paying for it, she figured Candy
would be more than happy to go and experience something new. They both needed a day of
relaxation and pampering. If Champagne had
to, she would force Candy to sit or lie back and
enjoy the occasion.

How they ended up at a hotel afterward Champagne couldn't figure out but they did. Perhaps
it was the being pampered, getting massages,

manicures, pedicures, and then going out for lunch and having drinks afterward that did it. They were so relaxed and had enjoyed each other's company so much that Candy brought up the subject of their tryst.

"How come we don't talk about what happened on the business trip?"

"What are we supposed to say about it?" It wasn't a topic Champagne felt needed to be discussed. It's not that she didn't feel anything for Candy, she did. Her attraction to Candy and Sharon, an author she met at a book signing, who later became a friend and more, wasn't going anywhere. She'd promised herself that she was going to chill on the whole making love to a woman thing. She and Zyair were in a good place right now and she wanted them to stay there.

"Did you enjoy it?" Candy wasn't letting it go.

"Of course."

"Would you do it again?" Candy boldly asked.

"With you?"

"Who else would I be asking about?"

Champagne looked at Candy and felt her pussy get moist. She closed her legs tight and tried to change the subject. "So what are you going to do while you're in DC other than be with your friend?"

Candy knew what she was doing. "Don't change the topic. Don't you want to feel my tongue on your pussy and in your pussy?"

Champagne wondered if those drinks Candy had were getting to her or if she was just saying how she felt. "Come on Candy, don't do this to me."

"Do what? Tell you how good you tasted to me? Tell you I would love to be with you one more time before I leave?"

"That's exactly want I'm asking you not to do to me."

"Let me make love to you again Champagne. Let me remind you how good I can make you feel. I'm leaving town after this and it could be my thank you and my good-bye."

Champagne did not recall saying yes but less than an hour later they were walking through the doors of Paradise, an upscale hotel. Champagne was lying on the bed with Candy lying on top of her looking into her eyes. She knew she should have felt guilty about being there but she didn't and she wondered what that meant.

"Tell me what you want me to do," Candy stated.

"Whatever you want to do to me," Champagne told her.

"You want my tongue deep inside your pussy?"

"Yes."

"You want my tongue inside your ass?"

"Yes."

"Tell me what else you want."

"I want your fingers inside me. I want my liquids to go down your throat."

Candy moaned from deep within her throat and put her mouth on top of Champagne's and pushed her lips apart with her tongue. She ran her tongue inside her mouth and Champagne kissed her back.

Champagne tried to wrap her arms around Candy but Candy knocked her hands down and held them to her sides.

She looked her in the eyes again and told her, "Keep your hands to your sides. I'm in charge."

What was there for Champagne to say other than okay?

Candy unbuttoned Champagne's shirt and caressed her breasts through her bra. She pulled Champagne's bra straps down and pulled the bra beneath her breasts and licked her nipples from one to the other and then bit down on them gently.

"Let me take my clothes off."

Candy ignored her and moved down below her belly with feathery, light kisses. When she got to Champagne's pants, she unbuttoned, unzipped and pulled them down just past her hips.

Again, Champagne said, "Let me take off my clothes."

Again, Candy ignored her. She pulled Champagne's pants down to her thighs and placed her mouth on top of her panties over her pussy.

Champagne tried to push her body up so she could see but Candy pushed her back down. "Relax Sweetie, let me do this the way I want to."

Champagne listened and laid back.

Candy pushed the panties to the side and started licking and sucking on Champagne's pussy lips.

"You're not wasting anytime?" Champagne asked not expecting an answer.

Candy continued to lick and suck, tasting the juices that were beginning to flow. She placed her hands on Champagne's thighs and pushed them open a little more and stuck her tongue as far up in Champagne as she could and then pulled her clitoris from its hidden spot with her teeth gently.

Champagne moaned and bit down on her lip to keep from screaming. Candy's lips then encircled her clitoris, drawing on it deeper and deeper, pulling, tugging, and sucking gently.

The next thing she knew, Champagne's body heaved into the air from the orgasm that was flowing like a river. She opened her legs wider and held Candy's head in place. She didn't let her up for air, until she felt that Candy had sucked and licked every bit of juice she could.

A few hours later when they departed from one another, Champagne felt like Candy was in her system. It was a relief to know that she was leaving town. Champagne was afraid of what she would do. She was afraid that she would not be able to keep the promise she made to herself and to Zyair about leaving the whole bisexual thing alone.

Coming back to reality and present time, Champagne shook her head and looked at her cell phone again. To receive a text from Candy threw her for a loop. *I'm going to have to think about whether I want to see her or not. I don't want to be tempted.* Champagne knew she would.

Lately, sex with a woman had been on her mind. And yes, she was trying to push it back, push it deep down into the crevices of her mind but it wasn't working. She needed something to distract her.

What I need to do is go home and sex the hell out of my man and call Candy back tomorrow.

Chapter 6

Sometimes You Have to Take a Risk to Know What Your Chances Are

This was Alexis' first time coming to Thomas' house and when she walked through the door, she had to admit that she was surprised that he had such good taste.

Champagne had told Alexis on numerous occasions that she had to see Thomas' house. What she failed to mention was that Thomas didn't just live in any kind of house. He lived on an estate.

"You live here by yourself?" Alexis asked.

This was a question Thomas was used to being asked by women whenever he invited one up to his place. By the look on some of their faces, he could tell they were making plans to try and snatch him up and move in. That was something he was not going to let happen.

Thomas was a "hit it and quit it" kind of man but that was growing old. He found himself wanting to settle down and maybe even start a family. All this playing the field, not knowing who wanted him for himself or his money was not the way he wanted to continue to live.

The thing of it was, as a child he never thought he would be the one living this way, financially successful and never having to worry about money again. His background and his upbringing until he became a teenager would have never predicted this outcome. If it wasn't for Ms. Dominique, or Ms. D as he liked to call her, he didn't know where he would be.

He still thought about that day she changed his life. The day she offered him a chance of a lifetime. The day he was put on the right track.

Thomas was laying in his room with his eyes closed and his arm thrown over his forehead, when his social worker walked in. It was one of the few times he had the room he shared with two others to himself and he was enjoying the peace of it.

"Thomas, I may have some good news for you."

Thomas sat up and threw his legs over the edge of the bed. "What type of good news?" He'd already come to believe at his young age that good news was hard to come by.

"I believe I have a family for you."

For a second there Thomas thought he'd misheard her. "Huh?"

"I think I have a family for you."

He did hear her right. Thomas stood up and looked her in the eyes. "I thought you said this was it for me. That I was going to be here at this group home until I could do independent living. Why would somebody want me now anyway? I'm almost a man, unless they're just in it for the money."

Ms. Dominique sighed. "Listen Thomas, I know what I told you but things have changed. This family isn't in it just for the money. They're in it to make a difference in someone's life. They're in it to change a life."

"Yeah right, I've heard that before." And he had. He'd heard that and so much more. He'd heard that all he's good for is the money, that he'll never amount to a damn thing, that he was worthless, and was even told don't get too comfortable.

So to hear that someone wanted to make a difference, it didn't faze him one bit. "That's what they all say initially, until I walk through the door and you leave."

"All I can tell you right now is that this family is different but if you don't want to give it one last try that's fine with me. I'll find someone else for them. Someone that would love this opportunity."

When Thomas heard those words, he had to admit to himself that he didn't want her to give this chance to another kid. What if this time, this one time, the people were being honest? He wanted it but he was scared. He was scared of it not working out and scared of being let down. If he got his hopes up and those hopes were destroyed once again, it would devastate him. But the look on Ms. D's face reassured him that wouldn't happen.

"Listen, I know you're scared," she told him.

"What! Ain't nobody scared?"

"It's okay to be scared Thomas. I can't say I blame you but I think you should give it one more try."

"Do they know how old I am? Are they prepared for a teenager? Did they specifically ask for a teenager?"

"Yes they do, yes they are, and yes they did."

"Did they say why they wanted an older kid?" He hoped they weren't going to try and slave him, have him keeping house and working the death out of him.

"This couple has another son your age. They work with at-risk kids and they're looking to give a teen a chance for a normal life, a chance to experience a family."

"Why me?" Thomas wanted to know. "You have other clients you could have picked for this family Ms. D. Why me?"

At this point, Ms. D was getting exasperated and Thomas could see it on her face and feel it in her energy.

"Listen," she told him, "If you don't want this, you need to let me know by tomorrow. That way, if I have to, I can pick someone else."

The truth was she didn't want to pick anyone else. There was something about Thomas that stood out from the other kids. He was smart. He had manners and although he had been abandoned, he didn't allow his heart and soul to harden like some of the other kids had. There was still hope.

"But I have to say this to you," Ms. D went on,

"I would be very disappointed if you didn't take this opportunity. Because that's what it is Thomas, an opportunity for growth. I also think you would be a good match for this family. You have the potential to be so much more than you think."

The thing of it was, Thomas did want another chance. He did want to be with a family. Just like any other human being on the face of this earth, all he wanted to do was be loved. *"I don't have to think about it, Ms. D. I'll do it. I'll go."*

Five days later he was on his way to what might be his new foster parents' home. He was scheduled to stay the weekend and if they vibed, he would move in. On the way there, he was quiet, in his own world, deep in thought. He was trying to get past the nervousness he was feeling.

As they turned into the subdivision, Thomas was immediately impressed. The houses were larger than any he'd ever seen. The lawns were manicured and kids were actually playing in their yards. He noticed quite a few white kids and realized he'd never asked if the family was white or black. Well, it was too late now because they were pulling into a cul-de-sac and as they pulled up into a driveway Thomas was relieved to see a black teenage boy sitting on the porch with headphones on. He appeared to be writing in a notebook.

"We're here," Ms. D told him as they pulled into the driveway.

That day changed Thomas' life. He walked in the door with an attitude of *"I'm going to make the best of this situation and I will make this work.*" And make it work he did. Along with the Turners' assistance, encouragement, and participation, they got along great. Not only did he excel in school, he ended up getting a scholarship for college and money for college from the system. After he graduated from college, he tried to reach out to Ms. D. He knew how proud she would be of him but she'd left the agency and there was no forwarding address. Thomas sometimes thought of her and wondered how she was doing. Then again, maybe it was best to leave the past just where it was and that's behind him.

The way Thomas figured it, had it not been for the Turners, had they not been there for him, pushing him and telling him he could do it, he would not be the responsible, grown ass man he is now and that's why once he began making money, he'd send them some sporadically. If he tried to do it any other way, they wouldn't accept.

So to go from having no place to really call home, to being able to purchase the home of his dreams was an accomplishment. To go from a place of poverty to a place of prosperity was an even bigger accomplishment, that of owning his own sports agency in which he was extremely successful.

Thomas looked at Alexis who was walking around taking in the art on his walls. She noticed that most of the paintings were by an artist named Antonio Pierre Hunter.

"So, you're a collector?" She asked.

Thomas stood next to her and looked at the painting she was standing in front of. "I wouldn't say all that. I just like what I like."

Alexis turned to face Thomas, "You're a sports agent right?" She already knew the answer to that. She'd heard Champagne and Zyair talk about Thomas' famous clients numerous times.

"Yes, and you're a counselor or a therapist, right?"

"Yeah, yeah, yeah." Alexis tried to blow off the rest of his inquiry. The last thing she wanted to discuss was the fact that she counseled some bad-ass, fast-ass teens. Teens, that when she tried to guide them and show them a better way gave her their ass to kiss. "Instead of discussing what we do for a living, why don't you show me your bedroom?"

"Huh?" That wasn't what Thomas expected to hear.

"Show me your bedroom. I want to see where the magic happens," Alexis joked.

Thomas was thrown off by her bluntness. This was definitely not the Alexis he knew. But he was a man and like any other man he was more than ready and willing to take the hint, if that's what she was throwing.

"Are you sure?"

Alexis smirked at Thomas' obvious discomfort. "Yes, I'm sure."

Thomas led the way upstairs. As they passed several rooms Alexis peeked inside and was surprised at how orderly everything was.

"Do you have a maid?" Alexis asked as they stepped in his bedroom.

"What, a brother can't be neat without any help?" Thomas joked.

"Not when they're as busy as you probably are."

"Actually, I do have someone that comes in twice a week, but I do cook my own meals."

When they entered his bedroom, Alexis was impressed. For some reason she imagined his room to be extremely masculine, everything in it being black, dark, glass or brass. She thought he'd have a big-ass television and a stereo system in it but there was neither. Instead the bedroom had a calming effect. The color on the wall was a soft pale blue and the bedroom set reminded her of the ocean. The carpet on the floor looked plush enough to sink her feet into. To her surprise, on the nightstand next to the bed were several books. The top of his dresser was covered in colognes and there was a little lounge area in the corner.

"You don't watch television or listen to music in your bedroom?"

"No, I use it to relax, sleep and for extra-curricular activities."

Alexis laughed. She could imagine what those activities were.

She looked at his oversized bed and walked over to it. She stood in front of it and turned toward Thomas who stood behind her watching every move she made.

"You think your bed is big enough?"

"I sleep wild," he told her.

Alexis sat on the bed and asked, "Do you do everything wild?"

Thomas hoped he wasn't mistaken or was being misled. He could hear the flirtatious tone in her voice. He'd wanted this moment to happen for so long. After all, Alexis was his dream girl and he'd fantasized about making love to her many times. After taking a long look at her, he took her hands and kissed them. He looked into her eyes and asked, "Are you drunk?" If she was he would not go through with this. He wanted her to be clearheaded and mindful of all he was going to do to her. Thomas didn't want any regrets.

"I'm as sober as you are," she reassured him. Although the two drinks she had were making her feel a little tipsy.

"I just wanted to make sure before I kissed you," Thomas told her.

Alexis didn't want to waste any more time. She placed her hands on each side of his face, pulled him down on top of her and lay back on the bed.

"Are you sure about this?" he asked.

Alexis was more than sure, she decided that this was going to be the night for Thomas to finally get his wish. In all her past relationships, the men had dictated the when, what and the how. No more, she was going to do this on her terms.

Plus, she was tired of waiting for Thomas to make his move. For some reason he was acting like a Mr. Goodie Two Shoes, all gentleman like. He wasn't being his usual aggressive self.

Alexis looked up at him, "Let's take a shower together."

Thomas was not expecting this at all. "OK," was all that he could utter.

"Well, you need to get up," Alexis told him.

He stood up and told her, "After you."

Alexis got off the bed and started taking her clothes off, leaving behind a trail of clothing.

Thomas, after the shock wore off, looked to the heavens and stated, "Thank you Jesus," and darted into the bathroom after Alexis.

Once in the bathroom, he followed Alexis' lead and took his clothes off while eyeing her body. He noticed that her body was flawless, almost creamy like a light coffee.

She turned the shower on. "Let's give it a few minutes to warm up."

Alexis could tell that Thomas liked what he saw. She immediately seized control by pulling Thomas close to her by his dick and started passionately kissing him.

Thomas' mind was blown. He never in a million years imagined that Alexis got down like this.

"Let's get in the shower," Alexis said.

After the kiss Alexis instructed Thomas to bathe her. She did this purposely so that he could enjoy every inch of her without fully experiencing her. Thomas quickly did as she requested and Alexis returned the favor.

Alexis turned the shower off and Thomas followed her out and into the bedroom. Alexis lay on the bed and opened her legs wide and gently ran her fingers up and down her pussy. She told

Thomas to stay where he was and just watch. She continued to play with her pussy for a little while longer then asked Thomas to come over to the bed.

Like an obedient puppy he complied. He was rewarded by Alexis sitting up and covering the head of his penis with her warm mouth.

"Damn, damn, damn," was all Thomas could manage to say. Alexis was licking and sucking the head. She was teasing the hell out of him and she knew it. He wanted her to put the whole thing in her mouth but instead she told him to lie on the bed and open his legs as wide as he could.

Thomas quickly assumed the position and Alexis went straight for the sides of his balls. All Thomas could do was squirm and moan.

Alexis continued to lick and suck Thomas' balls with expert precision. She then decided to try something she heard about on a cable sex show. The hostess said if you suck the area beneath the balls, and right before his asshole that the man will turn straight bitch.

She did it on Thomas and found that statement to be true. The second Alexis' mouth touched that area Thomas' body lost all control.

Alexis looked up and said, "You better not cum yet."

Thomas did not hear a word she was saying. He was in a place that only a few men experienced and he was loving every minute of it.

Alexis decided to run her finger gently over his asshole. When she did this Thomas jumped and arched his body up. He looked at Alexis and said, "Who are you?"

Alexis laughed and told him, "The girl of your dreams. Now lie back down."

"I will," Thomas told her, "but I felt that finger on my asshole, and I just want to let you know that there ain't no gay shit going on around here. I'm a secure brotha."

Thomas wondered if Alexis made love like this to everyone. He hoped not but if so he wanted to be the last. *Shit, I wish this had happened a long time ago.* Normally when a female gave it up so fast he wouldn't think twice about them but this situation was different. He knew Alexis was a different kind of woman. He knew she'd only had a few lovers. He knew this through Champagne because whenever he'd talk about he and Alexis getting together, Champagne would knock his fantasy down by telling him Alexis wasn't that experienced and was picky with the men she chose.

Well, tonight she chose him and he felt privileged.

Alexis started to masterfully work the head of his penis with her tongue. She slowly worked her way down to his balls, then onto his ass.

Thomas was wide open. He barely heard Alexis ask him to put his dick inside of her. She repeated herself as she climbed onto the bed and Thomas was more than happy to oblige her.

The best feeling in the world to Thomas was the moment the head of his dick first entered Alexis. He tried to delay the inevitable.

"What are you doing? What are you waiting for? Give it to me Thomas," Alexis demanded.

Thomas began to pound inside her.

"Yes, Yes!" Alexis screamed out.

Thomas was trying to be cool with it and make it last. But when he felt Alexis' pussy flexing, he didn't know how much longer he would be able to hold on. It's wasn't too much longer because before he knew it, he was yelling, "I'm about to come."

"Not inside me," Alexis told him, realizing they didn't use a condom.

He pulled out of her and moved his hand to jerk the cum out. Instead, Alexis pushed his hand away and firmly grabbed his dick, jerked and pulled out every ounce of cum.

Thomas was done, amazed, and in love.

Alexis looked at Thomas. "Now I need you to eat my pussy. Do you think you can handle that? And I know you have condoms right, because we are not done."

All Thomas could do was look up at the ceiling again and mouth "Thank you Jesus."

Chapter 7

People Only Do What You Allow Them To

The day after the drama at The Red Oak, Zyair hung up the phone and turned over to see if Champagne was still asleep. She was, but this was something he couldn't hold in, so he nudged her. Champagne didn't budge. He nudged her again and this time harder.

"What?" Champagne whined.

"You won't believe this." Zyair was like a kid with a secret.

"Zyair, come on now, you know I'm trying to sleep late. I'm tired."

"That's what you get for trying to hang out all night."

"I was with Alexis."

"And?"

Champagne turned over and tried to read the expression on his face. "Did you wake me up because you're upset with me for hanging out?"

Zyair didn't mean for her to interpret his

words that way. He wasn't upset about that at all. Hell, he was supposed to be out of town, although it was a surprise to come home and not find his woman there.

Champagne really wasn't one to go out and not call him and let him know she wouldn't be home. This time she did just that and it pissed him off just a little bit. It was called a matter of respect and respect was something they tried to have for each other in every way.

He did have to admit to himself that for a brief second, when he realized she wasn't home and hadn't left a message he panicked. *What if she's with another woman—that Sharon chick? Hadn't they let that moment go?*

Thankfully, before he could get any further into those thoughts the door opened and in walked Champagne.

"What Zyair? What is it that you want so desperately to tell me?"

He didn't like her tone, so he looked at her and wondered if she was still tired and horny. When she arrived home last night, she was ready to make wild passionate love but Zyair told her he was exhausted.

She gave him the look as though she didn't believe him. After all, when is a man too exhausted to accept the pussy? Of course, she tried to entice him by taking a shower and coming out with just a pair of lace panties on but he just couldn't get his energy up.

"Zyair, come on, I want to make love."

"I'm tired baby. I was at meetings all day and I don't think I'd be able to perform."

"Well, why don't we try to find out?" She wasn't giving up that easily.

Zyair really didn't want to turn her down but not being able to perform sexually was one of his biggest fears.

"How about I just eat your pussy?" he asked her.

He knew that some people believed that oral required more energy than penetration. But who would turn it down?

"Now we both know once you get a taste of this, you're going to want to stick it in," Champagne teased.

Little did she know he really was tired. When she lay on the bed he planned to pull her panties off and dive between her legs. He was going to head straight for the clitoris. He knew she was probably thinking she should take what she could get, since she was going to get hers.

However, she surprised him by saying, "I would love that and I promise not to hold back. I'll come as fast as you make me."

Zyair was relieved. As much as he might have wanted to do more, he knew his dick and it just wasn't going to happen. Zyair knew this happened to other men because his boys discussed it from time to time. It came with age and activity.

After Champagne came, they both fell asleep.

Early the next morning when Zyair hung up the phone, he had news to share so he woke her up.

"I have to tell you something," Zyair told her.

"Whatever it is, it'd better be good, because you're interrupting my beauty sleep."

"Snappy, aren't we?" Zyair said. He didn't know what her problem was. Shit, she got what she wanted last night, an orgasm, even with his ass being dead tired.

"I think Alexis stayed the night with Thomas."

He had Champagne's full attention on that note. She sat right up. "What makes you say that?"

"Because I just called his house and I could have sworn I heard her in the background."

Champagne lay back down.

Zyair nudged her again, "Don't you have anything to say?"

"That voice you heard could have been anybody's."

"Call her," Zyair said.

Champagne looked at Zyair and wanted to ask him why he was so concerned with whose voice he heard in the background. She already knew the answer. It wasn't concern. It was nosiness and she had to admit she was right there with him.

"All right, pass me the phone."

Zyair grabbed the cordless phone and watched as Champagne sat up and dialed Alexis' number.

Champagne placed her hand over the receiver and told Zyair, "It went straight to voice mail."

Zyair raised his eyebrow and said, "That's because they're fucking."

Champagne rolled her eyes and left a message for Alexis to call her. She looked over at Zyair who was smiling from ear to ear.

"What are you cheesing about?"

"He finally got that ass," Zyair said with pride. He felt good for his boy, after years of talking about her, he finally sealed the deal.

"Zyair, don't disrespect my girl like that."

Laughing, Zyair told Champagne, "I'm not trying to disrespect her. I'm just saying—"

"What are you saying?"

"That my boy finally got that ass."

Champagne rolled her eyes, turned over and tried to go back to sleep, but it wasn't working because now all she could do was wonder if the voice Zyair heard was Alexis'.

Chapter 8

Never Say Never Because You Just Might Be Right

Two days later Alexis looked at the phone and wanted to call Thomas but hesitated. *What if he thinks I'm sweating him? What if he doesn't want to talk? What if in his mind, he finally got what he's wanted from me for so long, that now he wants nothing else to do with me?*

Even as Alexis had these thoughts, she knew it couldn't be anything further from the truth. She knew that Thomas was crazy about her and had been for quite some time. Let Champagne tell it, he wanted her the second they met. That was over five years ago when he moved back to town and opened his office. What he felt was obvious in the way he made love to her.

The first time she was in charge. The second time, he explored her body with his hands and his tongue for her satisfaction and her satisfaction only. The third time was for his satisfaction. He took her with a gentle roughness. Afterward, every cell in her body was tingling and every muscle was sore. It was just what she needed.

I'll call him later, she decided. Alexis glanced at the clock and knew that what she needed to be doing was getting ready for work. Today was going to be a long day. Being a therapist at West Park High School was sometimes tiring. She could tell today was going to be one of those days.

Alexis had several conferences lined up with parents. Usually when this happened, someone almost always got indignant. They didn't want to hear anything negative about their child or they basically didn't care one way or the other. Those were the type of parents that made Alexis question why they showed up at all. What was the point? Whatever it was, she knew she had to be mentally ready for it.

Alexis stood looking in the closet trying to decide what to wear. Normally she took her clothes out the night before but laziness had set in. She already knew in the back of her mind that she was going to wear one of her pants suits. It was just a matter of deciding which color. She chose the cream colored one she ordered from the Victoria Secret catalog, with a brown camisole and some brown open-toed Nine West heels.

In the past Alexis' style was more conservative but because she was changing as a woman she would also change her style. Her appearance had never been an issue for her. She knew men found her attractive but like most women there was always something she'd like to change. She was short in stature, five feet three, but she wore three-inch heels most of the time. She was small in frame and wore a size five or seven. It depended on the quality and designer of the clothes. If she could change anything, she'd probably give herself bigger breasts and slice about an inch off her thighs. But those were things she could live with or without.

After laying her clothes on the bed, she glanced at the phone one more time. *I can wait to call him*, she reminded herself and went into the bathroom to take her shower. As she turned the shower on, she thought about her lovemaking session with Thomas and how just for that moment, she didn't think once about Khalil. Even if she wanted to, she couldn't have because what Thomas did to her body made her stay right there in the moment. Perhaps that would be what she has to do. Stay in the moment to forget about him.

Fifteen minutes later as she was drying off, she heard her phone ring. She wrapped the towel around her waist and ran in the bedroom. She snatched up the phone.

"Hello?"

"Hey sexy." It was Thomas.

Alexis almost breathed a sigh of relief. She had to admit that she was pleased to hear his voice and double pleased that he called her first.

"Good morning," she responded.

"I'm sorry I'm just now calling. I've been

caught up with some legal things for one of my clients."

"That's okay," she told him, although it really wasn't.

"No, it's not. I don't want you to think I just used you."

Alexis didn't respond. She didn't know what to say.

"Are you on your way out the door?"

"I'm just getting dressed. I have to meet with some of my students' parents today."

"Would you like to have dinner tonight?"

The word yes almost came out her mouth but she stopped it. She didn't want to appear too anxious. "How about I call you later and let you know."

"You make sure you do that," he told her.

After a brief pause, each of them looking for words to say, Alexis ended the phone call. "I don't mean to rush off the phone but . . ."

"I know. You have to go."

When they hung up Alexis felt a little lighter. *Why is that?* She did not want to get worked up over a man. She promised herself that she wouldn't set herself up for heartbreak. *That will not happen.* So his answer to dinner would be no, at least not tonight, maybe another night. She was not ready to rush into things. Yes, they'd made wild passionate love but that did not make them a couple.

Although she planned on doing her thing and playing the field, Alexis didn't want to play games or mess with someone's emotions. That wasn't her style, but her concern right now was herself and her heart. Any man she came across that expressed curiosity about her, that interest would be reciprocated. But she was also going to let them know up front what kind of party it was. So if that meant putting Thomas off for a little while because he thought this was the beginning of them, so be it.

By the time Alexis arrived at West Park High School, she was running late. Lateness was a quality in others she disliked but somehow time got away from her. Maybe it was because of the phone call but then again, maybe it was because of her thoughts, which somehow slowed her down. Whatever it was, she knew she had to get it together and fast.

She also felt a little nervous because it seemed like a car was following her. Every turn she took, they took. Maybe they were just heading in the same direction she tried to tell herself but still her gut told her otherwise.

She went into her office and shut the door. She turned on the light and proceeded to pull out the files of her students or should she say her subjects. That's what these teenagers of today were, subjects, something that needed to be looked at, taken apart, dissected and studied. Today's teenager could be one of two things, a disaster or a success. Sometimes Alexis wondered if she was reaching these kids and if they believed her when she would tell them they could achieve whatever they set their minds to. She wondered if to them she sounded like that old Army commercial, "Be all you can be."

Alexis sat down and looked through the files. She placed them in the order in which the parents were scheduled to appear. That was if more than half of them showed up. Sometimes she asked herself why didn't she choose a school in Newburg, the area in Jersey she lived in. It was nice and peaceful there and most of the families came from money, or the parents either cared or pretended to care. Instead, she chose to work in West Park, where some of the kids and most of the parents simply didn't give a damn. In her heart of hearts she knew why, it was because she wanted to make a difference.

There was a knock on her office door.

"Come in."

Ms. Maya McMillan stuck her head in. "Can I speak with you for a minute?"

Ms. McMillan was one of the few teachers she socialized with outside of school. Alexis preferred to keep her relationships at work in the workplace only. This was because she'd seen and heard the teachers talk in the lounge area. They talked about one another constantly and if you just happened to be the culprit of the day, the second you walked in the room, it grew quiet.

They also talked about the students as if they were students themselves, gossiping and what not. Very often, she'd hear words along the lines of "this one is pregnant," "that one has no home training," "this one is going to keep getting left back because she has no sense" and on and on it went. That was something she didn't want to be a part of.

After school that day, there was a meeting being held with all teachers and counselors present. Gossiping was one of the issues that were going to be discussed because the week before, one of the students overheard a couple of the teachers' conversation. It was also becoming obvious to some of the students that some of the teachers and counselors didn't really care about them and that they were just there for the paycheck.

Alexis closed the file she had open and asked Maya, "What's up?"

"I have someone I want you to meet," Maya told her.

"Huh?"

"I have someone I want you to meet," Maya told her again.

"Are you talking about as in a hook up?" Alexis didn't know how open she was to having a casual associate set her up.

"Yes."

Alexis had to ask, even though she knew this was not a situation she was open to at all. "Who?"

"My half brother."

Alexis wondered why Maya would consider her when it came to setting her brother up with someone. They didn't know one another that well. Yes, they had lunch together a couple of times but best friends, she and Maya were not.

"Why me?"

"Why you what?"

"Don't you have any other friends you could play matchmaker with?"

She did, but Maya's brother, Gavin, was over to her house a couple of days ago and he was looking through the yearbook.

"Are there any fine teachers teaching at your school?" he jokingly asked when he came across Alexis' picture.

"Who is that?" he wanted to know.

Standing over his shoulder and noticing who he was looking at, Maya told him, "That's Alexis. She's one of the counselors."

"I'd like to meet her."

"I don't know about that. She and I aren't really that tight."

Gavin laughed. "What's that got to do with me? I don't care if you're best friends or not. I think this may be my future wife."

Now that was something that made Maya laugh. "You know you're bugging right."

"I might be, but just ask her. See if she'd be willing to meet me."

"I'm going to have to think about it," Maya told him and think about it she did. She thought about her observations of Alexis and had to admit there was nothing that stood out that indicated she wouldn't be decent enough for Gavin. Not that he was the best thing since bread but he was her younger brother and he had a lot going for himself, a nice car, his own home and his own business.

Over the past year, Maya and Gavin had developed a close relationship. They had the same rolling stone father who never married either of their mothers and growing up they didn't really know one another. They knew of each other and maybe had a glance or two of one another but that was it. Maya barely knew their father. Her mother hated him with a passion because she felt like he had robbed her of her youth and was a rolling stone, sleeping around with everything and anything. She forbade Maya to see him. It didn't stop her though, because as she got older and was able to leave the house, she'd sneak down to "the avenue" where her dad hung out. Sometimes he'd have Gavin with him.

As they grew older, she saw less and less of her father and none of Gavin. It wasn't until her father's funeral a few years ago that she and Gavin got reacquainted. Gavin told her that they had several other siblings but she wasn't interested in meeting anyone else; she had all she needed in him.

Maya knew that Alexis was recently in a relationship that didn't work out. She also knew that last she heard, Alexis was a church going, God-fearing woman. Was that something she should warn her brother about? After all, he was an ex-hustler. Or did it even matter since that was no longer his profession and since Alexis wasn't one to go around preaching the word to people.

Heck, the more Maya thought about it, this matchmaking between Gavin and Alexis might just be a good thing. She just hoped Alexis didn't ask how old he was. Therefore, when Alexis asked Maya didn't she have any other female friends she could hook her brother up with Maya told her, "I do, but he wants to meet you."

"How does he even know who I am?"

Maya told her the yearbook story.

And just to think, I hated that picture. That wasn't anything new. Alexis disliked most pictures she took.

"Tell me a little bit about him," Alexis requested.

"Well, he's an entrepreneur. He owns several car detailing shops, property and—"

That meant he had money. Alexis wasn't slow in what Maya was conveying so she cut her off. "Does he have any children?" She was more concerned about that.

"Yes." That wasn't something Maya couldn't cover up. Plus, she loved her nephew. "And he takes good care of my nephew when he has him. He's a hands-on father."

Alexis wasn't keen on dating a man with children. But she also knew to find a man in his thirties that was childless, well, that would be short of a miracle. Thomas was one of the few exceptions.

"How old?"

"Six."

That wasn't so bad, Alexis thought, it wasn't like he was under five. Alexis had a rule; if a man had a child under the age of five, she would not date him. It was her belief that women with children that young by a man were still emotionally attached and with those emotions would come some mama drama and that's something she would not tolerate.

Maybe it's something that I wouldn't have tolerated in the past but now that I've made the decision to get out in the world, maybe I should rethink that, Alexis thought but said to Maya, "Let me think about it."

"Okay, that's fine. Just let me know and I'll have him stop by here one day, that way there's no pressure."

After Maya left Alexis' office, Alexis prepared herself for her first parent conference. Why she set up her conferences on a Monday, she didn't know. All she did know is that this was not a good way to start a week off.

The first conference was for a student named Rena Pugh and Rena was a piece of work. She was sixteen going on thirty and failing more than half her classes. She talked back to the teachers, cut classes, and was disruptive toward the other students. Alexis was concerned that something was going on in the household, neighborhood, or somewhere Rena frequented, because Rena now attended school when she felt like it and last year she was an A/B student.

Her intercom rang and the secretary informed her that her first appointment was there.

She looked at her appointment book and saw that Rena Pugh's mother was scheduled to come in. She was surprised because so far she'd missed every conference.

"Send her in," Alexis told her.

Alexis sat up in her chair and watched the door, when in walked one of the oldest looking thugs she'd seen in a long time.

"Who are you?" Alexis asked.

"Who the hell do you think I am? I'm Rena's father."

If Alexis wasn't mistaken, she could have sworn she smelled weed. If that is what she smelled, there wasn't anything she could do about it other than try to look past this man's ignorance and hope they could figure out together what was going on with Rena.

Alexis looked in the file for his name and saw that it was William Pugh, but it also stated that he was incarcerated. Alexis knew that she needed to ask him for ID and on instinct she could tell that this was going to be a problem.

"I'm sorry Mr. Pugh, but I'll need to see some identification."

"Identification! Identification! What the hell you need to see that for? I done told you who I was."

"Yes, you have, but here in Rena's file it says that her father is incarcerated. Have you recently gotten released?" If that's what the situation was, Alexis could now see what Rena's problem was.

As Mr. Pugh reached in his back pocket to pull out his wallet, he looked at Alexis and told her, "This is some pure bullshit. You know I'm her father; hell she looks just like me."

Alexis didn't even bother to respond. Rena was light complexioned and the man standing before her was dark as night. Rena had dimples and this man had a permanent scowl. Rena was tall and the man standing before her was short and stocky. If he wanted to think Rena looked like him, she'd let him.

"I come here to check on my daughter, to see how she's doing in school and I get harassed because I—"

Alexis didn't let him finish. "I apologize if you think I'm harassing you but this is procedure."

"Mmm, procedure my ass." Mr. Pugh pushed the wallet toward her.

"Open it please."

He snatched the wallet off her desk and flipped it open.

Alexis looked at the identification and indeed he was her father.

"Once again I apologize," she told him and handed him back his wallet.

Mr. Pugh was just the beginning of her drama with parents that morning. On top of that, Mr. Pugh, the weed head, had the audacity to ask her out on a date.

Later that day Alexis was sitting in the teachers' lounge sipping on a cup of tea when Maya walked in.

"You look stressed."

"Girl, these parents are a trip."

"You ain't telling me something I don't already know."

"I mean, don't get me wrong, there are some that genuinely care and are concerned but sometimes it seems like they are few and far in between."

Maya didn't respond as she poured herself a cup of tea.

"You know, I've been thinking . . ." Alexis decided that it wouldn't do any harm meeting Maya's brother, maybe for lunch or after work for coffee or something. However they met, it would be someplace casual. "I'm open to meeting your brother."

"Cool," Maya responded. "I don't normally do this, hook people up, because if it doesn't work out, I don't want to be the blame."

"I can understand that."

"Instead of me inviting him to the school, why don't you come by my house Saturday? My book club is getting together and I'll tell him to stop by."

Alexis' plan was for something more casual, but hey, a book club was something new. There was a time she was thinking about joining one. At least this way, she'd get to see what it was all about.

"Can I bring a friend?" Alexis asked. She was thinking about Champagne.

"A female friend?"

"Of course."

"That's fine with me." Maya turned to walked out but stopped in her tracks. "In case you want to pick up the book we're reading, it's called *Sister Girls 2* by Angel M. Hunter.

"I just might do that," Alexis told her.

* * *

When Alexis returned to her office, she called Thomas like she said she would. She wanted to let him know that they would have to do dinner another night. She was glad to catch his voice mail because she really didn't feel like making up an excuse. She then called Champagne and left her a message to meet her at "their new spot" for an early cocktail. This was a new thing for her, having a cocktail after work. She didn't think it was out of hand because she only had one or two.

Throughout the day, Champagne had left numerous messages on her cell and office phone and she sounded anxious to speak with her. Before meeting up, Alexis wanted to hit the gym and run a few errands. She wasn't looking forward to it but the sooner she got them done the better.

Looking at her cell phone, Alexis noticed a text from Champagne as well. *I wonder what that's about?*

Chapter 9

Some Things Are Best Kept to Yourself; Just Figure Out Which Ones

Champagne and Alexis were seated at a table in The Red Oak sipping on Martinis once again.

"So," Champagne started, "what's up with you not returning a sister's phone call, making me stress out? I was worried about your ass."

Alexis didn't answer right away; she continued to sip on her drink and glance around the room.

"What's up? You keep looking around? Are you looking for anyone in particular?"

Alexis turned to focus on Champagne. "I'm sorry. It's just that while I was running my errands today, I just had this weird-ass vibe. Like someone was following me. And, it's not the first time."

"For real? Who?"

"That's just it. I don't know." Alexis shook her

head. "You know what, maybe I'm bugging. Maybe I'm just on edge."

"Girl, you need to go with your instinct. If you think someone is stalking you—"

Alexis threw up her hands, "Whoa . . . I didn't say all that." The thought of a stalker was scary to her. She did not want to put that in the universe.

"Well, that's what someone following you means."

"You know what," Alexis requested, "let's change the topic."

"All right, how about giving me the dirt." Champagne was ready to find out if it was Alexis' voice Zyair heard.

"The dirt on what?"

"You know, you and Thomas."

"There's nothing to tell."

Champagne could tell that Alexis was holding back. They'd known each other long enough to be able to read tone, mannerisms, and inflections. Honestly, it kind of pissed her off that Alexis wasn't sharing.

Normally, they told one another everything, but ever since the incident with Khalil, it seemed like their friendship was changing. Alexis still hadn't said anything about the apology she made to her. Champagne wondered if that meant she didn't forgive her. That she was holding onto the hurt. They weren't communicating as much as they used to and she really needed to talk out this whole bisexuality issue. She would have preferred to do it with her best friend but if that couldn't happen, she'd talk to Sharon.

Champagne and Alexis being distant with one another had happened before. This time it felt different. They were definitely going to have to talk it out.

Champagne knew they were grown women and that life often took over but she still felt somewhat abandoned. Especially since she thought that the whole fiasco with Khalil was going to leave Alexis in need of her best friend. Well, it was obvious she guessed wrong.

"There's really nothing to tell. We hung out, I stayed the night and we're friends."

Champagne caught the "I stayed the night" part immediately. "Excuse me? Did you just say you stayed the night?"

Alexis kept a straight face, not wanting to give anything away. "Yes."

"Stayed the night as in slept over? Slept in the same bed and didn't leave until the morning?" Champagne couldn't believe what she was hearing. Alexis having a one night stand, those words didn't even sound right in a sentence. She wondered if her mouth was wide open from the shock.

"Yes."

"So, did y'all do the do?"

Alexis started laughing. "Listen to you." She mocked Champagne. "Did y'all do the do?"

"Well, did you?"

Alexis smirked and if Champagne wasn't mistaken, it even looked like she blushed when she replied, "That we did."

"Get out of here. You did not. I don't know what to say." Champagne was at a complete loss of words. She just knew Zyair was wrong when he said it was Alexis' voice.

Alexis motioned for the waiter to come back over. "There is nothing to say."

"How was it?" Champagne asked. On several occasions Champagne would overhear Thomas brag on his sexual skills and Champagne had to admit she wondered if it was just words or if he could back it up.

Alexis leaned across the table. "Girl, it was so good. I couldn't believe it myself."

"Get out of here."

"I'm telling you, Thomas put it down and quite well."

"Details girl, you know I want details."

Alexis' gaze looked like she was taking herself back to the moment and she was.

She was thinking about the way he turned her over and ran his hands over her ass. She thought about the way she spread her legs wider and waited for him to enter her. What he did instead took her by surprise. He licked her down her back slowly all the way down to the crack of her ass and to her pussy, opening it from behind and entering her with his tongue. She moved her hips back and forth and wondered if she was smothering him.

She thought about how he stood up and put the head of his dick on her pussy and ran it on the inside of her lips and finally just when she thought she couldn't take it anymore, slammed inside of her so hard that she yelled.

"Do you want me to stop?" he asked her.

All Alexis could do was shake her head. She didn't want him to stop. She wanted more.

He pulled out slowly and slammed inside her once again.

She looked between her legs and could see his balls. She reached for them and started massaging while he grinded inside of her.

"Deeper," she told him. "Deeper."

Deep inside her, he pressed harder and pulled out slow and slammed back in. She wondered if he could feel her body trembling.

"Come Thomas, I want you to come." At this point, she wondered if it was even possible, he'd already had an orgasm.

She looked behind her and saw that he had closed his eyes and was starting to slide in and out of her real slow.

"That's right baby, concentrate, focus."

Before she knew it, his body got stiff and he pushed deep inside of her and exploded into the condom.

"Come on, girl, details." Champagne could tell by the look on Alexis' face that whatever took place was beyond words.

"Girl, he was gentle and rough at the same time. It's like he wanted me to remember every touch and every inch of him." She shook her head, "and his coochie eating skills were out of this world. I came so hard, I thought I was going to have a heart attack."

Champagne laughed and asked, "So what does this mean?"

"What does what mean?"

"Is this the beginning of something serious for you and him?"

"Girl, please no. I'm just having fun right now. As a matter-of-fact, remember Shamel?"

"The guy we met at the club?"

"Yes, the one and only. We're having a late dinner together Friday night."

Champagne didn't know what to say. She just wasn't used to Alexis acting this way. She also didn't know if she should say anything at all because Alexis was grown and she could do what she wanted to do.

"Really?" Champagne asked, not really sure what else to say.

"Yes really." Alexis looked Champagne in the eyes and could tell she was holding something back. "Why are you looking like that?"

"Like what?" Champagne didn't think she was looking any kind of way. Yes, she was holding her tongue but she didn't think that was being relayed on her face.

"Tight."

"I apologize, girl. It's just that I'm surprised that's all. I just want you to be careful. I mean you don't know this man at all."

"The only way I can get to know him is to go out with him."

"I know, I know."

"What else is on your mind?" Alexis asked.

Might as well come out with it, Champagne thought. "Our friendship."

"What about our friendship?"

"I feel like it's changing. I feel like you haven't forgiven me for interfering in your love life."

Champagne watched as Alexis took a deep breath before speaking. She watched as Alexis reached her hand across the table and placed it on top of hers.

"It's not that I haven't forgiven you. It's just that I don't understand why Khalil's betrayal had to come out the way it did, at the airport around a ton of people. I don't understand why you would want to humiliate me that way."

"I'm so sorry about that Alexis. I wasn't thinking. I just knew that I didn't want you to be made a fool out of and I would do anything to keep that from happening. I do wish I would have handled it differently and if I could go back and do it again, I would. I just hope that this doesn't put a strain on our friendship. You mean so much to me."

"You mean a lot to me as well and it won't affect our friendship. You're still my sister in spirit. I just needed time."

They both stood up and hugged one another and told each other "I love you."

When they sat down, Alexis looked at her watch and said, "You know I can't stay too long. I've got to go shopping for my date Friday night."

*   *   *

Earlier that day, Alexis received a phone call from Shamel who told her he hadn't stopped thinking about her since they met.

"Oh you haven't, have you?" she asked, pleased to hear this.

"Can I take you out to dinner tonight?"

Since she didn't have any other plans for the evening she initially told him yes. But after some thought, she called him back and told him they could have dinner Friday.

"Okay, I'll pick you up."

Alexis told him that she'd meet him at the restaurant of her choice instead. There was no way she was going to let a man she just met pick her up at her house.

Alexis brought her attention back to Champagne, "Enough about me, let's talk about you and the wedding we need to start planning."

Now, that was a topic Champagne had been procrastinating on for quite some time. Yes, she wanted to marry Zyair and yes, she knew they had set a tentative date six months away but something was holding her back.

"What's up with the look?" Alexis asked.

"What look?"

"The tight-faced look," Alexis observed.

Champagne hadn't realized she was tight faced as Alexis so eloquently put it but she told her, "Girl, I'm scared."

"Of what?" Suddenly, it hit Alexis, "Are you scared to get married? You and Zyair have been together forever and I thought this is what you wanted. Shit at one time, you were stressed the hell out because you didn't think it was ever going to happen."

"I know, right?" Champagne shook her head. "I don't know what's up with me and this fear I have all of a sudden."

"Don't tell me you're having second thoughts."

Was this the time to tell Alexis what went down with her and Sharon? Was this the time to tell Alexis that she believed she was bisexual?

Champagne wanted to tell someone and who better than Alexis? She was keeping a secret from her best friend and wanted to share it. She needed to talk about the mixture of emotions. Her only fear was what Alexis would think. She recalled that at one time Alexis thought homosexuality was a sin but that was when she was an avid churchgoer. She also knew that although she thought this, Alexis had become more tolerant since learning that a couple of the teachers in her school were gay and even a few church members.

"I have something to tell you and I'm nervous about telling you. I'm afraid of your reaction."

"What could you possibly have to tell me that would make you nervous?"

Champagne opened her mouth to say the words and closed it. She wasn't sure whether to blurt it out or build up to it.

"Girl, now you're making me nervous, just say whatever the hell it is you have to say."

Champagne took a deep breath. "Remember when Zyair and I went to Hedonism, the all nude resort in Jamaica a few months ago?"

"Yes."

"And prior to me leaving, we joked about me and Zyair hooking up with other people?"

Alexis hoped Champagne wasn't going where she thought she was going with this. "What? You got with another man and now you want to leave Zyair?"

"That's not it."

"Then what is it?"

"I slept with a woman in Hedonism and I've been with someone since I've been home and I think I'm bisexual."

Alexis almost choked on her drink. "What the . . . What the hell are you talking about?"

"I've slept with a couple of women."

"I heard that part, I'm talking about the bisexual part. You need to explain that part to me!"

"What's there to explain? I'm attracted to women and men."

Alexis didn't know how she was supposed to react. This was not something she expected to hear. Hell, Champagne was her best friend and she would have thought that if Champagne had been feeling this way, she would have told her a long time ago.

Curious to know, Alexis asked, "How did this all happen? Are you sure you haven't just been experimenting?"

"'Girl, you know I'm in my thirties. I'm too old to experiment. "

"What about Zyair? Does he know about the women?"

"Yes."

Alexis' eyes opened wide, "He does?"

"He does." Champagne didn't feel the need to reveal everything and tell her how they went on the hunt for a female lover. She also didn't feel the need to tell her about Sharon and Candy and how once Zyair got his wish of observing her and another female, he realized he bit off more than he could chew. What she shared so far was enough.

"Wow." Alexis looked at Champagne stunned. "I don't know what to say. I don't even know if I should ask you any questions."

Champagne didn't say a word. She figured Alexis needed a second or two to adjust to what she just told her.

"Is this something new? How long have you been feeling this way?"

"I don't know girl. I'm wondering if it was always in me." Champagne paused. She was about to bring up something and she had no idea how Alexis would react. "Remember when we were younger and we used to mess around with each other?"

It was a memory Alexis tried to forget as she got older. So she said nothing, she just listened.

"Well, maybe I was bisexual back then."

Alexis had to laugh at that one. "All kids experiment, it doesn't mean anything."

"How do you know?" Champagne asked.

"You don't see me interested in women, do you?"

Champagne laughed also. "I guess not."

"Is that why you haven't started planning the wedding?" Alexis asked.

"I don't know." Champagne was ready to get married but she also wanted to do her thing, see where this whole being with women could go. She didn't feel like she was done with it and she didn't want to go behind Zyair's back and sleep around, but it was starting to look like she had no choice.

Champagne thought about Sharon, the woman she felt most connected to and how she would call her every now and then to invite her to lunch. Champagne kept putting it off until Sharon called her out on it.

"What's the deal? Why won't you meet me for lunch?"

"I've just been busy," Champagne lied.

Always one to be blunt, Sharon told her, "Don't lie. I think you're afraid of me."

"Afraid? Why would I be afraid?"

"You're afraid of your feelings, your desires, your wants, and maybe even your needs."

Sharon was right so Champagne kept silent.

"You see, your silence is my answer. I know I'm right."

"If you know you're right and if you know what I'm afraid of, then why keep calling?"

"Because I like you Champagne. Not just as a lover but as a friend and I was hoping that if we couldn't be anything else, then at least we could be friends."

So Champagne agreed to lunch the following week.

"I think maybe you're having some kind of mid-life crisis. My psychology books say sometimes it happens earlier than expected. Maybe you and Zyair need to take another vacation. Perhaps have a weekend getaway and talk about the whole marriage thing," Alexis offered in the form of advice.

"You think so?" Champagne asked.

"Yeah, I do."

"I just might take that suggestion," Champagne said knowing she was telling a bold-faced lie.

They both sat silent consumed in their thoughts, then they looked at one another and started to laugh.

"Girl, we're both a mess," Champagne said.

They continued to sit and talk for a while about nothing in particular until Alexis stood up. "I need to go shop before the stores close."

Champagne stood up too. "Call me."

"I'll do that." Alexis leaned over and kissed her on the cheek. "You make sure you talk to Zyair about what's on your mind. Shit or better yet, see that counselor you used to see, maybe she can help you sort things out."

"We'll see."

An hour and a half later after shopping Alexis was driving home. She reached over to get her cell phone out of her purse, when she felt someone hit the back of her car. She pressed on her brakes and looked out of her rearview mirror only to find that someone had run into the back of her.

"What the hell?" She turned her car off and opened her door. Before she could even climb out of her seat, the driver of the other car was standing by her door. He scared the mess out of her. *What if he's the one following me?* She instantly regretted opening her car door.

"I'm so sorry miss, are you okay?"

"I will be the second you back up and give me some space," she snapped.

"Is that really necessary?" he asked as he took a step back.

Alexis looked up to see who the hell this man was talking to. After all, he was the one that ran into her.

"How did you run into me? The light was red."

The man didn't answer. He just stood there staring at her through his sunglasses.

Alexis got out of her car and waved her hands in front of his face. "Hello, I'm talking to you. I asked you a question."

"Did you attend Seashore High?"

Alexis looked at him and tried to place the face. She was hesitant in answering yes.

"Alexis?"

She took one step back and looked him up and down. Whoever he was, he was handsome, but this wasn't the time to be checking someone out. She needed to see if there was any damage done to her car.

She stepped past him and walked to the back of her car, which was a black BMW M3.

"It's just a little scratch," he told her, "I'll take care of it."

I bet you will, Alexis thought to herself. She looked at him again and tried to place the face. Behind the shades he looked handsome. *But even handsome men are crazy.*

"You do look familiar," she told him, "but you know it's been over fifteen years since I've been in high school."

"Maybe this will refresh your memory," he told her as he took off his shades.

The second she saw his grey eyes, she knew who he was.

"Finn?"

"The one and only."

Alexis was more than surprised to see him. Hell, she'd heard he went to prison right out of high school. Not only was he an ex-convict who went to jail for armed robbery, but he was also her childhood crush. Alexis reached out to give him a hug and he hugged her back and held on to her a second too long.

After she pulled away, she looked him up and down. He was still in shape, *probably from the jailhouse workout* and he was dressed in a suit.

"You know this doesn't excuse the fact that you just ran into me?" she told him.

"I didn't expect it to, but like I said, I'll take care of it."

Alexis looked at her car and saw that there was a small scratch and a tiny dent.

A second later Finn was standing beside her. "Give me your contact information and I'll call you. We can get that fixed this week."

Alexis couldn't even be mad because she believed he would do just that.

"Let me give you my card," she told him, "and you give me your contact information and we'll go from there."

After exchanging information, he told her he'd call her that evening. She told him she wouldn't be around.

He then asked her if he could take her to dinner.

I don't think I can handle seeing another man right now. She had sex with Thomas, now she had a date with Shamel and was going to be meeting Maya's brother. "We'll see," she told him and walked back to the front of her car and climbed inside.

The second he pulled away, Alexis pulled out her cell phone and called Champagne. She got the answering service.

"Girl, you won't believe who just ran into me, literally. I'm talking about ran into the back of my car. Finn, girl! You remember fine ass Finn with the pretty eyes? Anyway, I'll call you later. Oh and don't worry, I'm fine. Love you."

Alexis hung up and continued to drive home while reminiscing about her first real tongue kiss and it just happened to be with Finn.

They were at a party at Shana Lewis' house. Shana was one of the most popular girls in school. Normally Alexis would not have been in-

vited to a party of hers but since she helped her pass several of her Algebra tests, Shana felt obligated to invite her.

That night as Alexis got ready for the party, she was nervous as hell because she knew if Shana was throwing a party, anybody who was somebody was bound to be there. That list of people included some of the girls she couldn't stand; the crew who thought they were the shit and took great pleasure in belittling others.

"It's going to be what it's going to be. If I have to smack a bitch, then I will," she told herself while getting dressed for the party. She even called Champagne to see if she could go with her but Champagne had to work.

"I don't think you should go," Champagne told her. She was afraid that it was a set up. "I'm going, if things get out of hand, I'll just leave."

"Well, you make sure you call me."

"I'll do that."

That night wasn't a bust. No one bothered her. She had a good time and got to kiss a boy.

About an hour later when Alexis returned home, she was surprised to see flowers on her porch. Thinking they were from Thomas, she smiled, walked over to them, bent over, pulled the card out and read it. "I'm watching you closely."

I'm watching you? What the hell does that mean? Alexis looked around to see if she saw anyone in the vicinity. Her heart was racing a mile a minute. Maybe her instinct was right and maybe what Champagne said was true, that she was being stalked. Again, she looked around. There was no one. She picked up the flowers and unlocked her door.

Alexis sat the flowers down on the table near the door and went into the kitchen to call Thomas. She placed her purse on the counter and dialed his number.

"Hello?"

"Hey, Thomas. It's Alexis."

"What's up baby?"

"Did you send me some flowers?"

Thomas hesitated in answering because he had not, and that meant some other man was trying to get her attention. "No. It wasn't me."

When Thomas told her no and said it wasn't him, it scared Alexis. For one, she didn't play that secret admirer shit and two; it scared the hell out of her. Just knowing that her intuition was right, that someone was following her and knew where she lived made her anxious.

"Hello?" Thomas said. "You still there?"

"I'm still here."

Thomas could hear something in her voice and whatever it was, he didn't like it. "What's wrong? What's going on?"

"I don't know."

"What do you mean you don't know?"

"Well, lately I've felt like someone's been following me."

"What! Who?"

"I don't know, and then when I arrived home

there were some flowers on my porch with a card that said, 'you are being watched' and there was no signature."

Thomas didn't like this at all. "What! I'm on my way over." Zyair had mentioned to him where she lived before and for this he was grateful.

Alexis liked the fact that Thomas was ready to jump up and come to her rescue. But what was he going to do, come look at the card and wonder who left it like she was did? There was no name or any information to indicate who sent it.

"That's okay. You don't have to do that."

"I know I don't have to, I want to."

"There's nothing you can do."

"I can look around."

Alexis could see that Thomas wasn't going to let up and she didn't want him to come all the way to her house for nothing.

"I said you don't have to do that." She made sure her tone implied that she was serious.

"Well, if you change your mind, just let me know."

"I will," she assured him.

"I got your message about dinner, how about Friday? Would you like to have dinner Friday?"

"I can't," she told him.

"You sure, I heard of this new restaurant and—"

Tired from the day and feeling thrown off because of the flowers, she told him, "Thomas, I'm not going to be home Friday night."

He didn't want to ask, he knew it wasn't his business but he couldn't stop himself. "May I ask you where you're going?" *Please don't let her say on a date.*

"I'm going out with a friend."

"A male friend?" Thomas knew he was acting like a pussy and he also knew that he wouldn't care if this was someone else, but it wasn't someone else, it was Alexis.

No sense in lying. "Yes," Alexis told him.

"Is that why you won't go out to dinner with me, because you're seeing someone else?"

Alexis told him that wasn't the reason. She couldn't go out with him tonight because she was exhausted and that during the week it was just a challenge, period, but that she did want to see him again.

"Well, you make sure you call me tomorrow so we can figure out what to do about us getting together." Thomas hoped he didn't sound as heartbroken as he felt. *Damn it. What is this girl doing to me?*

"I promise. I will."

The sincerity in Alexis' voice made Thomas feel a little better.

When they hung up the phone, Alexis sat down and thought about Thomas and her feelings for him.

She had to admit she was feeling him. The little time they spent together showed her who he really was and that was the opposite of what she thought.

Truth be told, Alexis could actually see the

two of them together as a couple but she wasn't ready for that just yet. Khalil had ruined it for other men. *Is that who's watching me? Is it Khalil?*

Alexis shook her head to get the thought out of it.

Chapter 10

Keep Your Eyes Open at All Times: You Never Know Who You Might Run Into

Friday finally arrived and as Alexis prepared for her date with Shamel, she admitted to herself she was a little nervous about going out with someone she just met. Hanging with and being around Thomas was one thing because he was part of her circle via Champagne but Shamel, well, that was another story.

What would they talk about over dinner? Would they click? Would she be comfortable around him? Was he going to try and get her to his house? Would she go? There were a million questions running through Alexis' head.

Get it together, girl. Don't worry about it, it's just a date. Enjoy yourself, make small talk and ask him questions about himself; men love that.

Alexis looked in her closet and pulled out the red wrap dress and her red stiletto boots that she'd purchased not too long ago. She showered, rubbed her body down with a vanilla body cream and got dressed. She wore her hair pulled back to show her face. She'd decided to let it grow down her back. Right now it was just a few inches past her shoulders when pressed. Alexis preferred to wear her hair natural. *Thank God it's naturally curly*, she thought as she looked in the mirror. Wearing her hair back also showed her cheekbones which were sharp like Angela Bassett's. Alexis liked to say they were from the same tribe. She then put on the diamond studs she'd just bought herself as well.

After she finished dressing, she looked in the mirror, liked what she saw and said, "The lady in red, that's what I am tonight, hot, on fire and ready to take on the world." Yes, she was trying to psych herself up and looking good was one way to do it.

Alexis and Shamel were going to meet at this new lounge/restaurant that just opened up downtown called, "Lovers Lane." To Alexis that was an odd name to call a lounge but hey, whatever worked for the owner worked for her.

It was almost 8:00 P.M. and she had to be there by 9:00 P.M. She was on her way and she would be on time, the question was would he be prompt as well.

As Alexis approached Lovers Lane she saw that they had valet parking. That suited her fine because it meant she wouldn't have to drive around looking for a place to park. She pulled up in front of the building and a young man walked up and pulled open the door.

The young man seemed surprised to see her, "Ms. Oliviá?"

She recognized his face and recalled that this would be his first year in college. She glanced at his name tag.

"Michael, how's college treating you?"

"It's all good. I probably would not have made it out of high school had it not been for you."

Hearing something like that is what made her job worth going to. That's why she did the type of work she did. She wanted to make a difference. Most times she didn't think that she was but hearing Michael's words told her she thought wrong.

"Thanks, sweetie, but all the credit goes to you."

She stepped out of the way so he could park her car and walked in the lounge.

From first glance it appeared to be full to capacity, but not to the point where the service might lack. There was a band playing that sounded like old school R&B in the back of the club on a small stage. A small number of people were dancing which was all that would be able to fit on the dance floor anyway. Even though the kitchen was upstairs along with seating for those who wanted dinner, Alexis could still smell the aroma of barbeque in the air.

Alexis glanced around and her eyes fell on Shamel at the bar. He was looking her way and smiled when she located him.

Am I going to have to walk up to him or is he going to come to me? Alexis' question was answered when he started walking her way.

She could tell he was taking her in from head to toe as she was him.

"You look dapper," she told him. The off-white linen slacks and shirt he wore made him look very put together.

"And you," he took her hand and kissed it, "you look beautiful." He released her hand. "Come on, let's go to our seat."

As they were moving from the front door, Alexis felt someone tap her on the shoulder. She turned around and saw that of all people, it was Thomas.

Did I tell him where I was going when I spoke with him earlier? She knew she didn't and she was certain he didn't follow her because from the time she hung up and got dressed there was no way he could have made it her house, so a coincidence this was.

"Thomas?"

Shamel turned around as well. They recognized one another immediately.

Shamel put out his hand. "Well, well, we just keep running into one another, us three."

Thomas, not wanting to seem like a jealous asshole, shook it. "Thomas," he said by way of introduction.

"Shamel."

Alexis just stood there looking from one to the other.

"Can I speak with you for a minute?" Thomas asked.

"She's on a date," Shamel told him.

"I'll let her come back."

Alexis frowned when she heard the word *let*. "You won't let me do anything. I'm a grown-ass woman and . . ." Before she went on, she looked at Shamel. "Please, just give me a minute." *Is he following me?* She hoped not. Thomas didn't strike her as that kind of man, but she was going to find out.

Shamel frowned. "This is the second time you've done this to me. Are we going to make this a habit?"

Alexis stood on her toes and kissed him gently on the lips, "Of course not. Please, just give us a minute."

Shamel decided to give her just that, especially after the kiss.

"One minute." He tapped his watch to let her know he meant it and took a couple of steps back.

Alexis turned toward Thomas, "Just what in the hell do you think you're doing?"

"You look sexy," Thomas told her.

"Are you the one following me?"

Thomas just looked at her.

"Well, are you?" she pressed.

"You'd really stand there and ask me that, when I was the one who offered to come rushing to your house because you thought you saw someone earlier?"

"It's just odd that I'm here meeting with Shamel and you're here as well."

"How many spots are there in this area for us?"

Alexis knew that "us" meant African Americans. "Well, I guess you're right."

"What's up with you kissing him, didn't y'all just meet?"

Alexis sighed and didn't bother answering. "You said you needed to talk. What Thomas? What do you need to talk to me about?"

He had to think of something quick. "About the flowers and the note that came to your house and about us."

"And you have to talk to me about that now and here?"

Thomas didn't answer. Alexis knew what he was doing. "You just don't like me being out with another man."

Thomas didn't even try to deny it. "You're right, I don't."

"But you do know you have no control over that."

"I know." Thomas looked over Alexis' shoulder and saw Shamel heading their way.

"Come home with me."

Alexis laughed gently. "We're not going there again."

Before Thomas could respond Shamel was up on them.

"Your minute is up," Shamel informed Alexis.

"Listen, you just be careful, okay, and promise to call me so I know you got home safe." Thomas told Alexis.

That was not a promise she was going to make. "How about I call you tomorrow instead?" Alexis responded.

"I'll be waiting," he told her before he walked away.

Shamel followed him with his eyes. "Do you and him have a thing going on?"

"No, we're just friends."

"Is it something I need to be concerned about?"

Alexis looked up at Shamel and asked, "Now why would you be concerned? After all, this is our first real date."

Shamel placed his hands around her waist and pulled her to him. "And I hope it won't be the last."

Alexis looked him in the eyes. "I'm sure it won't."

Shamel was still holding onto her when she told him, "You can release me now."

"Did you make reservations?" Shamel asked as he let her go.

Shit! Alexis knew she forgot to do something. "Oh my god, do you know I forgot."

"I'll see how long the wait will be."

Shamel walked away and when he returned a brief moment later he told her, "Forty-five minutes."

"Damn," Alexis said. "I apologize for forgetting."

"Listen, let's leave this place and go to my spot. I can order something for us to eat and have it delivered there."

"Are you sure?" Alexis asked.

"Yeah." Shamel nodded toward the right. "Plus, your boy can't seem to stop looking our way and I'm two seconds from stepping to him."

Alexis definitely didn't want that to happen. "What's your spot?"

"Dreams."

The only Dreams Alexis heard of was the strip club in North Jersey. "Are you talking about the strip club?"

"Yes."

Alexis took a step back and stared at him.

"Why are you staring at me like that?"

"You don't look like the type of brother that would own a strip club."

Shamel just laughed because he'd heard this before. "And what does that type of brother look like?" He knew that most people expected black men that own strip clubs to look like thugs or shifty characters but no, not him. He liked to keep his goatee tight at all times, have his hair cut low, almost bald and he stayed dressed in designer clothes. He liked for his style to speak volumes and money.

They were walking toward the door. "I don't know, but not like you. You look more like a . . . a . . . Actually, I don't know what you look like."

"I don't know whether I should be insulted or not."

"I'm definitely not insulting you."

They were outside and Michael approached them.

"Ms. Oliviá, you're leaving so soon?"

"That I am."

"I'll get your car."

When he walked away, Shamel looked at her. "You know him?"

"Yes, he was one of my students." During one

of their prior conversations, she'd told him her profession. "Shamel, is your club a dive?"

"Sweetie, do you really think I would own or associate myself with some bullshit?"

"That's just it, I don't know. Plus, I've never been to a strip club before."

"Don't worry. Dreams is classy and I have only the best-looking girls there with the best bodies."

"Do they show their coochies?"

"Not on the dance floor they don't. I have a rule and that's if the women choose to be nude, it's their choice but there's where it stops. There's no opening of the pussy or doing tricks with bottles and all the other shit that brought the riff raff in." What Shamel didn't tell her was whatever goes on in the back rooms was another thing altogether. What's done behind closed doors, stayed behind closed doors.

It was at that moment Michael drove up with her car and another young man was behind him in Shamel's car, which was a Mercedes G-class truck.

"Don't drive too fast," Alexis told him.

"Don't worry, I won't."

Less than a half hour later, they pulled up to Dreams. Every parking spot on the street was full as was the lot across the street. The only spots that were open were the two directly in front of the club. It was obvious that those two spots were for them. Shamel waved her into the first spot and then pulled in behind her. Before she could even turn off her engine, one of the bouncers was at her door assisting her out of the car.

Shamel was getting out of his car at the same time.

"What's up, boss?" the bouncer greeted.

"How's business?" Shamel asked.

"Busy as usual. A couple of troublemakers got out of hand but you know it was handled."

Shamel took Alexis' hand and together they walked in.

Alexis didn't know what to do when they first walked through the door. She didn't know where to look first. There were people everywhere. Near the bar, on the floor standing and sitting at the tables throughout the club. A couple of men were getting lap dances and there were two dancers on the stage.

On one hand she wanted to sit down and take it all in. On the other hand she felt like she wanted to place her hands over her eyes. She felt like she was somewhere she wasn't supposed to be, and seeing things she wasn't supposed to see. But that's how a good Christian lived. *Wow, I've really sheltered myself.*

Shamel was watching her look around. He wondered what she was thinking. Was she turned on, was she turned off or did it not bother her one way or the other? He couldn't tell from the look on her face.

"Come on. Let's go to the bar and get a drink. Then we'll go to my office and I'll have something delivered to eat."

Eating was the furthest thing from Alexis'

mind. She started to tell him this when she thought she saw someone that looked familiar getting on the stage.

Alexis hoped what she was seeing was not real. She knew something was going on with Shay but she would have never thought it was this. Shay was one of her students that seemed to be going through some changes. Alexis had summed it all up to hormones. Okay, maybe she was mistaken, after all there is someone that looks like everyone and hopefully this was the case.

"Alexis, you okay?" she heard Shamel ask.

She didn't answer. She took another look at the girl. *She looks just like her, I'm going to have to get closer to the stage and see if my eyes are fooling me.*

Alexis started to take a step away from Shamel. He stopped her by taking hold of her arm. "What's up? I'm trying to order you a drink and you're not paying me any mind. Again, are you okay?"

"I don't know."

"What do you mean you don't know?"

"I just see someone that's looks familiar."

"Really? Where?" Shamel glanced around the club to see who she could possibly know.

"The girl on stage." In her heart of hearts Alexis knew it was Shay but wanted to be in denial. She took in with her eyes what Shay was wearing and that's barely anything. All she had on was a white sheer G-string and a stringy looking bra that barely covered her nipples. She also had on tons of makeup to obviously make herself look older. Alexis watched as she moved her hips in a circular motion that suggested and hinted at a good time, maybe even the best time of a man's life.

"Who? Diamond?"

Alexis looked at him, "Is that what she calls herself?"

"Yeah, why? She's one of our best dancers," he told her.

"I also think she's one of my students."

Shamel put down the drink he was holding and told the bartender, "Pour it out, I'll be back."

He took Alexis' hand. "Let's go in the back."

Alexis looked at the stage once again before following Shamel into the back where his office was located.

Once inside he closed the door. "Have a seat."

Alexis looked around and saw that he had four mid-sized screens on the wall. Showing on the screens was the stage; the front door and what looked like two rooms inside the club. "You always know what's going on huh?"

"Sweetie, you have to in this line of business. You never know when someone is going to try to get out of hand. I don't want any trouble and I don't take any bullshit." He pulled open his desk drawer and pressed a button, the screen with the view of the stage got closer.

"Is that your girl?" Shamel asked.

Alexis looked at the screen and saw that her eyes weren't playing tricks on her, it was Shay. "Yes, yes it is."

Shamel shook his head. "Damn." He picked

up his phone and told someone to have Diamond come into his office when she left the stage. "I didn't know she was underage," he told Alexis.

Alexis looked at the screen again and seeing Shay up there naked and gyrating, she could see why Shamel would have no idea she was underage. The way these teenagers looked today was a damn shame. Sometimes there was no way to tell their age unless you asked for identification.

"Have a seat," Shamel told her as he sat behind his desk.

Alexis sat in the chair across from him. She felt like she was being interviewed with the way he was looking at her.

"Why are you looking at me like that?"

"Because you are a beautiful woman."

Just like any other female, Alexis appreciated the comment. "Thank you."

Relaxing back in his seat, Shamel asked her, "So, tell me, how come a lady like you doesn't have a man?"

What was she supposed to say? Should she tell him the last one she had ended up being married, a pimp and dishonest. "I just recently got out of a relationship."

"What happened?"

Before Alexis could respond there was a knock on the door.

Alexis could feel her heart racing; she figured it was going to be Shay.

"Come in," Shamel said as he looked toward the door.

Alexis didn't turn around and face the door. As much as she wanted to, she figured her face shouldn't be the first one Shay saw.

The door opened and in walked Shay wearing a robe. "You wanted to see me?" Shay glanced at the back of the woman's head that was facing Shamel.

"Yes, as a matter-of-fact I did."

Shay was standing between the door and Alexis. "Yes?"

Not one to beat around the bush, Shamel asked her, "How old are you?"

"Huh?" That was the last thing Shay expected to be asked.

"I asked how old are you?"

"I'm twenty," Shay replied with a straight face.

On that note Alexis turned around.

The look on Shay's face when she saw who was sitting in the chair could only be described as shocked, embarrassed and busted. "Ms. . . . Ms. . . . ." Shay couldn't even get it out.

Alexis stood up and with disappointment in her voice said, "Shay, what are you doing?" Shay tried to get her emotions together. Alexis asked again, "What are you doing?"

Shamel wasn't saying a word. He was just sitting back letting the scene play out.

Shay looked from Shamel to Alexis. What was there to say, she knew she was busted. She knew she could not lie about her age with her school counselor sitting right there but what she felt she could do was act indignant.

"It's none of your business what I'm doing

here. What I do outside of school is my personal business. You don't run my life. I do what I have to do."

Alexis knew Shay was acting ignorant because there was nothing else she could do, so she let her have her moment. Shamel was just the opposite, he wasn't hearing it.

"Well, it is my business," he told Shay/ Diamond, "and you've jeopardized it by being here. What I think you need to do is leave, bounce, get your shit and go."

"Please Shamel. You know I need this job." If Alexis wasn't sitting there, Shay would have been willing to give him her body for exchange. Yes, she could go be a stripper somewhere else but she would not be treated the same. Here at Dreams the girls were treated with respect by the clientele, if not, they were thrown out.

"You know damn well, I don't play that underage shit in my club. As a matter-of-fact, if any of the other girls are underage, you need to let them know, I will find out over the next couple of days. I am not trying to have the cops run all up in my shit."

Shay looked at Alexis with so much hatred that it threw Alexis off. She couldn't understand where that look was coming from. All she'd done in the past was try to help her, to be there for her, to offer advice from time to time. When she did, it appeared that it was appreciated. Alexis wondered again what was going on in Shay's life, if there was something in the family that was disrupting everything. Even though the look made her pause, what the look didn't do was stop her from standing up and walking toward Shay.

"What's going on Shay? Why do you need this job so bad?"

Alexis noticed that Shay was tearing up. This was a sure sign that something was definitely not right in Shay's life. Shay wasn't one of those students that showed emotion. If anything, she was one of the girls that walked around with attitude all on her face, one of the girls who appeared to be frowning even when they weren't.

"I ain't telling you my business," Shay told her but didn't move. After all, she felt that Alexis should know what's up. They'd had enough counseling sessions in the past.

Shamel was looking at both of them. He decided he should leave them alone but not before giving Shay a look that Alexis caught. *What was that look about?*

He stood up. "You know what? I'll be right back."

They watched him leave the room. Once he closed the door behind him. Alexis turned toward Shay and asked her, "So, do you want to tell me what's going on? Why you need to work in a place like this?"

"Again, it's not any of your business." Shay turned her back toward Alexis but again didn't leave the room.

"Obviously you need someone to talk to or you would have left the room by now."

Shay said nothing.

"Listen," Alexis stepped in front of her so

that they were face to face. "We can talk now or we can talk later."

Shay brushed past her and walked out.

Alexis turned and sat back down. She looked at one of the screens and noticed Shamel talking to Shay who appeared to be pleading. *Why would she plead to be a stripper?* Alexis wondered. She knew she wasn't going to be able to let this go and that was because she knew that Shay had potential. If a student stayed in school nowadays it was because they wanted to at least try, even if it was half-heartedly. At least that's what Alexis wanted to believe.

When Shamel returned, Alexis asked him, "What did she say?"

"It's not important. What's important is that she's leaving the premises."

"But I'm worried about her."

Shamel stood in front of Alexis and pulled her up and into him. She didn't fight it. "This is our night. Let's focus on getting to know one another and then tomorrow when we aren't together you can focus on Diamond, Shay or whatever her name is."

Feeling the closeness and the heat that was flowing from Shamel, Alexis could only agree. After all, she was out to have a good time and this was her first night in a strip club and she wanted to make the most of it.

"Do you want to get something to eat?"

The last thing that was on Alexis' mind was eating. What she wanted to do was go out and explore the club. "Not really, I want a tour of the club. I want to see what's behind those closed doors I saw when we came to your office."

What was behind those doors were private parties and private lap dances. "I can show you on the screen but you have to keep it between you and me," Shamel told her.

"Of course, but let's go out on the floor first. I want to check out the dancers up close."

"Come on," he told her and she followed him out of the door.

"Where do you want to sit, at a table, the bar, or a booth?"

Alexis looked around. Most of the tables and seats surrounding the bar were full, so she chose a booth. They not only looked comfortable but they also were located on the side of the stage where she could see mostly everything.

Shamel waited for Alexis to sit down and he slid in next to her. "I might leave you here a time or two. There are a couple of things I have to take care of. Is that okay? Would you mind?"

"Not at all," she told him.

"The dancer that's coming up next, her name is Blue. At least I know she's old enough to work here."

"After Shay, how can you be so sure?"

"Because she's one of my boys' wife."

"Get the hell out of here. He doesn't have a problem with his wife being a stripper?"

"When they met she was a stripper. Of course he tried to change her mind but she wasn't hearing it. She loves what she does."

Alexis looked at the stage and the second Blue walked on the stage, Alexis felt herself get moist. *Oh hell no, this is not happening.* Alexis could feel her heart racing. This shit had never happened to her before. The little incidents Champagne reminded her of; not that she'd ever forgotten, she just chose to push them so deep and so far away from her mind that it didn't' mean anything—didn't count. Why the hell was her pussy getting wet over a female? Was it because of what Champagne had told her? Was it because she told herself that she was now a new woman ready to make changes? Well hell, that change didn't include being attracted to women.

Okay, okay, just because she was sitting here getting wet, didn't mean she was ready to sex down a female. It just meant her libido was up. At least that's what she wanted it to mean. Because now she was thinking about something she hadn't thought about in years. As a matter-of-fact; decades. She tried to put out of her mind the times she and Champagne used to play around with each other. After all they were in their preteens and early teens. She didn't think it really counted. She did wonder what would have happened had they been caught. By that she meant touching each other, lying on top of each other hunching and fingering each other. It was their secret then and it was their secret now and a secret it would stay.

Alexis watched Blue as she bent over while wearing a thong and noticed that on each of her ass cheeks were butterfly wings. She was entranced as Blue made them clap and made it appear as if the butterflies were flying. She watched as Blue stood up, faced their direction and placed her hands on her breasts. Alexis found herself wanting to reach out and touch. Hell, she wanted to experience a lap dance. However, wanting something and getting it were two different things. She wasn't ready for that.

Alexis turned to face Shamel only to find him watching her intently.

"Why are you looking at me like that?"

"You like Blue?"

"What?"

"You were so intense when you were watching her."

Damn, Alexis didn't think she was going to be that easy to read. "I think she's sexy." Those words were not supposed to come out of her mouth.

"Want me to call her over here?"

She wanted to say yes but was afraid to. What would happen if he did call her over? Would everyone look their way?

"You can always go into one of the rooms."

She really wanted to experience this moment to the fullest but she just couldn't bring herself to admit it out loud. At least not here while she was supposed to be on a date.

"No, you don't have to do that. As a matter-of-fact, I'm ready for the tour of the club."

Shamel stood and helped her up. "Come on, I'll show you around."

Before they got far, Alexis heard someone say

her name. She and Shamel turned around. It was Finn.

"Finn, hi." Alexis gave him a hug.

"Wow, I didn't expect to see you here," he told her.

Shamel cleared his throat.

Alexis turned to face Shamel. "Oh, I'm sorry. Shamel, this is Finn, an old friend."

Shamel knew who Finn was; he'd thrown him out a time or two. As a matter-of-fact, Shamel wondered what he was during there now, he was told not to come back up in there.

They gave one another the head nod.

"I haven't heard from you about your car. I told you I'd get it fixed for you."

"I know. I planned on calling you this week actually. I've just been so busy." Actually she hadn't been thinking about it at all. She was going to take care of it herself. She didn't feel like dealing with him asking her out and her having to turn him down. Two and possibly three men were enough. There was that, plus the armed robbery charge that scared the mess out of her.

Shamel placed his hand on the small of Alexis' back and it did not go unnoticed by Finn. "You ready?"

"I'll call you this week, okay."

Finn looked at Shamel who was shooting daggers. He wasn't stupid; he knew that meant to get the hell out of the spot. "Make sure you do that. I always pay my debts."

"I will." Alexis turned to walk away but stopped when Finn said her name again. "Yes."

He couldn't help himself, so he asked her, "Can I get another hug?"

Shamel stepped in front of Alexis, "Get the fuck out of here."

Finn started laughing, turned and left.

"Damn Shamel, was it that serious?" Alexis asked.

"How well do you know him?"

She had to admit not well, she hadn't seen him in quite some time.

"Well, I don't think you should get to know him any better. He's trouble and I've had to deal with him on a number of occasions."

Alexis thought about what Champagne said when she told her to be careful and that there are some crazy men out there.

"What debt is he talking about?" Shamel asked.

"He hit my car the other day and he's going to get it fixed."

"I have someone that can do that for you."

Alexis didn't bother responding to that. It was something she was going to have to think about. Although she'd told herself she was going to "get what was hers," she was well aware that to men, when they did something for you that required their finances it became something else. It was almost like you owed them and she needed to figure out a way to get it and not feel obligated. So she told him instead that she was ready for her tour of the club.

Take her around he did. Dreams was bigger than it appeared and it was obviously upscale and done in good taste. There were several rooms and only a few were empty. There was a room where people were just sitting and having conversation. There was a cigar room, a room where what appeared to be a bachelor party was going on, but she wanted to see more. Alexis was shocking herself because all of a sudden she felt like a voyeur.

Alexis turned to Shamel, "Let's go back in your office. I want to see what's going on in one of the rooms where the door is closed."

"You sure about that?" Shamel asked. She'd already told him this was her first time at a strip club and he didn't want to run her off.

"I'm sure," Alexis told him.

"Okay, but I have to tell you, it be some shit going down in those rooms."

"I understand that."

"And you also need to understand that whatever you see stays here."

"I understand that also."

Shamel didn't normally do this, let someone look at what was for his eyes only. Only a few knew that he had cameras everywhere except the bathrooms and those who knew wouldn't say a word because they feared him. The reason he was doing it now was because he was hoping it would lead to them being physical.

There was something about Alexis that turned him on the first day they met. Normally, if a female walked away from him to talk to another man, he would have embarrassed her ass and his, but this time he didn't. He let it slide because he wanted to see her again.

Later that night his boy even called him out on it. "Man, you let that girl play you. That ain't you, what's going on?"

"Ain't shit going on, there's something about her, something different about her."

Of course True wasn't trying to hear that. "Ain't nothing different about no pussy. Pussy is pussy. The end."

Normally that would have been true but for the first time in his life, he was feeling like he wanted more with a woman and not just to fuck her. Don't get it twisted, he did want sex but he also wanted more.

Oh shit, does that mean I'm ready to settle down? Shamel wondered. In a way he thought he was. After all, he was in his mid-thirties. He was ready to have kids and when he looked at Alexis, not only was she so fine that he knew their babies would come out pretty but she also had a head on her shoulders. There was also a quiet innocence about her. He'd been around enough women to know a thing or two. He was more than capable of reading them and summing them up.

Once they were in his office, he closed and locked the door. Alexis sat down and waited anxiously with her heart racing.

Shamel walked behind his desk, turned on the screen, opened a drawer and pressed some buttons. All four screens came on. One obviously was on the main floor. Another showed a man getting a lap dance. One showed a group of women in a room together with a couple of dancers. The last room was one of a stripper sitting across from a male patron. They appeared to be talking and she appeared to be rubbing his dick through his pants. Alexis didn't know what to focus on.

"I'll be right back," Shamel told her.

Alexis just nodded as she watched the screen with the woman and man. She wanted to see how far it would go. She wanted to ask Shamel if he had sound so that she could hear what they were saying but she held back.

"Want me to turn it up?" Shamel asked.

Damn, is he reading my mind? "Yes." *I wonder what he's thinking? Is he thinking I'm a freak?*

"Which screen?" He already knew which one because she couldn't take her eyes off it. It was the one with Jada and one of her regulars. Shamel knew that some of his girls did extras for the patrons but that was their choice. It wasn't something he asked them to do, they did it because they wanted to and those extras included anything from masturbating, to touching and sucking. There were even a couple of the girls who let the men eat them out. Jada was one of the girls that had a special talent when it came to her mouth. He knew because he'd experienced it a time or two.

"The one with the woman and man." Alexis continued to watch as the woman stood up and started circling him.

"That's Jada," Shamel told Alexis as he walked out of the office.

Jada was now behind the man and she asked him, "What do you want me to do?"

"You know what I want you to do," he told her and he started to unzip his pants.

Jada placed one of her hands on top of his. "Not so fast. What's the hurry?"

"Come on girl, stop playing."

She stepped in front of him.

"You want me to suck your dick," she told him. "That's all you ever want me to do."

"That's because you do it so well." The man reached for his zipper again and Jada pushed his hands away.

"Let me do it." She got on her knees and started to unzip his pants as she licked her lips.

Alexis was all into it, she had forgotten about the other screens.

Jada unzipped his pants, reached inside and pulled his dick out. She then got on her knees.

"Damn! I always forget how big you are."

Alexis noticed it too.

"And thick," Jada said as she licked the head like a lollipop.

"Let me pull my pants down some," the man said.

"No. I want your dick only. Not your balls but this right here," Jada told him as she gripped his dick and took the whole thing in her mouth.

Alexis couldn't believe what she was seeing as Jada's mouth went down the whole length and width of him and came back up. Alexis wanted to put her hands on her pussy so bad but she knew she couldn't because Shamel could come back into the office any minute. *Am*

I really sitting here watching this and getting turned on? Alexis was shocking herself. Watching other people have sex was not something she was into and it definitely wasn't something she'd thought she'd ever be into, but now she knew not to say ever or never. In the past, she'd never even considered watching porn, now she might give it a second thought.

Alexis watched as Jada slowly licked the man's dick, taking it all in. She watched as Jada licked and sucked on the head of it as the man closed his eyes. She watched as he threw his head back and tried to push Jada's head down.

Jada pulled his pants down farther and told the man to spread his legs. "I changed my mind," she said as she started licking his balls and placing both of them in her mouth.

Alexis watched as the man raised his ass up off the chair and she could feel her mouth water from the excitement.

Alexis was so busy watching Jada that she didn't hear Shamel enter the room.

"She's good isn't she?" he asked causing Alexis to almost fall out of her chair.

She turned around, looked at him and almost choked out the words, "Yes, yes she is."

"Have you ever watched someone do this before?"

"No, this is my first time."

"Well, you might want to turn back around and watch her make him come."

Alexis didn't want to continue watching in front of him but she couldn't help herself, she was drawn in. She turned back around and

watched as Jada moved her head up and down
the length of his penis. When she got to the top
she'd lick around the head of it and go back
down. The man started moving his hips up and
down. It looked like he was trying to push his
dick down her throat.

"I'm going to come," he told her.

Alexis wondered what Jada was going to do.
She didn't have to wonder long because suddenly Jada replaced her mouth with one of her
hands and cupped the other to catch the semen
as it flowed out.

Shamel was standing behind Alexis rubbing
on her shoulders. Alexis was trying to catch her
breath. Shamel was giving her time.

When she got up the nerves to, she turned
and looked at him. "I can't believe I just watched
that. I'm embarrassed."

Shamel stood in front of her and she let him
pull her up. "Ain't nothing to be embarrassed
about." They were standing so close to each other,
Alexis could feel the need for sex radiating off
their bodies. *I'm a whore . . . I'm a whore,* Alexis
couldn't help but think to herself. *Okay, I know
I'm being ridiculous but it's like all of a sudden
my libido is out of whack.* Alexis wondered if
making love with Thomas had opened up a
whole new world for her. Or had she always
been a freak in disguise?

"How do you deal with seeing this every day?
Does it excite you or are you immune to it?"

"It depends on the moment."

"What do you mean?"

Shamel placed his hands on Alexis' waist and

pulled her into him. She could feel that he was hard. "I mean like now, watching you watch them and get excited turned me on."

It was at this point that Alexis asked herself how far she wanted to go and the truth was she didn't know.

Alexis cleared her throat and took a small step back.

"Am I making you uncomfortable?"

Alexis looked up at him and he could see that a kiss was coming.

Shamel normally didn't kiss, it wasn't his thing. He always thought kissing was for wifey, only this time he did. He bent his face down to meet hers, while pulling her back into him and placing his mouth on hers. He let her lead the kiss and was surprised at how much he enjoyed it.

When they finally broke apart, Alexis looked at him and told him, "I should go."

"Why?"

"Because I might do something I'll regret."

"Why would you regret it? I'm grown. You're grown. We can do what we want to do."

Alexis hesitated before answering. "This is true but it can wait. We can wait."

To Shamel that meant she had already made up her mind to let him make love to her. It was a known fact that a woman knows almost immediately if she's going to allow a man inside her and it appeared Alexis was.

"I understand," he told her, "but you don't have to leave."

Alexis shook her head, "No, I think I'd better leave."

Shamel looked at one of the screens and spotted Shay still in the club. "All right, I understand. Let me walk you out."

Alexis stepped back and let him lead the way while thinking, *what the hell am I getting myself into?*

Chapter 11

Let the Haters Hate: They're Just Mad Because They Know Your Power

Saturday finally arrived and Alexis was exhausted. Between seeing Thomas the week before and then hanging out with Shamel at Dreams the day before, she'd had a busy two weeks. And, it wasn't slowing down. This was the night she was going to Maya's for the book club meeting and Maya's brother was supposed to show up. Truth be told, Alexis didn't feel up to dealing with another man. Two were enough.

She had an hour left before her day was over. She wanted to hit the gym and call the contact numbers for Shay. She wasn't calling to reveal what she'd learned about Shay. She was going to say she was calling because Shay had not come to school with the hopes of speaking to her. Alexis needed to find out what was going on and if there was anything she could do.

Alexis picked up the phone and dialed the

main number that was on file. It said it was the house phone. She wasn't surprised when there wasn't a ring and she heard the operator saying the number was disconnected. She hung up and tried the other number, which said it was the number of an uncle. That number was also disconnected.

Alexis now had to make a decision. Was she going to take the next step and drive to the address that was in the files or was she going to let it go. Before she could make up her mind there was a knock on the door.

"Come in," Alexis called out.

In walked Victoria, one of her favorite students. Victoria was on the honor roll for the first time that school year. She was a sophomore trying her hardest to get a scholarship. So when she walked through the door with a long face, Alexis was concerned.

"Hey sweetie, what's wrong?"

Victoria plopped down in the chair in front of her desk. "My mom is driving me crazy."

This was nothing new to Alexis. Most mothers drove their teenage daughters crazy. "Why, what's going on?"

"I don't know. She's been talking about killing herself and killing this man she used to see."

"She actually said that, those were her exact words?" As a therapist whenever Alexis heard the word suicide or whenever someone hinted around about it, she knew to be alarmed and she knew it was a call for help.

"Yes, and I don't know what to do about it."

"Do you know what man she's talking about?"

"I have an idea but she won't really say. All I know is she's scaring me and I need you to go speak with her."

"Me?" What the hell was Alexis going to say to a grown-ass woman? All she could do was give Victoria a number for her mother to call and a card of a woman who would actually come to their house.

"Please Ms. Oliviá . . . Please will you talk to my mother?"

"That's not what I do Victoria. I don't counsel parents, I counsel teenagers. I can refer you to someone else."

"So you're just going let my mother kill her- self."

Alexis wasn't stupid. She knew what Victoria was trying to do. She was trying to guilt her but that wasn't going to happen. "No, what I am going to do is call a friend of mine that special- izes in this kind of thing and have her call you."

"But I'm asking for your help."

Shit, this was the kind of thing that came with the job. She knew that she would come across parents who had less sense than their kids but that wasn't her fight. Her fight was for the kids.

Alexis opened her desk and pulled out a card, she handed it to Victoria. "Call her and tell her what's going on with your mother. She can help you."

Victoria didn't even bother to answer. She just snatched the card out of her hand and marched out of the office, slamming the door behind her.

Alexis did feel bad about it, but what else was she suppose to do? She had over 500 students a year that she dealt with. If she stepped in and dealt with the parents when they had their issues as well as their children, she wouldn't have a life. If she did it for one, she would have to do it for everyone. That's why she had referrals and other numbers she could give the students. Especially when there was something going on in their life that someone else could deal with better.

Yes, she'd call the home and check on the student. Yes, she'd talk to the students when and if they were pregnant and needed to make decisions, such as having a baby or having an abortion. Of course she didn't make the decision for them. She just listened and yes, she'd gone to rehab centers with students to support them when they first entered but that was different; that was a part of her job.

There was another knock on the door interrupting her thoughts. Alexis did not have the energy for another dramatic scene.

"Come in." She called out bracing herself and was relieved when she saw that it was Maya.

"Girl, what the hell is wrong with Victoria? She's in the hall calling you all kind of bitches."

Alexis just shook her head and waved her hand as if to say, *girl please.* Plus it wasn't her place to tell the business of students. "You know these kids when you don't do something they want you to do."

"Don't I know it. Just the other day, my student Tina—"

Alexis interrupted her mid-sentence. She didn't feel like hearing it. "Is the book club meeting still on?"

"Yeah, I came to give you my address." Maya placed a piece of paper on Alexis' desk. "Call me if you have any trouble finding my house."

"That's what MapQuest is for," Alexis told her.

"I know that's right." Maya turned to leave but stopped. "Don't forget my brother is going to stop by."

"I won't forget." Alexis really didn't feel like doing this but she made a promise. She was so glad she invited Champagne.

It was finally time to leave work. Alexis had just enough time to hit the gym for an hour, go home, shower, and call her father.

As a matter-of-fact, right now the person Alexis most wanted to see was her daddy. He'd called her the other night and sounded kind of down. When she asked him what was wrong, he told her nothing, but she didn't believe him; she could hear something in his voice. After all, she was his "baby girl" as he liked to call her and she was his only child.

Alexis' parents divorced once she graduated from college. That was something she didn't understand, why wait until then. If you were unhappy prior, you should have divorced sooner.

When she asked her mother about it, her mother told her, "We still love each other; we're just not in love with each other sweetie. We grew apart a long time ago."

When she asked her father, he told her, "Baby, sometimes people know when it's time to let go and move on. We've known it for quite some time but we wanted to make sure you would be okay."

She had to admit, even though she didn't understand, she was grateful they waited to divorce. Because had they done it when she was in high school, she might have starting acting like a wild child. Had they done it while she was in college, she might have flunked out because she would have been worried about both of them.

She spoke to her mother who lived in Georgia about once every week but she spoke to her dad who resided in Florida more often. That wasn't anything new because even as a youngster, she went to her dad about most things. They were close and she loved it. Sometimes she even thought her mom was a bit jealous.

Alexis picked up the phone to call him then hung up. She decided to wait until she had some real time to talk. She didn't want to rush through a phone call with her daddy. Actually, a phone call wasn't good enough. She was going to make plans to go see him. She was even considering telling him about Khalil but he'd wonder why she never mentioned him in the first place. She wondered the same thing. Was it because she knew something was off? Perhaps.

* * *

An hour later Alexis was at the gym. She'd just left the locker room after changing and was headed toward the treadmill. She planned on doing twenty-five minutes on the treadmill, elliptical and stair master, and then she was out. Accelerated Sports was a new gym that had just opened up a little over a year ago. It was a predominantly white gym and almost everyone there was either fit or close to it. That's why she chose this gym, it motivated her. She also chose it because she didn't think she would be harassed by men trying to hook up like they did at her old gym.

The second she stepped on the treadmill, she felt someone tap her on the shoulder. Alexis turned around only to find Khalil staring in her face. The last time she saw him was the week before at the club.

"Go away," she told him as her heart raced.

"I need to talk to you."

The last thing Alexis felt like doing was talking to or seeing Khalil's face. She was not in the mood. "Khalil, there is nothing for us to talk about."

He wasn't going to give up that easily. "Please, just ten minutes, that's all I'm asking."

Alexis didn't know what to do. She could tell him to go away again and if he didn't she could always cause a scene. But what would that do other than embarrass herself. She could leave the gym or she could hear him out to try and get some closure.

She chose the closure. "Ten minutes," she told him with her hands on her hips.

"Well, can we at least leave the floor and go in the café?"

"No." Alexis looked at her watch. "The clock is ticking."

Khalil saw that he had no choice but to say what he had to standing right there and he had no problem doing that. After all, he really cared for Alexis when they were together. His intent wasn't to hurt her or play her. Actually, he didn't know what his intent was. When he first met Alexis, he was seriously feeling her. His wife Suzette had left him and was begging to come back home. At first he was on the prowl, then he started considering it, then he realized he didn't want to be with her anymore anyway.

According to Suzette, she went to find herself. To him, that meant it was over. No, they hadn't divorced but in his mind they weren't together. Shit, his whole marriage was a sham. He met Suzette at a damn swingers club. Her family came from money, she was willing to share it and she gave good head. What was he to do other than take advantage of the opportunity? Hell, she proposed to him, it wasn't the other way around.

Khalil knew he was wrong for proposing to Alexis while legally he was still married but he wanted her to himself. That was the only way he figured he could guarantee it. When he and Alexis came back from their trip to Cancun, his plan was to hunt Suzette down and divorce her ass. That Thomas motherfucker got to her first and ruined everything by revealing the marriage before he had a chance to.

Eventually Khalil was going to make sure that Zyair and Thomas got theirs. He wasn't stupid. He knew they were boys and he knew Thomas was into Alexis. He knew that even though Zyair was the one who brought Suzette to the airport that Thomas was behind it. However, for now, he wanted to try and make Alexis understand and maybe even forgive him.

"I'm waiting," Alexis said, interrupting his thoughts.

"Alexis, please I need more than ten minutes."

Alexis tried to walk past him. She was no longer in the mood for a workout.

"All right, all right," Khalil said. "First off, I want to apologize for hurting you. I didn't mean to. I was in the process of getting divorced when we met."

"And you couldn't tell me that," Alexis said.

"I was afraid you wouldn't want to date me."

"Were you afraid I wouldn't date you or were you unsure as to whether or not I was going to give you the ass?"

Khalil was taken aback by what she said.

"You know Khalil, you hurt me, plain and simple. You weren't man enough to be honest with me then, why should I think you're being honest with me now?"

Khalil reached for her arm but she snatched it back. "All I'm saying is I apologize and that I want to make it up to you. You never gave me a chance to explain my situation. You wouldn't take my calls—"

Alexis cut him off. "Answer me one question."

"Anything."

"Are you still married?"

Khalil hesitated a second too long because Alexis placed her hands on his chest and pushed him back. "That's what I thought."

She walked away and this time Khalil didn't bother stopping her because he knew it wouldn't make a difference. However, he was not going to give up that easily.

"I will get her ass back, one way or the other," he said out loud.

Chapter 12

Obsession and Love Are Not That Far Apart

Thomas and Zyair were sitting in Thomas' office. They were going out to shoot pool with the boys but there were a couple of things Thomas had to settle. One of his clients had gotten themselves arrested on a DUI. Although his attorney was able to keep him from being locked up, Thomas had to see to it that his client handled the press the correct way and not end up acting like an asshole. That was something a lot of his clients that were young did; acted a fool. It was like money made them three things; cocky, crazy, and overconfident.

Into the phone, Thomas said, "I'm not even going to ask you if you were drinking and driving, because I already know the answer." It was going to be one of the two answers they almost always gave; *I only had one or two drinks or I don't know why they pulled me over.* It was always one excuse after the other. Well at least this one didn't do what another one of his clients did a few months back; try to switch seats with his passenger real quick. There is no "real quick" in climbing over someone when you're damn near seven feet tall.

"Tomorrow you're going to issue a statement I'm putting together, donate some money to a charity, and we're going to move on from there."

Thomas listened to what his client had to say, which must not have been much because a few seconds later he'd hung up the phone.

Zyair just shook his head. "I don't know how you do it."

"I do it for the money," he half joked. Thomas loved his job. He loved anything sports related. He loved being able to help young men make it and of course he loved the financial rewards that came with it.

"And that makes your job much easier, huh?"

"And you know this." Thomas shut down his computer. "Let's get out of here."

"Man, aren't you going to loosen up some? You all in a tie and shit. We're going to play pool remember."

"Yeah, I remember. What? You think I forgot? I'll be right back." Thomas always kept a couple of sets of clothing at his office in the closet. His office also consisted of a private bathroom, a conference room and a small kitchen with a seating area. He also had two people that worked for him, a receptionist and an assistant.

* * *

When they stepped outside, Thomas noticed that Zyair was following him. "Where did you park?" he asked Zyair.

"I had my driver drop me off. I figured we could ride together," Zyair told him.

"How do you know I don't have plans afterward?" Thomas had tried earlier to reach Alexis with no luck.

Zyair stopped in his tracks. "Oh shit, my bad, I didn't even think about that. I'll call my driver."

Thomas bumped Zyair's shoulder with his. "Man, I'm just playing with your ass. You don't have to call your 'driver'."

"Did you think this would be us?" Zyair asked.

Thomas had no idea what he was talking about. "That what would be us?"

"That we would be two successful black men." Although Zyair didn't come from the streets, both his parents who were deceased had worked and left him with the restaurant business, he was proud of that fact that he'd made it into the success it was on his own. He knew they would be proud of him. His father wanted him to be a responsible man and that's just what he was.

Thomas looked at Zyair and smiled. "Hell yeah, I knew it. Shit, I didn't know how it was going to happen or when it was going to happen, but I knew it."

"Really?" Zyair wasn't asking in disbelief. He was asking because even though Thomas had confidence oozing out of his pores when they were in college, it seemed like when they were first starting their businesses everything was a struggle for them both. To make one another feel better they would quote to each other Frederick Douglass who said, "Without struggle there is no progress."

"Yep, that's why I tried so hard. I knew eventually it would pay off."

"I hear that," Zyair said. Zyair knew of Thomas' meager beginnings. After all, he was his best friend; therefore he knew that Thomas beat the odds.

As they were putting on their seat belts, Thomas said, "But you know what?"

"What?"

"There was a time when as long as I had money, as long as I could buy whatever I wanted and whoever I wanted, I was happy, but that's getting old man. I'm ready to settle down and be with one woman and share what I have with one woman."

"And you want that woman to be Alexis?"

"I do, man. I sure do."

"What is it about her, man? You've been feeling her for a couple of years. She never gave you the time of the day, yet, that didn't deter you. I'm trying to figure out what kind of voodoo she put on your ass."

Thomas laughed. "Nah man, there's just something about her that gets me going."

Zyair didn't respond, because although Alexis was fine, he knew that in the past Thomas' women were finer, sexier, and more experienced.

They drove the rest of the way to the pool hall in silence, each consumed with his own thoughts.

Zyair was thinking about what transpired the night before, when Champagne's cell phone was going off. She was in the bathroom taking a shower and normally he would just let it buzz. But for some reason, a reason he still couldn't put his finger on, he picked it up and saw *missed call.* He knew he should have just put the phone back down but he couldn't stop himself. He pressed the button to see who it was. On *received calls* Sharon's name showed up over four times.

Why the hell is she calling my woman so much? Champagne told me they rarely speak and here she's called her four times in one day.

Zyair couldn't decide if he wanted to bring it up and ask her what the deal was because then she'd know he'd been snooping.

When Champagne came out of the bathroom, she didn't even bother to look at her phone. She was looking so sexy in one of his T-shirts that he decided to leave it alone, at least until after they made love. And, the way he was going to make love to her, if she even had an inkling of wanting another woman, it wouldn't be for long. Sometimes he regretted sharing the fantasy of seeing her with another woman because seeing how much she enjoyed it brought up some insecurities he wasn't even aware of.

"Come here," he told her.

Champagne was able to tell by his voice that it was about to be on. "Why?" she teased.

"I want to taste you."

Zyair didn't have to say another word, because the next thing you know, Champagne was lying on the bed, legs spread and ready to go.

Zyair laughed. "Aren't you eager?"

"I've been thinking about this all day actually."

I wonder why? Is it because of Sharon? Zyair wondered as he pushed Champagne's legs apart and bent his head down between her thighs to take in her scent.

Champagne grabbed his head as she tried to force his face into her pussy, but Zyair resisted. He continued to kiss and nibble on her thighs.

"Stop playing," Champagne told him.

Zyair snickered and placed his tongue on the inside of her labia, running his tongue up and down. He then pressed his chin on the bottom of her pussy, applying pressure. He knew that drove her crazy. Then he put his tongue as deep inside her pussy as he could.

Champagne's hips started shaking and he knew that his tongue had hit one of her spots. He pressed on the spot with his tongue and then brought the tip of his tongue to her clitoris. Zyair knew that the clitoris had hundreds of nerves so he licked her clitoris from underneath to the tip and back underneath.

Champagne tried to grab his head and pull his mouth off her. "I don't want to come yet."

Zyair wasn't listening. He was in control and

he planned on staying in control. He grabbed ahold of her wrist and held on tight until he felt her body begin to buckle. He knew the time was near, so he placed one of his fingers inside her just barely. He moved it in and out and continued to lick.

"I'm about to come!" Champagne moaned.

Zyair waited until he could feel her juices flowing down his chin. When she finished quivering he looked up at her, smiled and thought to himself, *Ain't no need for a woman. Shit, I am the man.*

Chapter 13

Follow Your Gut Instinct (you never know where it may lead you). It Might Take You Right Where You Need To Be

When they pulled into the neighborhood, Alexis couldn't help but wonder how Maya could afford to live in an upscale area on a teacher's salary. Baldwin Estates homes started at 300 thousand dollars. Alexis looked around and noticed that most of the driveways were empty. She wondered if everyone was out running errands on a Saturday afternoon. Normally that's what she did, especially when it was warm outside. Fall was here and winter was just around the corner. Alexis quickly wondered if she'd have someone to cuddle up with in the winter.

"Damn, your girl must have it going on," Champagne said.

"I know right. I wonder how she does it?"

"Shit, ask her."

"Now you know I don't be all up in people's business like that."

Champagne was looking at the house numbers. "There it is right there." She was pointing straight ahead toward a brick home that from the outside if one had to guess was over 2500 square feet.

"Damn, her shit looks better than mine," Alexis noted as she parked the car.

"You sure this girl is cool?" Champagne wanted to know, "because you know how women are, especially when they don't know you."

"Girl, don't start with that. That's the problem right there with us women. We talk about one another instead of to one another. We're suspicious on each other instead of being—"

"Oh Lord, there you go on with your sisterhood, can't we all just get along speech."

Alexis laughed and opened her car door, "Girl, come on."

As they walked up the walkway, Champagne asked her if she'd talked to Thomas lately.

"Yes, we talk briefly almost every other day."

"And?"

"And nothing, we're just friends."

"Well, according to Zyair, he wants to be more."

Changing the subject, Alexis told Champagne what transpired between her and Khalil at the gym.

"He's such an asshole. Don't get caught up in his web again girl."

That was something Alexis didn't have any intention on doing.

It was at that moment that the front door opened. Standing before them was one of the finest, yet thuggish men Alexis had seen in a long time. He was over six feet tall and had on a white T-shirt that fit so you could see every muscle, every cut and some of the packs on his stomach. His hair was in cornrows and his face hairless. His complexion was like chocolate and just as smooth.

"And there she is," he greeted them. "Just the lady I wanted to meet."

He pulled Alexis into him giving her a hug, which caught her by surprise. In the meantime, Champagne was standing there wondering what the hell was going on and who was this fine specimen standing before them.

"And you," he pulled Champagne into his arms giving her a hug as well. "I won't leave you out."

After he finished giving out hugs, he ushered them in.

"I take it you're the brother," Alexis said.

"Gavin," he told her.

"Champagne", Champagne said, "and it's obvious you know that this is Alexis."

Alexis nudged Champagne.

"They're having the meeting in the living room. It's straight ahead. Alexis, I'll speak with you afterward."

Alexis and Champagne watched him walk off. All Champagne could say was "Wow."

When they entered the living room, all the women looked up. Alexis did a quick count of twelve and that included Maya who was walking up to them. "Everyone, this is my coworker, Alexis and . . ." She looked at Champagne, who told them her name. "Alexis and Champagne, this is everyone. Y'all can introduce yourselves."

Everyone went around the room and introduced themselves. Maya noticed a couple of women from work but there were several she didn't know. As the introductions took place, Maya took in the room. It was obvious "Black Pride" was in abundance. There were paintings of Malcolm X, President Barack Obama, and Langston Hughes on the wall. There was a bookshelf that didn't have a space left on it. Finger foods were on a table that was against the wall along with a few bottles of wine and juice.

Alexis and Champagne listened as Maya proceeded to give a rundown on the procedures for the meeting. She asked Alexis if she had a chance to read the book, *Sister Girls 2* by Angel M. Hunter.

The truth was she hadn't had a chance to finish it, with her busy schedule and all.

"I started it but didn't get an opportunity to finish."

"I read all of it," Champagne told them.

Alexis looked at Champagne, "You didn't tell me you finished it."

"Was I supposed to?" Champagne joked.

"When did you have time?"

"I didn't have to make that much time. It was a quick read. I read it in like two days."

"Good, then let's get started," Maya said.

An hour and a half later, when they were wrapping up, Alexis was surprised to how much she enjoyed the meeting. Even though she hadn't read the full book, she now intended to read the first *Sister Girls* and *Sister Girls 2*. From what she could tell, the books focused on friendship and overcoming obstacles that most women may have had; obstacles such as rape, drug addiction, single parenthood, and their sexuality.

It was also obvious that Champagne had enjoyed herself as well because she was standing with a few women on the other side of the room deep in conversation.

Just as Alexis was about to walk up to them, she felt someone tap her on the shoulder.

"Hey beautiful." It was Gavin, Maya's brother. "Come in the kitchen and talk to me."

Alexis looked in Champagne's direction. She wasn't paying her any mind, so Alexis followed Gavin into the kitchen. At first glance he reminded her of Morris Chestnut, chocolate, muscular and intense looking with a pretty-ass smile.

Once inside, he poured himself some orange juice and asked Alexis if she wanted something to drink.

"No, thank you."

"So, my sister told you I wanted to meet you?"

"Yes."

"And you decided to come."

"Yes." *Damn, why is that all I'm saying?*

"Why?"

"Why what?"

"Why did you decide to come?"

What kind of question is that? "Because I had nothing better to do," she told him with a smirk.

"Damn, it's like that?"

"Well, don't ask a question you might not want the answer to."

"Duly noted."

They sat there for a few seconds looking at one another.

"How old are you?" Alexis asked breaking the silence.

"Old enough."

"No, for real."

"Does it matter?"

"Yeah, it matters."

"I'm twenty-nine."

Had Alexis been drinking she would have choked. She turned to walk away.

"Where are you going?"

"I can't go out with you. You're too young for me."

"You're in your thirties right?

"Yeah." She was thirty-two.

"Then what's the big deal? Age ain't nothing but a number and I can do just as much if not more for you than a man twice my age."

"Oh really?" Alexis was feeling his boldness. She didn't know about this dating a younger man thing. Even though it was only by a few years, she still wasn't feeling it. She felt like younger men had to be tolerated a little more and she didn't have the energy to do that. However, he was so good-looking she was willing to hear him out.

"Let me take you out one time and if you don't enjoy my company then you don't ever have to see me again."

"Oh, there you are." Champagne walked in the kitchen. "You ready?"

Gavin didn't let her answer. "So what's it going to be?"

"Let me get your number and I'll think about it."

He reached in his pocket and pulled out a card. He opened one of the drawers in the kitchen, got a pen and wrote down a number on the back. He handed the card to Alexis. "This is my personal number. Call me with your decision sooner rather than later. I'm not a man that's waits around."

"I'll do that."

Once Champagne and Alexis were in the car, Champagne asked what was up with Gavin.

"Nothing. He saw a picture of me and asked Maya to introduce us."

"Damn girl, look at you. Thomas, Shamel and now Gavin. You're on a roll."

Alexis didn't respond, she was too busy asking herself what the hell was she doing. This wasn't her. Although she was trying to be this bad bitch, did she really want to be that person?

"Just be careful sweetie, because there are some crazy-ass men out there," Champagne told her as she'd told her a time or two before.

"You ain't said nothing but a word."

Chapter 14

A Day with Someone Special Can Make Up for a Week of Hell

It was Sunday and Alexis didn't have any plans. All she wanted to do was relax. Maybe she would read *Sister Girls* and go to the movies. It was going to be a day just for her. The past couple of weeks had been hectic. She'd had a few dates, busted one of her students working as a stripper and had to deal with an irate student. She deserved a day of doing nothing.

After grabbing her book and cell phone off the kitchen table, Alexis went and sat on her porch, in her rocking chair. Just as she was getting comfortable, her cell phone rang.

She looked at the caller ID. It was Thomas.

"Hey there."

"What's up beautiful?" Thomas asked.

"Nothing. Just sitting on the porch reading."

"Are you doing anything today?"

"Nope, and I don't plan on doing anything. Today is my day for me."

"Well, you have to eat, let me take you to lunch."

Alexis hesitated because she really didn't intend to leave the house at all. She wondered if he sensed this.

"How about I bring you lunch instead?"

That suggestion perked Alexis right up. "Now that sounds like a good idea," she told him.

"What would you like?"

Alexis had no idea what she wanted so she told him to surprise her.

"What's a good time to come by?"

Yes, today was supposed to be a day by herself but like Thomas said, she had to eat. Alexis looked at her watch. It was just 11am. "Come around 1:00 pm." That would give her enough time to read a couple of chapters and take a shower.

After hanging up, Alexis gave herself one hour to read. That was hard to do considering her mind kept drifting to Shay. She'd made the decision to go by her apartment. The thing is she didn't want to go alone. Shay lived in "The Grove," which was a bad neighborhood and you just never knew what could happen. The drive to get there was around thirty minutes. The second you turned the corner in the neighborhood, you knew you were in a place where you had to be careful. The houses looked run-down. People stood on corners looking for the next customer to sell drugs to. The apartment buildings and the yards were unkempt. All over the place, there was trash, graffiti, bottles, and other signs of people not caring. Alexis knew this because when started working at West Park High, she drove around to the neighborhoods of the kids she would be counseling, to get a sense of their background.

I'll wait and see if she comes to school Monday and if not, I'll have Champagne or someone go with me.

A few chapters and a shower later, Thomas knocked on the screen door.

When Alexis went to let him in, she saw that he was carrying a picnic basket.

"What's this?" she asked as she led him to the kitchen. "We're having a picnic?"

"Yes, right in your kitchen," he told her as he placed the basket on the counter.

"So what's inside?" Alexis was starving.

"Can I have a hug first?"

She gave him one and took in his scent. "You smell good," she complimented. "What is that?"

"It's an oil I bought from some Muslim guy. It's called Blue Nile."

"I like it."

"I'll pick you up some." Thomas opened the basket and pulled out a bottle of Moscato wine.

"I love that wine."

"I know." He knew because he called Champagne and asked her what type of food and wines Alexis liked. He then pulled out some containers.

"Can I look inside?" Alexis asked.

"Of course."

When Alexis opened them, she saw that he'd brought a cucumber, tomato and cheese salad, with what smelled like sun-dried tomato dressing, some sort of quiche and there were a couple of slices of cake. She took a sniff and could tell immediately that it was her favorite kind, lemon.

"Okay, you need to tell me how you knew that Moscato is my favorite wine along with lemon cake and quiche."

"I have contacts," he told her.

"And do those contacts include someone named Champagne and Zyair?"

Thomas threw up his hands, "You got me."

Alexis was touched that he put this much effort into their lunch date and impressed that he did it in under two hours. She walked around the table and gave him a quick kiss on the lips.

"What was that for?" Thomas asked, pleased that he'd scored some points.

"It's for being thoughtful. You sit down while I set the table."

Thomas looked around and told her, "Your kitchen is so . . . so—"

"So white?" Alexis finished the thought for him. It's something most people commented on when they came over. Her cabinets were white, her floor was white, her refrigerator was white and her accessories were white.

"That and clean. It's so crisp looking, I'd be afraid to cook in here."

Alexis laughed, "Oh believe me, I cook. Maybe not often enough, but when it's just you, there's really no need to, especially when you can just pick stuff up and throw it in the microwave or go out and eat."

"I know just what you mean, I eat out often and I have to tell you, I'd love a home-cooked meal every now and then, by someone other than myself."

"I'll take that into consideration," Alexis teased. "Sit down," she told him again.

Thomas did just that. He sat and watched as Alexis set the table and made their plates. They made small talk while eating but Thomas could tell something was on Alexis' mind.

"So, what's going on?" Thomas asked.

"Nothing."

"Are you sure?" Thomas wasn't easily fooled.

"Well, actually there is something going on but not with me. It's with two of my students."

"You care to share?"

"Well, one of my students came into my office and asked me to talk to her mom because she believes she's suicidal over a man and the other I found out is a stripper."

"Wow. How did you find out about the one that's a stripper."

Did Alexis really want to tell him about her going with Shamel? She didn't think so. "It doesn't matter, what does matter is that she is and when I confronted her, she walked out on me and hasn't been to school since. I'm concerned. I'm almost thinking about going to her house to see what's up."

"You don't think that's a bit much? The way these teenagers are today, you can't tell them shit, they know more than us."

"I know but I still feel like I need to do something. The only thing is where she lives is not a welcoming area. It's the hood of all hoods."

"Where does she live?"

"In The Grove."

"Oh hell no, you will not be going into that neighborhood by yourself. Should you decide to go, I'm going with you."

That was all Alexis needed to hear. "All right, then let's go."

"Today?"

"Why not?" Although the plan was to do nothing, she might as well do something productive and meaningful.

Before Thomas could respond, his cell phone went off. "Excuse me," he told her as he unhooked it from his belt.

"I'll be right back," Alexis told him and walked out of the kitchen to go to the bathroom.

When she was reentering the kitchen, she heard Thomas saying, "I asked you not to call me anymore and I mean that shit," then he hung up.

"Someone stalking you?" Alexis asked.

"It's this female I used to see. She'll call, then she'll stop calling for a while and then it starts up all over again."

"Block her number from your phone," Alexis told him.

Thomas looked at her and frowned.

"What?"

"I don't know why I didn't think of that shit."

"That's what we women are for, to give you men the answers."

Thomas stepped toward Alexis and pulled her into him. "I can't believe I'm finally spending time with you."

"Well, believe it," she told him.

"Can I kiss you?"

"Yes, you can do more than that if you want to."

Thomas stepped back and looked at her.

"Just not today," she teased.

"Girl, don't play with me like that. Shit, I was ready."

"I bet you were. Let me go get my bag and put some shoes on so we can go."

"Go where?"

"The Grove."

Thomas looked at his watch. He didn't think she really meant doing it today. He'd made plans with his boys to play basketball around 4 pm.

"What? You have other plans?" Alexis asked.

"I did but I can postpone for you."

"You don't have to do that."

"I want to."

"Damn, you're racking up the points today."

Thomas hoped so. He was trying his damnest to be sensitive, caring, and attentive. This was a new experience for him, but hell, he'd do whatever it took to win Alexis over.

Thomas called Zyair and told him to let the others know that either he'd be late getting to the gym or he wasn't going to make it.

"It's going that good?" Zyair asked him. They'd spoken earlier that day when Thomas called to find out what types of food Alexis liked.

"I'm going to run an errand with her."

Zyair thought this was the funniest thing he'd heard in a long time. He could not stop laughing.

"What's so funny?"

"You man, being all domestic and shit."

"Whatever," Thomas told him, and hung up.

A half an hour later they parked in front of the building Alexis had on record for Shay. The appearance of the outside had not changed much. It still looked dingy and worn. The graffiti or tags as some called it were still everywhere.

"You sure you want to get this involved?" Thomas asked.

Alexis' answer was to start walking toward the building. Thomas followed behind her while making sure he was aware of all that was around him. What that consisted of was young wannabe thugs hanging on the corners and on the bench that was in front of the building. It was obvious some of them were drug dealers.

Little did either of them know that right across the street was one of Shamel's boys. He recognized Alexis from when she came to Dreams. He quickly pulled out his cell phone and dialed Shamel up.

Alexis and Thomas were now in the building, looking for apartment 3B. When they found it, Thomas stood close behind her as she knocked on the door.

"Who the fuck is it?" someone on the other side of the door yelled.

Alexis looked at Thomas, who said to her, "What's the girl's name?"

"Shay."

"I said who the fuck is it?" the person yelled again.

"We're looking for Shay," Thomas yelled back.

The door swung open and standing before them was a woman that was drunk as hell. You could smell the liquor coming out of her pores.

"Don't no Shay live here."

"Are you sure?" Alexis asked.

"What the fuck? You think I don't know who lives in my damn house."

"This is the address I have for her miss."

"Well, it's the wrong fucking address," she told them and slammed the door in their faces.

Alexis looked up at Thomas who took her hand. "Come on. Let's get the hell out of here."

When they were walking out of the building, Shamel's boy watched their every movement and he made sure to snap a picture with his cell phone.

When they pulled off, he called Shamel and all he got was a voice mail. He left a message telling him the honey he was with at the strip club was in The Grove with some other dude.

Chapter 15

People Are Not Who They Seem All The Time (but they are always who they tell and show you they are).

Shamel was sitting a few houses down from Alexis'. It didn't take much to find out where she lived. He had Michael, the guy who set up the computers in his establishment search her name on the Internet. Not only did Michael find out where she lived but he found out her credit score, her history, who her parents were and a whole bunch of other shit.

This was not Shamel's style, to be stalking a female. To him, he wasn't stalking her. To stalk a woman was to scare her, to leave her notes, to threaten her. He wasn't doing any of that, he was just staking his claim and trying to find out as much about her as he could. Was he becoming obsessed with her, he wondered? Maybe, but he had set it in his mind to make her his and for her to be the mother of his children. He'd even dreamed it and as a believer that dreams often had a meaning, he'd decided to put it into action.

A couple of days ago, his boy called him and told him that he saw Alexis in The Grove. Later he showed him a picture that he snapped. When he saw the picture of the dude she was with, he recognized him as that Thomas character.

This motherfucker was getting on his last nerve popping up everywhere. Not only that, but Shamel wanted to know what the hell was she doing at The Grove. That used to be his old stomping ground when everything he did was illegal but since he was now on the up and up, it was his boys' spot.

Shamel also found out some information on Thomas; found out he was a well-known sports agent and not a fuckup like he was hoping. He was going to have to come up with some sort of plan to get him out of the picture. Shamel wanted Alexis to himself. He was not one to share.

Because he'd been watching her for a few days he learned her schedule and knew that she would be home shortly. He had one of his boys farther down the block waiting for her car to turn the corner and when she was close by, the plan was for him to go set flowers, candy, and a teddy bear on the porch. He would be walking away when she pulled up.

His cell phone beeped, there was a text message from his boy, *Now, now, go now.* Shamel got out of his car with gifts in hand and placed them on the stairs. He could hear her car pull up into the driveway. He wondered what she was thinking when he turned around and they were looking at one another through the windshield.

What she was thinking was *what the hell?* Alexis didn't recall telling him where she lived, but just because she didn't recall it doesn't mean she didn't do it.

The thing is she didn't like him showing up uninvited. Something about that didn't sit right with her. Her inner alarm was going off especially since she sensed someone following her. Should she call the police she wondered? But what would they do, she had no evidence that it was Shamel, Thomas, or anyone else. All she had was her intuition. Alexis looked at Shamel and noticed he was smiling. He didn't look threatening or like he'd come to do her harm. So she made the decision to trust him and turned off the engine, grabbed her purse off the floor and climbed out of the car.

Shamel noticed that she did not look happy to see him.

"What are you doing here?" she asked him.

"I thought I'd bring you a gift." He moved to the right and she noticed the flowers, candy, and teddy bear on the porch.

Alexis would not have taken Shamel to do something so sweet and she almost swooned but first she needed to let him know that she didn't like pop-up visits.

Before she could say a word Shamel told her, "Listen, I apologize for showing up unannounced. I just wanted to surprise you. When we talked the other day you sounded stressed."

Well, he wasn't lying about that, she was stressed. Shay still hadn't come to school. Alexis was starting to feel like she was missing and that concerned her. Victoria also came by her office again asking for her help.

"I have been," she told him as she walked around him to pick up the flowers. Like almost every woman on the face of this earth, she loved receiving flowers. She placed them up to her face and took a sniff. "Although I don't like when people just pop up, because you came bearing gifts, I'm going to allow you to come in."

"Let me." Shamel took the flowers out of her hand and picked up the candy and the bear while she opened the door and he followed her inside.

"How did you find my house? I don't remember telling you."

"You did during one of our conversations," Shamel lied.

Alexis accepted it as the truth because she just might have.

"Have a seat. I'm going to go throw on something more comfortable."

Shamel sat down in the living room and waited for her to return while looking around. He noticed that she liked neutral colors and didn't like clutter. On the coffee table were numerous books that appeared unread. One in particular caught his eye. The title was *The Art of Seduction*. He glanced through it and before he knew it Alexis had returned wearing leggings and a T-shirt.

"You have a nice place here," he told her.

"Thanks. Do you want anything to drink?"

"Like what?"

"Well, I have some wine and cognac."

"Cognac? What are you doing with cognac?" Shamel wondered if it belonged to that Thomas fellow, if he was the one she originally bought it for.

"It's my dad's."

He was glad to hear that, although he hoped it wasn't a lie. "I'll take some cognac."

"I'll be right back," she told him and returned shortly with a glass of wine for her and cognac on ice for him.

She sat next to him.

Shamel picked up *The Art of Seduction*. "Interesting read," he acknowledged.

"I just bought it, I haven't had a chance to read it yet. Actually, I just bought all those books." She handed him his drink.

"So you like to read?"

"I just joined a book club. I'm trying to catch up with them."

Shamel took a sip of his drink, draped his arm around her and turned to face her. "So, tell me what has you so stressed?"

"Shay."

"Diamond?"

"The one and only. Since that night I busted her at your club, she hasn't been to school."

"I'm still bugging over that fact that she's in high school," Shamel said.

"I even went to her house to talk to her."

"You did? Where does she live?"

"In The Grove."

So that explains why she was there. "Did you go alone?"

"No, a good friend went with me."

He already knew who that good friend was but knew not to push.

"Have you seen her? Has she come back to the club?" Alexis asked.

Actually, she came back the next day and pleaded with him to give her another chance. There was no way in hell he could do that, especially now with Alexis being in his life. "No, I haven't seen her since that night either." Shamel had other uses for Shay. Alexis didn't need to know that. The only person that needed to know was Shay and he let her know that prior to her leaving the club the night after the confrontation.

"I'm really thinking about calling the police and reporting her missing. The apartment I went to, 3B, the drunk-ass woman who answered the door all but cursed me out and said she doesn't live there. I don't know if I believe her."

He was going to remember that number, "3B" and have someone check it out.

Alexis was surprised to see that she had drunk her whole glass of wine. *Damn, did I gulp it?* "I'm going to get another glass of wine. As a matter-of-fact, I'll bring the bottle in here."

She wasn't acting like she wanted him to leave and that pleased him. When she came back in the room she was carrying the wine and the cognac. To him, this meant make yourself comfortable.

After she put the bottles down, she picked up the remote control and sat down, while turning the television on.

"So Mr. Shamel, tell me about yourself."

"Haven't I done that already?" After all, they have spoken on the phone numerous times.

"You told me surface stuff. I want to go deeper."

"Let's do this, you ask me a question and I'll ask you one." Shamel wasn't one to tell all his business.

"So, you're into games?" Alexis teased.

With seduction in his voice, he told her, "It depends on what kind of game you're talking about."

"Have you ever been in love?" was her first question.

The only time Shamel could remember being in love was when he was around seventeen. The girl's name was Melena. They broke up when she got pregnant and went against his wishes and aborted the baby. For the first few weeks before she'd made the decision to abort, Shamel thought he was being attentive but she told him he was smothering her. Smothering her? He asked her how could she say such a thing, after all, he just wanted to take care of her and the baby. That's not what Melena felt he was doing; she felt that he was crowding her; that he was being controlling. When she woke up, he wanted her to call him. If she didn't by nine o'clock, he'd call her, and then proceed to call her every three to four hours. If he didn't reach her, he'd just pop up. Her parents started to become concerned

*about him and questioned her. When she re-
vealed that she was pregnant, it was her father
who pointed out that if he was acting like he
owned her now, how did she think he would act
once she had the baby?*

*When Melena tried to talk to Shamel about it,
he lost control and grabbed her and yoked her up.
It's when she felt that he could become violent
that she decided she could not have the baby. Of
course, she didn't tell him of her decision. It's
when her mother took her to the clinic that he
found out. Little did she know, one of his home-
boys was following her. When he figured out
where she was going, he called Shamel who
barged into the clinic and caused a scene that
was so frightening to the other young women
that were there, they called the police. Afraid of
what he would do to her, Melena's parents placed a
restraining order on him and she tried to stay as
far away from him as possible.*

*There was also one other time a few years ago
when he was in deep like and lust and what he
thought was love with this chick named Lavonne. Now years later he knew that it was the
sex that had him bugging out. She put it on him
and did things with and to him that no other girl
had done up to that point. She licked his ass,
swallowed his come like it was water and even
let him have her anally whenever he wanted to.
He was strung out and thought she was too because she was so open to him sexually. It wasn't
until she told him that she wanted to see other
people that he lost his mind. He beat her so bad
that she ended up in the hospital. Because by*

then, he'd been in trouble with the law and was not about to go to jail, he told her if she told anyone it was him who put her there, he would ruin not only her life but her brother's, who was a drug runner for him. Of course she didn't tell and after she got out of the hospital she moved and convinced her brother to move with her.

That was an incident he put out of his mind and it was also one he was not going to share.

"Yes," he answered, "I was in love once when I was a teenager."

"What happened?"

"We were young. She got pregnant and had an abortion when I begged her not to."

"So you broke up with her because of that."

"That and other reasons." This was not something Shamel felt comfortable talking about, so he asked her, "What about you, have you ever been in love?"

Alexis was on her third glass of wine. She knew she needed to slow down, but she was not only stressed the hell out but tense as well. She rolled her shoulders and placed her hand on her neck and started to rub.

"Let me do that for you," Shamel volunteered.

Not one to turn down a massage, she did just that.

Shamel stood up, went behind the couch and started rubbing on her shoulders. "So have you?"

For a second there Alexis forgot the question. She really didn't want to go into the whole Khalil thing, but because Shamel was working magic with his hands, she found herself telling him about how they were engaged and she found out he was already married. "Remember the night we first met?" she asked him.

"How could I forget?"

"Well, he was in the club that night."

"Not that Thomas character?"

"No, the other guy."

Shamel recalled all that had happened that night and knew who she was talking about because he'd seen him in his club after that incident.

The longer he massaged her neck and shoulders and the more wine she drank, the more Alexis found herself getting relaxed.

"How come you don't have any kids now?" She'd asked him that question during one of their phone conversations. She was surprised to hear him say no.

"I don't know. After my high school sweetheart got pregnant, it just never happened again." There was an alleged pregnancy but once the baby was born, he had a blood test done only to find out that it wasn't his. He came close to beating the female's ass for trying to play him like that.

"Can you have kids?" Alexis asked.

Shamel didn't even bother to answer that question because it was something even he didn't want to think about. He's a man and he was positive that there were a number of kids swimming around in his sperm.

"Let's talk about something else," he told her as he moved his hands down her back.

Alexis closed her eyes, "Well, what do you want to talk about?"

"Let's talk about how you like to be made love to."

She kept her eyes closed and asked him, "Why should I tell you?"

"I'd think you'd want me to know."

"Why is that?"

"Because when we make love, I'll already know your likes and dislikes."

Alexis still had her eyes closed. "So, you think we're going to do it?" she joked.

"Honestly?" Shamel asked growing serious.

Alexis opened her eyes, "Yes, honestly."

"Yes, I do."

Alexis moved his hands off her shoulder and looked up at him. She knew he was right and was considering letting it happen today.

For some reason, she was getting turned on. Was it the wine? Was it his hands? Or was it the situation and his bluntness? Her body was screaming *yes, make love to me now* but her mind was saying, *slow down, you're getting out of hand*.

In the past her mind would have won out but the past was no more, this was the new aggressive Alexis. The Alexis that wanted to do what the hell she wanted to and not be afraid. The Alexis who if she wanted to sleep with one, two, or three men, she could do so. She didn't give a damn what or how anyone else thought, said or felt.

"Come sit next to me," Alexis told him. She'd

made up her mind about sleeping with him but she wanted to be as honest with him as possible. She didn't want him to think that their getting physical meant she was his exclusively. She didn't want to mislead anyone.

"What's up?" Shamel was aware that her mood had shifted slightly.

"If we decide to make love, it doesn't mean we are a couple." Alexis decided to be blunt with it, to keep it as real as possible.

That's what you think, Shamel thought to himself but said out loud, "I'm not a young kid. I know sex does not equal a relationship." After his experience with Lavonne, with other women and with him being thirty-five, he wasn't slow. He was intelligent enough to know this but it wasn't going to stop him from pursuing Alexis.

"I'm just letting you know because I'm not ready to be in anything serious. I want to date, I want to be free to be me and do me. I don't want to have to answer to anyone and you really need to know that."

Shamel put his finger against her lips. "Shhhh, we're not kids. I think we can handle whatever comes our way."

He moved in closer and waited for her to move closer before he initiated a kiss.

"Do you have any condoms with you?" Alexis asked.

"They're in my wallet in the car. Don't move, I'll go get them and I'll be right back."

"I'll go freshen up while you run out."

Shamel stood up, "Don't change your mind,"

he said it as though he were joking but he wasn't, he was serious as hell.

Once Alexis heard the door close, she ran to her room and picked up the phone. She dialed Champagne's number. She wanted someone to talk some sense into her because she knew she was out of control but she wasn't having any luck with this phone call.

She put the phone back down and went into her bathroom. She stood in front of the mirror and stared at herself. "Do you really know what you're doing? Do you really know what you're getting yourself into?" she wondered out loud. "Well, it's too late to back out now."

"Alexis?" Shamel called out. He'd just walked back in the house.

"I'll be out in a second," she called out.

"How about I come to you?"

For a reason that she couldn't explain even to herself, she didn't want to invite him into her bedroom, which was odd because she was inviting him into her body. "No, I'll be right out. Make yourself comfortable."

He was doing just that. He took off his shoes and relaxed onto the couch, but not before he poured himself a shot of cognac and downed it.

"Hey there," Alexis said as she walked into the room this time wearing short-shorts and a camisole.

To have sex this time of day was different for Shamel. It was early evening and sexually he was a night man. When he went out to his car to get the condoms, he popped one of his "just in case" pills. The pill that promised to keep your dick hard longer than usual. Not that he needed it but for Alexis he wanted to put it down and let her know he was a man of stamina.

Shamel patted his lap and Alexis took the hint and sat there. She must have had a look on her face because he asked her, "What's wrong, are you nervous?"

She was just that because getting with someone new was always nerve wracking. "Shut up and kiss me," she told him.

He was more than happy to oblige. Alexis turned to straddle him, her breasts touching his chest. He had his hands on her ass and pulled her pelvis into him, so she could feel how hard he was.

Alexis knew she needed to slow this whole process down, but she couldn't. She was too turned on. She started to grind up against him as they kissed deeper. Shamel moved his hands from her ass to her breasts. He started sucking on her nipples through her shirt.

"Take it off me," she told him.

Once it was off, he placed his mouth on her nipples again and nibbled, a little too hard. She pulled away, stood up and pulled off her shorts. He stood up, took the condoms out of his pocket, pulled his shirt over his head and his pants down as Alexis watched.

She couldn't help but notice the thickness of his dick and the slight curve. It wasn't long but the way it was shaped, she knew that if he knew how to work it, pleasure wasn't too far behind.

"Sit back down," she told him as she waited for him to put the condom on.

He did as she demanded and waited for her to straddle him. She held her pussy lips open with her hands as she lowered herself onto him, taking it all in. Alexis was shocked when Thomas' face flashed before her. She shook her head from side to side to get the image of him out.

Stay in the moment she told herself. *Stay in the moment*.

Once he was deep inside her, he placed his hands on her hips and told her, "Don't move, stay right there." He started moving his hips in circles, going deeper and deeper inside her, so deep that she pulled back.

"Where are you going?" he asked, holding her steady.

Finally he moved his hands and let her control the movement. He filled her up as she moved up and down and rocked back and forth while touching her clitoris.

"I want to come with you inside me," she told him and come she did at the same time as Shamel.

It was close to midnight when Shamel left Alexis' house. While they were making love, her cell phone had rung a number of times and she'd ignored it. It was now time to see just who was trying so hard to reach her.

Alexis climbed out of the guest bed, where they ended up making love and walked into the living room. Her cell phone was on the floor next to the lounger, which was odd because she could have sworn she'd left it in the kitchen. Then again, she did drink a whole bottle of wine by herself.

Alexis looked at the caller ID and saw that Champagne and an unknown caller had phoned numerous times. Who the hell was the unknown caller, she wondered. She hated shit like that. If you had to call a person, let them know who you were. Don't be a damn coward about it.

"A shower, I need a shower," she said out loud. On her way to the bathroom, she thought about Shamel and his lovemaking skills. As far as foreplay was concerned he definitely wasn't Thomas but he didn't lack in the pleasure department either.

Champagne left a couple of messages saying, "Call me back. I saw that you had called. Where are you? What's going on? Okay now I'm starting to worry."

Alexis dialed Champagne's number. The phone was picked up on the first ring.

"Girl, it's after midnight and you're just now calling me back. Where the hell have you been?"

Alexis almost told her but for some reason stopped. "I was out and about, doing what I do."

"What does that mean?"

Alexis laughed. "Girl, I don't know, it's something kids say all the time. I went and ran some errands and then came home and fell asleep. I didn't mean to make you worry."

"Well, you did."

"I apologize."

Alexis heard Champagne yawn. "You go back to bed. Let's talk tomorrow."

Not one to argue, Champagne said, "Okay."

Zyair, whose back was facing Champagne, turned over and asked, "Is everything all right?"

"Yeah, it was Alexis."

"Oh okay."

"Something is going on with her," Champagne said.

"Oh, here you go with that shit again."

Champagne nudged him, "What shit?"

She didn't even have to ask, because she knew what shit he was talking about. He was talking about her being up in Alexis' business but shit, if she wasn't she'd still be with that married asshole Khalil.

Zyair gave her a look that said *do you really have to ask*. He then turned back over. "Let that girl live her life how she sees fit, Champagne, you can't keep interfering."

"I'm not interfering. I'm being concerned."

If she wanted to mistake the whole thing about her investigating Khalil with being concerned instead of interfering, he'd let her, so he didn't say a word because he knew better.

Chapter 16

Everyone That Comes to Your Door Should Not Be Welcomed In

Thomas was sitting across from his secretary, Lisa, giving her instructions on what needed to be done for the gathering he was having. It was something he did every year for his clients to show his appreciation and for morale.

"Please make sure the caterer is there on time."

"I know, I know," Lisa told him. They went through this every year. He'd repeat himself over and over and Lisa would just sit and nod her head or say I know, I know.

"Oh and close the door behind you. I'm not to be disturbed for a couple of hours." Thomas had some contracts he needed to review before discussing them with his clients. Prior to him getting settled, he wanted to call Alexis and see what was up with her. Before he even had a chance to do that, Lisa came running into his office.

"Didn't I tell you I don't want to be disturbed?"

"You did Thomas, but the car attendant called and said someone damaged your car."

Thomas was out of his seat in less than a second. His car was his baby and one of his favorite vehicles. It was a midnight-black Jaguar and it was one of his pride and joys. He spent a great deal of money on getting it suped-up.

Thomas brushed past Lisa who decided to follow behind him to see what was going on. He was so focused that he didn't say a word. Once in the hallway, Thomas hit the elevator button and didn't give it any time to hit his floor. He decided to take the stairs. It was only six flights and with the shape he was in he'd get there sooner. That's where Lisa drew the line though. She and stairs did not get along.

Once Thomas entered the parking garage, he could hear his car alarm going off. *What the fuck happened?*

When he finally reached his car, all he could do was stand there with his hands on his head, like it was about to explode. He looked around to spot the attendant, Jimmy, who was nowhere in sight. Instead some young boy who didn't look over twenty was standing there watching him, looking scared as hell in an attendant's shirt.

"Who the fuck are you?" Thomas was so angry he was trembling.

"I'm Sean, the new attendant?" The boy answered with fear in his eyes and fake bravado.

"How old are you?" Thomas couldn't believe the garage was hiring kids to look after his shit.

"Eighteen."

"Where the fuck is Jimmy?" Thomas asked, looking around.

"He's on vacation."

Thomas started pacing. "Vacation? Vacation? I don't believe this shit. You didn't see this happen?"

The boy opened his mouth to speak but Thomas cut him off. "You didn't see this shit happening? Where were you when it was happening!"

By now Thomas was up in the boy's face, who kept backing up.

"I . . . I . . . I—"

"You what? Do you know how much this car cost?"

Thomas walked around the car touching it. The windows were broken out and there were several dents on each side of the car as though someone kept hitting it with a bat.

"Where were you?"

Sean felt Thomas' anger and knew there was no way he could tell this man where he was and that was getting his dick sucked.

Sean was sitting in the booth, chilling and thanking God for this easy-ass job. He'd just gotten fired from a fast food joint because he cursed out one of the customers. He had his music playing, his feet up and was considering smoking some weed, wondering if he could get away with it when this cherry red Benz with tinted windows pulled up. The driver rolled the window down and it was the finest female Sean had seen in a long time. He was ready to spit his best game.

"What's up beautiful?" he asked as he tried to see who was on the passenger side. He didn't have to try too hard because the other female who was just as fine as the first leaned over and said, "Hey handsome, can we park in here for a little while?"

"It's twenty-five dollars."

"What if we don't have it?"

Everything in him wanted to just tell them to go ahead but he didn't want to lose this job as well.

"Listen," the driver said, "I have to run inside this building for a brief meeting. If you let us park for free my girl here will take care of you."

Sean could not believe what he was hearing, shit like this never happened to him. There had to be a catch to it, but he couldn't stop himself from wondering just what would she be willing to do.

"How about give you the best head in town?"

The next thing Sean knew the girl was climbing out the car. Not only was she fine but she had some big ass titties too.

"Come on; let's go in your booth."

Sean led the way and the driver pulled off.

They went inside the booth where Sean sat down on the chair and the girl got on her knees. "You're really going to do this?" Sean could not believe his luck, his boys would not believe this shit.

"Yes, now shut up."

Sean prayed in his head that no one would show up to park.

She pulled his pants down and knowing that she wasn't going to have that much time because they came there to do a favor for a friend, she immediately started sucking his dick She moved her tongue back and forth over the head of it and she went up and down his shaft. She placed her right hand on the base and as she moved her hand up she squeezed and she did the same thing as she moved down, while making sure her mouth was moist.

She could tell he was enjoying it because he grabbed the back of her head and kept saying over and over, "I don't believe this shit, I don't believe this shit. I'm going to come soon. I'm going to come soon."

It was a good thing too, because less than a second later she heard a car alarm going off and she knew her job was just about done.

She started sucking faster and squeezing harder and right when she could tell that he was going to explode she moved her mouth and grabbed the towel she saw on the counter to catch his cum.

By the time he caught his breath and got himself together the car was pulling up.

"Somebody's alarm is going off," the female who was driving said as the other one got in the car and waved.

Before he could get a number or say anything more they drove off.

It was after they pulled off that he went to check on the car to see whose parking spot it was. When he saw how busted up it was and

*while he waited for Thomas and the police, he
knew his ass was fired from yet another job.*

"Where were you?" Thomas asked again.

"I was in the bathroom."

Thomas looked him up and down and noticed his zipper was down.

"Zip up your fucking pants and call the cops."

Sean zipped up his pants and told him, "The police are already on their way."

While Thomas waited for the police to arrive, he called Zyair up to tell him what happened.

"And you mean to tell me the attendant didn't see a thing or see anyone come in and out?" Zyair wanted to know.

"He claims he was in the bathroom."

"What about cameras?"

Thomas hadn't thought about that but you best believe he was going to do his own investigating. If he had to go around and ask every street hustler he knew that's what he was going to do. Between him, the cops, a private investigator, and the street, he would find out who did this shit.

Chapter 17

Charity Can Come in Many Forms; Two of Them Are Time and Money

How she put herself in this position, she didn't know. Maybe it was because Victoria kept coming to her. Maybe it was because she was cutting classes and when Alexis asked her why, she told her she had to go home and check on her mother. Or maybe it was in the plan all along and she just wasn't listening. Nonetheless, here she was a week later pulling up in front of Victoria's house with her in the passenger seat. Unlike Shay's neighborhood, Alexis felt safe here. It was a community of small homes. Alexis recalled hearing about this neighborhood some time ago. When the homes were first being built, there was a special for first-time home buyers in this area. There were also a couple of kids outside playing kickball in someone's yard, using two trees and what looked like telephone books as bases.

Neither of them said a word. What was there

to say? Alexis couldn't make any promises. She couldn't say I'm going to save your mother's life and she couldn't make a guarantee to Victoria that everything would be all right.

Once the car was parked and the engine off, Victoria reached over and took Alexis' hand. "You don't know how much I appreciate this. It means a lot to me."

Alexis moved her hand. "That's okay sweetie."

"And I'm sorry I called you a bitch."

Alexis looked at her. "You should be."

When they got to the porch, Victoria took out her key and unlocked the door. She peeked inside first to see if the house was a mess. It wasn't, so she opened the door wider and stepped through with Alexis following behind her.

"Ma!" she called out.

She didn't get any response. "Ma!" she called out again with panic setting in.

"Girl, what the hell are you yelling for? I was in my room."

The woman walking toward them didn't look suicidal to Alexis. As a matter-of-fact she looked saner than Alexis felt sometimes. Her hair was cut short; almost pixie style and she looked to be in her twenties, although Alexis knew they were around the same age. Alexis also noticed that she was very attractive. Her skin was flawless, her breasts had to be a D-cup and she had ass for days.

Victoria was standing in front of her mother with her mouth wide open. She was expecting her mother to look unkempt.

Her mother placed her hand under her chin.

"Close your damn mouth girl, and who is this?" She nodded toward Alexis.

"I'm Alexis, the school therapist."

"I'm Shondell, Vicky's mom." She looked at Victoria. "What the hell have you done?"

"Actually Ma, I brought her here for you."

"For me? Girl, ain't nothing wrong with me. I was just going through a little something and now I'm over it. Shit, I'm past that mother-fucker. Well, I'll be past him when I fuck up his life and take all his money when he finds out I'm having his baby. When he realizes that this good ass. . . ."

The more Shondell spoke, the more Alexis realized that her initial impression of sanity may have been incorrect.

"Maybe I should leave," Alexis said.

Shondell grabbed her arm. "You don't have to leave. I haven't had company in weeks. It'll be nice to have some company."

Alexis looked at Victoria who was mouthing the word "please."

"Come on. Let me get you something to drink."

Alexis followed her into the kitchen. Victoria wasn't far behind. As they walked down the hall, she noticed that her mom must have been cleaning all day. When she left for school that day, newspapers and magazines were all over the place. Dishes were scattered about, the floor looked like it needed to be swept and the pullout couch was unmade. For some reason her mother had taken to sleeping on it. But now, nothing was out of place, the floors had been swept and even had the appearance of being waxed or mopped. No dishes were anywhere, not even in the dish strainer. There was even the smell of Pinesol about the house. Maybe she was getting better. Normally when Victoria came home, she'd have to put some order to the house.

When they stepped in the kitchen, Alexis noticed pictures on the table ripped up. Shondell walked over to the refrigerator and took out a gallon of water.

"You know, I loved that man with all my heart, with my everything and he just used me. Fucked me all he wanted to and then all of a sudden he's telling me he don't want me no more. Me!" Shondell put the gallon of water on the counter. "Okay, maybe just maybe, I should have listened when he told me he wasn't ready for a relationship but he sure acted like he was."

Alexis looked over at Victoria who was just sitting there taking it all in with a look of pity.

Shondell went on. "You see that's what men do, use you and I got tired of being used. I was like, is this it? Is this what I have to live for? I was ready to go hurt that motherfucker but then this morning after my baby. . . ." She stood up and walked over to Victoria and kissed her on the cheek. "This morning when my precious baby left for school, it hit me. I have her to live for and I have this baby inside of me to live for and you best believe that motherfucker will pay some child support."

Shondell walked over to the table, forgetting

all about the water she was supposed to be pouring. She picked up one of the pictures that wasn't cut yet. "Yeah, and it's going to be a pretty baby too."

When Shondell flashed the picture in front of Alexis she could have sworn . . . No, it couldn't be.

Alexis put her hand out. "Can I see the picture?"

Shondell handed it to her. When Alexis looked at the picture she couldn't believe it. The motherfucker this crazy-ass woman was talking about was Thomas. He was looking good as usual. He was standing by himself, distracted, as though he was unaware that there was a picture being taken.

Chapter 18

Sometimes Things Get Worse Before They Get Better: Just Hold on and Learn the Lesson

"You've got to be kidding me?" Zyair said.

"Man, I wish I was. That young motherfucker was getting his dick sucked while my car was being vandalized. What's real crazy is that my car was the only one damaged which basically means I was targeted, that this whole thing was a set up. Even when we tried to look at the video, I couldn't see shit. It's like the motherfuckers had their backs turned the whole time. Whoever did this had obviously been to the garage and knew where the cameras were located."

"Who would do some shit like that?"

"I don't know. Even when the police pulled the video and tried to enhance it, we couldn't make out faces and there was no license plate on the car."

"And it was two women?"

"Yeah." Thomas slammed his hand down on the table. They were in his den. "I still can't believe this shit."

"You see man, I told you not to be fucking with those money-hungry females you meet at the games and shit."

Thomas looked at him like that was the last thing he wanted to hear. He pulled out a chair and sat down.

Zyair stepped to the side of him and placed his hand on Thomas' shoulder. "Come on, get up and get ready for your party."

Thomas shook his head. "I don't even feel like having that shit."

"And that's what whoever did this wants. They want to fuck up your day. Shit man, a car is a material thing, you can always get. . . ."

Zyair knew when he'd said enough by the way Thomas looked up at him. "All right, all right, I'll shut up, but know this man, I got your back."

"I know you do."

They gave each other daps.

"But damn," Thomas said, "I wish I knew who it was."

"You need to figure that shit out later. Right now, you need to get ready for tonight."

Thomas stood up and looked at his watch. "You know what, you're right. Let me go get ready for tonight and I'll deal with this shit tomorrow." He knew it was easier said than done but he had a houseful coming and needed to be prepared.

They half hugged one another and Thomas walked Zyair to the front door. "Don't be late."

"Tell that to the little lady," Zyair said, talking about Champagne. "Shit, you know how women are."

That Thomas did.

"Did you invite Alexis?" Zyair asked.

"You know it. At least that's something to look forward to."

"All right man, I'm out."

Once Zyair was gone, Thomas went to make a couple of phone calls. He'd had his car towed before coming home and needed to let his insurance company know what happened. He also needed to get a referral for an investigator to find out who fucked up his car.

Thomas knew that Zyair was right when he talked about his past choices of women. He usually picked the ones that were out for a party. The ones that just wanted to have a good time, sex, and money. Yes, he knew that most of them were all about the dollar. That didn't really bother him much because money came and went. If a few hundred dollars meant less of a headache, than so be it.

He went into his room and pulled out his phone book and his photo album. He went through them both trying to decide which one of these women were out to get him. This one female, named Shondell, he'd dealt with some time ago had taken to calling him, cursing him out and leaving obscene messages on his phone. He wondered if it was her. He doubted it because he could tell she was all talk. However, one could never be sure. He was going to have someone pay her a visit. Better yet, he was going to pay her one himself.

Chapter 19

Just Ask a Person What You Want to Know; Don't Assume They Know What to Tell You

Champagne was on the phone with Alexis when Zyair walked through the door.

"Are you serious," she asked, motioning for Zyair to come sit next to her.

"Yeah, what do you think? I had the picture in my hand."

"Are you sure it was Thomas in the picture, Alexis?"

"Didn't I just tell you that?"

When Zyair heard Thomas' name, he mouthed "What? What?"

Champagne put up her hand and told him to calm down.

"Are you going to his party tonight?" Champagne asked. Zyair had told her earlier that in light of Thomas' feeling like someone was out to get him and not knowing who to trust, he decided, with Zyair's support, to go through with the gathering.

"Hell no!"

Even Zyair heard that through the phone.

"Well, I think you should go. You need to tell him what you saw and ask him what's up."

Zyair looked at Champagne and waited patiently for her to get off the phone.

"Listen," Champagne told Alexis, "Zyair just came in and we have to get ready."

"Don't say anything to him about this," Alexis told her. "I want to talk to Thomas first."

Champagne lied and said, "Okay, but you need to handle this as soon as possible and not wait around. You know like I know, you care for him more than you want to admit. And for all you know, that chick could be straight lying."

"I know, just don't say anything to Zyair."

Champagne didn't respond because she knew the second she was off the phone, she was going to tell Zyair.

"What's going on?" Zyair asked the second they hung up.

"Does the name Shondell ring a bell?"

"Shondell? Shondell?" He repeated the name, knowing that it sounded familiar but he couldn't place the face. "I don't know babe, it sounds familiar. What does this have to do with Thomas?"

"Supposedly, she's pregnant with Thomas' child."

Zyair stood up. "Who told you that shit? Ain't nobody having his baby. He would have told me some shit like that." That was not something Thomas would keep to himself and if Zyair was sure of anything, this would be it.

Thomas always talked about how he wanted children and if he was about to become a father, Zyair would be the first to know because he would be the godfather. "How did Alexis hear about this?"

Champagne went on to tell Zyair about Victoria coming to Alexis and asking her for help. She then told him what took place when she got to Victoria's house.

Zyair just shook his head. "Damn! Thomas is having a bad-ass fucking night." He looked at his watch. "Come on. Let's get dressed and I'll fill you in on what happened to him earlier."

Alexis was sitting on her bed feeling all emotional and shit. She was stuck somewhere between anger, disappointment, and jealousy. Anger because she felt played once again, disappointment because she really thought Thomas was trying to change and jealousy over actually seeing one of the women he was dealing with. She didn't expect to feel that way at all. *Does this mean I care more than I want to admit? Does this mean I'm falling for him? What about Shamel? Why would I sleep with him if I have feelings for Thomas?*

"Shit!" Alexis said out loud. Her emotions were starting to become confusing. The last thing she wanted to do was develop more than friendly feelings for Thomas. What she thought she wanted from him was to be friends with benefits. Could it be that she wanted more?

"Call him, talk to him," Champagne told her. "There are two sides to every story."

Alexis would do just that after she calmed down and got hold of her emotions. What she wanted to do right now was lie down and get some sleep. She was mentally drained.

She walked into her bedroom and lay across the bed. On the nightstand next to the bed was the *Sister Girls* book, she was almost finished reading. She reached over and picked it up because she recalled putting Gavin's card inside. She pulled it out and looked at it.

You know that boy is too young for you, she told herself. Alexis was not into young boys but she had to admit he was charming and maybe he'd help her get her mind off Thomas.

Alexis looked at the card. "Damn, why he gotta be under thirty?"

She decided to call him anyway, after all, what's a three to four year difference?

Chapter 20

Ask Who When Meeting, Ask What Beforehand and Ask Why When You're Doing It

He was kissing her between her thighs, running his tongue up the insides, stopping short of just where she wanted him to be.

"Why are you stopping?" Alexis asked him.

He didn't answer her. He just continued to let his tongue travel in circles on her thighs. As his tongue got closer and closer to her spot, Alexis started thrusting her hips toward his mouth, but he'd pull away.

"Stop playing," Alexis told him while feeling her vaginal walls clench and tremble. He'd been playing with her for over ten minutes and she was ready for him to either bring her to an orgasm with his mouth or get inside her, but he wasn't paying her any mind when she told him to stop.

His whole focus was on what he was doing. Suddenly, she felt his tongue on her clitoris, flicking back and forth.

Gavin surprised the hell out of Alexis. She didn't think he'd have skills like this, but he proved her wrong. Before she knew it, his fingers started to go inside her, first one and then another. He then climbed on top of her body and replaced his fingers with what she'd been waiting on, his dick.

"Wait," she stopped him. "Do you have a condom on?"

He pulled out so she could see that he did.

Damn, he's slick as hell. Alexis didn't even know when he'd put it on. She placed her hands on his buttocks and pushed him deep inside her.

"Put your legs up," he told her.

She bent her legs up until her knees were pressing against her chest. She closed her eyes and felt him even more as he lifted up and entered her. Their bodies slammed together repeatedly until she felt him stiffen and look in her eyes. He didn't even have to say it, she knew he was coming, she could feel him pulsating.

It was now official; she was a whore. She'd slept with three men in less than a month, something she never would have done before. If someone else had done it, she'd probably talk about them.

"What I am is in control," she said out loud.

Gavin turned over and yawned, "What did you say?" He asked with his eyes closed, taking in the moment.

"Oh nothing," Alexis said.

He opened his eyes and said, "Yes, you did, you said something about control."

Alexis threw the covers back. "Are you hungry, you want something to eat?"

She wanted him to say no, to just leave but she didn't want to be the one to initiate it.

"And she cooks too."

Alexis just looked at him. Obviously she was going to have to help him along with leaving. She'd do so right after a quick breakfast.

"Are you going to serve me breakfast in bed?" he asked.

Alexis gave him the "you have lost all your mind" look and Gavin got the message because he started climbing out of the bed.

"Can I have a towel and wash rag?"

"Look in the hallway in the linen closet. It's near the bathroom. There's also an extra toothbrush in there." Alexis threw on a robe and went into the kitchen to make a quick breakfast.

As she was cooking she tried to recall how the conversation went from "Hey, I was hoping you'd call" to him eating her pussy, to him being inside her.

Damn, was his game that good? The obvious answer was yes.

"Hey beautiful." Gavin was standing in front of her looking like he was dipped in fudge. All he had on were his jeans. They were hanging slightly off his hips, not low like the youngsters but low enough where she found herself asking, "Aren't you uncomfortable without drawers on?"

Gavin just laughed. Before she could stop him, he was up on her hugging her from behind.

"Stop," she said playfully, while slapping his hands away. "Let's eat."

"What did you make?"

"Vegetable omelets."

"What, no meat?" Gavin couldn't imagine a breakfast without bacon or sausage.

"I don't eat meat."

They took their plates off the counter. Alexis grabbed two water bottles out of the refrigerator, handed him one and they sat down across from one another.

Alexis found that she couldn't look him in the eye. Suddenly she was embarrassed. Damn, how was she going to be a woman of the world if she couldn't handle what she was doing and what she was becoming.

"What's going on Alexis?"

She looked up at him. "Huh?"

"What's going on?"

"Why do you think something is going in?"

"You won't look at me. Are you regretting last night?"

"I . . . I. . . ." What was she going to say? *This is not me, this is not something I do often, sleep with a man on a first date. I've only done it a couple of times.* Hell, his being here in her home wasn't even a date, what it was, was a booty call. "This is not something I do often," she went ahead and told him anyway. "I'm not a whore."

Gavin took a sip of his water and sat back in

his chair with his arms crossed. He looked her in the eyes, "I didn't think you were."

"How could you not? I call you to talk and next thing you know I'm asking you to come over and we're going at it like two horny teenagers."

When she said that, he laughed.

"What's so funny?" she wanted to know.

"Nothing."

"Then why are you laughing?"

"Because you're serious." He sat up in his chair and told her, "Sweetie, you need to relax. We are both adults and what happened, happened. Why dwell on it?"

Alexis decided she'd do just that, move on; pretend it wasn't a big deal. At least she had enough sense to use a condom.

After they finished eating, Alexis stood up, picked up their dishes and put them in the sink. "I have a lot to do today."

"Are you putting me out?" Gavin asked. Before she could answer he told her, "That's okay, I know you need to think."

She turned and looked at him. She started to stay something but he stopped her by stepping to her and kissing her on the lips.

"Don't say another word, just know that next Sunday, I'm picking you up and we're going somewhere fun."

She wanted to protest, but the word fun was something she hadn't heard in a while and it sounded like something she needed at this exact moment.

* * *

Ten minutes later, Alexis was standing on the porch watching him get in his Navigator and pull off. She looked down the street and noticed a car with someone sitting behind the wheel. The windows were slightly tinted, so she couldn't see inside the way she would have wanted to but she could have sworn they were looking her way. She put her hands up to her eyes to shield the sun and to see better but it didn't help.

Girl, you are seriously bugging, ain't nobody watching you. You just have a secret admirer, that's all. She tried to convince herself.

But someone was and he'd been paid to do it. He picked up the cell phone and dialed a number. He listened to it ring.

"Did she stay in last night?" the voice on the other end asked.

"Yes, but she wasn't alone."

There was a slight hesitation, then, "Find out who she was with."

It wasn't with Thomas, that was for sure, because last night he'd been arrested.

Chapter 21

If You Doubt It, Ask; If You Don't Believe, Do Research: Take Only Your Word

Alexis was about to get in the shower, when she turned on the television. She was about to turn around when she saw a familiar face and that face belonged to Thomas.

What the hell? She picked up the remote and turned the volume up.

The newscaster was saying, "Thomas Wade, the agent for several well-known athletes was arrested early this morning around 3:00 A.M. for solicitation of minors."

Alexis dropped down on her bed staring at the television. *What the hell is going on?*

The newscaster went on—" The police received an anonymous tip that Mr. Thomas was having a gathering at his house and underage call girls were present when they arrived. They found several underage girls drinking, partying, and soliciting."

At that point, Alexis stopped listening. She was

in shock. As she looked around for her phone, she heard it ring. It was under the bed. Alexis bent down to pick up the phone. She didn't even bother to look at the ID.

"So, your boy was locked up last night?" It was Shamel.

Not catching the tone in his voice, she said, "I know. I can't believe this. It can't be true. There must be some kind of mistake."

This was not what Shamel wanted to hear, he wanted to hear outrage and disgust. "How do you know it's not true? Shit you never know what someone is capable of."

She knew he was right but her gut told her in this instance something was off. Even though Thomas was a known womanizer, there's a difference between being a womanizer and dating women in your age range than being a pedophile and dating women that were underage. She just couldn't see it. She'd heard about his history and how he grew up in foster care. She knew that he donated money to children's homes and she knew that he could get almost any woman he wanted. He didn't have to succumb to dating woman that were too young.

What Shamel was saying, Alexis wasn't trying to hear. She needed to get off the phone and find out what the hell was going on.

"Listen Shamel, I don't have time for this. Let me call you back."

"Call me back?" Shamel looked at the phone. He couldn't believe this shit. He wanted to go off but he quickly pulled it together and asked, "Can we get together later?"

The last thing Alexis wanted to do was get together. "Not today."

"How about Sunday? We can go to brunch."

Alexis, unable to hold it in told him, "Shamel, I want to find out what happened with Thomas. Please let me call you back."

Shamel didn't respond. He just hung up.

Alexis then dialed Champagne's number, which was busy. *How the hell can a phone be busy when there is call waiting?* She hung up and tried again. This time it went to voice mail.

"Champagne, call me. I just saw the news. What's going on?" She hung up and sat on her bed. She looked at the ceiling and said a silent prayer for Thomas while wondering, what had he gotten himself into. She refused to believe even for a minute that he knew these girls were minors.

While Alexis was wondering what the hell was going on, Thomas was sitting in a cell wondering the same thing.

The gathering had started like all the other gatherings he'd had in the past. Him at the door, greeting people, Zyair mingling, making people feel at home, his assistant making sure she kept up with who came with whom so she could send out thank you cards, which was always important in the business he was in.

On the guest list were several well-known athletes, Neal Jones, Louie Ali Muhammad and quite a few up and coming athletes who were looking for new or better representation. Some came alone and some brought their wives.

There was also a list of women that were invited to these types of functions. It was a secret list that only a few agents had and only a few knew about. These women were high class, sexy and fine. They knew how to entertain and make a man feel special. They knew how to make him feel like he was the only person in the room. They knew how to stroke a man's ego.

Everyone was on the bottom floor spread out between the dining area, the conversation room and the game room which had two pool tables and some old school video games like *PacMan.*

A couple of the women had just come in and asked him if they could get in the pool and the Jacuzzi.

He'd told them yes, but not to let things get too carried away. He then gave one of the security men the look which meant, *watch their asses.*

Thomas was walking behind the bar when the bartender told him, "I'll make your drink, that's what you're paying me for."

"Nah, I've got it," he told him. He needed to do something other than talk to occupy himself and to keep from noticing that Alexis hadn't arrived. They needed to talk. He'd tried calling her several times but hadn't gotten an answer. Zyair had informed him earlier that Shondell somehow had gotten to her and fed her some bullshit.

Out of all the women from his past for Alexis

to run into, she ran into the craziest one out there.

Shondell was the craziest and the freakiest. She could suck dick for hours, fuck for hours and take it in every hole on her body. For a second there, Thomas thought he was in love with her. Until she started calling him all hours of the night, insisting he tell her where he was and who he was with. That shit got old real quick and he had to let her go. Initially, she still continued to call and he wouldn't give her the time of day. It wasn't until he told her if she didn't stop calling he'd get a restraining order on her, that she finally stopped but not before cursing him out.

When Thomas first met Shondell he never would have taken her to be a crazy one. As a matter-of-fact, his first impression was of someone that was sophisticated and had her head on her shoulders.

She ran game on him like it wasn't anything. Obviously she knew he grew up in a foster home. That would not have been to hard to find out being that his clients are high profile and he'd given a few interviews himself. She talked about how she was raised by a lady she called her aunt, when the woman was really just a friend of her mother. Her mother was a schizophrenic who had lived in a mental facility since Shondell was a child. Knowing what it's like to grow up without parents, Thomas felt for her and after learning that she herself was a single parent he started to provide by giving her money here and there.

So between the sex she was giving him, which up until that time had been the best he'd experienced and his feeling like her hero, he got caught up. It's when she became sort of a stalker that he had to let her go. He hadn't heard from her in over three months when he ran into her at a night club. She was looking good as hell. Some kind of way; it may have been because of all the liquor he'd consumed, he ended up at a hotel and that night the sex was out of this world.

The second they walked through the door, she was on him, damn near ripping his shirt off his back. He had to tell her to hold up. She took a step back and looked at him while licking her lips. "Don't you miss having your dick in this mouth?"

That he did.

Then she had the nerves to turn around, pull up her dress, bend over and show him she wasn't wearing any panties. "What about this ass? Don't you miss having that dick in this ass?"

That he did.

Before he knew it, his pants were down and he was stepping to her. His mind was saying, "Thomas, what are you doing? Thomas, stop this nonsense right now. You know her ass is crazy." But his dick was saying something entirely different. His dick was saying, "Go for it."

When she started wiggling her ass, he knew that was just what he was going to do.

He was holding his dick and rubbing it on the crack of her ass while she held her cheeks apart. He was teasing her. As much as he wanted to go there right at the moment, there was no way he would do that without a condom.

"Dip it in my pussy," she begged.

He wasn't ready to do that yet and especially not without a condom.

"I thought you wanted it in your ass." That was where he wanted to put it.

"I want it there too." She pushed two fingers inside her pussy and pulled them out and rubbed her clitoris.

Thomas reached into his back pocket and pulled out a condom. He'd taken to carrying them everywhere he went, just in case.

He bit it open, threw the wrapper down and placed it on his dick. Once it was on, he dipped his dick in her pussy and pulled it out while sliding it down the crack of her ass. He then put just a tiny bit of his dick in her ass, causing her to wind her hips around, allowing her to open up wider and he'd pull out and dip it back inside her.

"Oh, you're trying to play with me? Is that what you're doing?"

Thomas pulled his dick all the way out and this time slammed it inside her pussy. They hadn't even gotten to the bed yet, she was bent over a table.

"Oh fuck!" she cried out. "Fuck my ass like that."

And he would because he knew she could take it. He knew she would take whatever he gave her like a champ and want more.

He pulled his dick out her pussy slammed it in once again and pulled it out real slow. He entered again until he had just the head in. He took one of his fingers and started playing with her asshole, circling it, dipping his finger in and out, he kept the tip of his dick in her pussy, moving slightly as he opened up her ass more and more with his finger.

Shondell was moaning and moaning. She was loving every minute of it. "Damn, I'm glad I ran into your ass," she told him. "Come on and give it to me."

This was the shit that got him in trouble with her before. She could talk shit and back it up but she was also mental.

At that moment, he knew he needed to hurry up and do what he came to do so he could get the hell out. He pulled his dick out and opened another condom and put it on, threw the old one down and placed his dick on her asshole and pushed it in causing her to scream out.

"You knew it was coming baby, don't scream,'" he told her. "Take it, take it like you want it."

Take it she did. She pounded back on his dick like it was in her pussy, while rubbing on her clitoris and rubbing on his balls. Once he was all the way in and she could feel his balls on her ass, she started to grind.

"Give it to me," she demanded. "Give it all to me."

Thomas did just that. Before he knew it, his body started trembling.

Shondell started bucking even harder and ruined the moment talking about "I love you Thomas, I love you so much."

The second he came inside the condom, he took it off and held it in one hand, pulled his pants up with the other and walked to the toilet to flush it down. When he came out of the bathroom, Shondell was sitting on the edge of the bed totally naked.

"Come on, we're not done yet."

That I love you shit threw his game off and he was ready to go.

Thomas made the mistake of looking at his watch and that set her off. "Oh, so now you're ready to leave? You done fucked me all up in the ass and got your nut and you're ready to go. That's fucked up Thomas."

It was and he knew it.

"The least you can do is let me get mine and I promise I won't bother you again. All that love shit I said was in the moment. I'm over your ass. I just want your dick."

Thomas said the only thing he could think of to say, "I don't know if I could get hard again."

"I know how to make it happen."

Then Thomas and his weak ass allowed her to pull his pants down once again and suck on his balls.

"I only had two condoms," he told her.

"Don't worry about that I got it covered."

She reached over, opened her purse, pulled out a condom, opened it and put it on him.

"We can do this real fast. Just fuck me hard, while I play with my clit."

He did as requested and it was over before it started, with both of them exploding with him inside her.

"Your work is not done," she told him while taking the condom and heading toward the bathroom. Normally he would have been the one to take control of the used condom. Working with athletes had taught him a valuable lesson. He'd heard one too many stories. But this time he slacked off. It wasn't until the next day when he replayed the scene in his mind that he realized what he'd done. All he could do at that point was hope she wouldn't do anything stupid.

That was the last time he saw her or heard from her until recently, when she started calling, hanging up or breathing into the phone once again.

When Zyair arrived a few minutes before everyone else with Champagne in tow giving him the evil eye, he had to know why.

"Man, that psycho chick you used to mess with knows Alexis and told her she was having your baby."

"What? Who?"

"Shondell."

"What! Where's Champagne, let me talk to her."

"Nah man, she went to the ladies room and I promised her I wouldn't say anything."

"Now why would you promise some stupid shit like that?"

"Because I want some pussy tonight."

Thomas just looked at him. He had to get in touch with Alexis and soon.

After calling Alexis for the fifth time and accepting she wasn't going to call him back or come to the gathering, he gave up. He needed to mingle with the guests. He'd visit her tomorrow unannounced. She was going to talk to his ass.

However, that wasn't what was in the cards for him.

For the past forty-five minutes, Thomas had been in his office talking to a potential client when he realized how late it was. It was almost 2:00 A.M. and he was ready to start sending people home. Any other time, it would have been over by now but he'd been so preoccupied with his thoughts and trying to conduct business that the time flew by.

The second Thomas arrived from the back office, his front door burst open with men in uniforms following.

"What the. . . ." Everyone stopped in their tracks to see what the hell was going on.

One of the officers stepped up. "Thomas Wade? We're here for Mr. Wade."

Everyone turned to face Thomas who had stepped up. "What is it, Officer?"

"Are you Thomas—"

"Yes, yes I am."

"And this is your residence?"

At this point Thomas' attorney stepped up. "Excuse me, Officer. I'm his attorney and I would like to know what's going on."

Several of the officers by now had dispersed and were moving throughout the house. The officer who was speaking pulled out a search warrant.

"We have reason to believe that there are minors under the influence at this residence and that they are here soliciting." He waved his hands around to indicate the numerous men who were standing and watching what was taking place.

Thomas laughed at this. "I can assure you gentlemen that all the ladies here are of age."

From behind Thomas, he heard women fussing and talking about, "Get your hands off me. What do you want? I want my lawyer."

Thomas turned around to see what the ruckus was about and was shocked to see some women he didn't even know. Not only didn't he know them but he had no idea who let these women into his home.

He took a step forward toward the girls. "Who the hell are you?"

One of the girls popped the gum she was chewing. "You know who the hell we are. You sent for us."

"All right, all right," one of the officers said.

"Oh, hell no. I don't know any of you. Who the fuck let these girls up in my house?"

No one answered. He looked at the girls again. If you looked hard enough and was experienced enough to see under the makeup, it was obvious these girls were either just eighteen or slightly under.

"You are under arrest. . . ." and so the story went.

So here Thomas sat, wondering just like Alexis "What the fuck was going on and who the hell would set him up like this?"

Chapter 22

Sometimes There Is Nothing You Can Do But Wait

Alexis hung up the phone. She'd just spoken to Champagne, who had informed her that Thomas' attorney was working on getting him out of the holding cell. It might not happen until Monday, depending on if they could find a judge.

"Fuck!" Today was Sunday, the day she'd told Gavin she would go out with him. That was the last thing she felt like doing but Champagne told her maybe it would be the best thing to get her mind off what was happening with Thomas.

Shamel tried to call her numerous times but she just let the phone go to voice mail. She had some other shit she was trying to deal with and he wasn't a priority.

Alexis went into her bathroom and turned on the bath water. She sat on the edge of the tub and questioned what she was doing. Alexis had contemplated calling Gavin all day and canceling their date. She would have if she hadn't misplaced the card with his cell phone number and she forgot to save it on her cell phone.

She wanted to stay home and find out what was going on with Thomas but Champagne already said there was no more information to give *and I kind of do want to go on this date. Shit it ain't like I can concentrate on anything anyway.*"

Alexis settled down in the tub, letting Calgon take her away.

Across town Gavin was finishing up a conference call at one of his shops. He was looking forward to this date since earlier this week.

Dating older women never made Gavin nervous. Successful older women were more his preference. They were more secure in themselves, comfortable in their bodies and less likely to beg. They also had fewer inhibitions.

That night when she'd called him up, he was surprised. He was almost positive that he wouldn't hear from her after he gave her his number but thankfully he was wrong.

Tonight he planned on taking her to Dave and Busters, a game lounge for adults and kids. He wanted to do something fun and different, to show her that life did not have to be so serious all the time. But first he told her to meet him next door at the bar called Honeys. On Sundays they had open mic and he had a treat in store for her."

A few hours later Alexis was walking into Honeys. The plan was for them to meet inside.

On her way there, Gavin was kind enough to call and let her know that he would be running a few minutes late and that he'd left her name with the hostess.

Alexis had never been there before. That might have been because this whole hanging out thing was new to her. When she stepped through the door, she noticed that the crowd seemed to be professionals in their mid-twenties and early thirties. On the walls were pictures of African American heroes, artists, writers and musicians. There was no doubt that this place was black owned. The lights were low with a yellow undertone, giving the patrons a glow, and the tables were small and round. You could only seat four. Along the back wall was a plush-looking couch that was the length of the wall, obviously made for this location. There was also a bar and a stage.

When Alexis gave her name at the door, the hostess smiled and stated, "We were expecting you."

She then led her to a table that was in the center of the floor with the best view of the stage.

As she took her seat she noticed that the people at the surrounding tables were looking her way and whispering. It made her self-conscious. She stopped a waitress and asked her, "Do I have something hanging from my skirt? Why are these people staring at me?"

The waitress laughed and told her, "They're trying to figure out who you are because that table is usually reserved for celebrities."

Alexis felt a little uncomfortable with all the stares and hoped that Gavin would hurry and join her.

"Would you like a drink or an appetizer?" the waitress asked.

"As a matter-of-fact, I'd like a Mojito."

The waitress nodded and walked away.

Alexis turned her attention to the stage where a band was setting up. *I wonder if Thomas is okay. I hope no one is doing anything to him. Okay girl, get him out of your head, you are here waiting on another man.*

Speaking of the other man, Alexis looked at her watch and wondered when he'd be there. He said a few minutes late it was now more like fifteen, damn near twenty.

The waitress returned with her drink. She placed it on the table. Alexis went to reach for her purse which she sat on the chair next to her but the waitress stopped her and said, "Oh no sweetie, it's taken care of."

"By who?" She looked around to see if another man was looking her way.

The waitress tapped her on the shoulder and pointed to the stage where Gavin was standing with a white rose and looking directly at her.

"I'd like to sing this song for the sexiest girl in the club."

"Who me handsome?" a voice yelled out in the crowd. Everyone started laughing.

"You too, but I'm talking about that lady sitting right there." He looked directly at Alexis, which made everyone look her way.

He will not embarrass me this way.

That's just what he did when he started singing "Sweet Lady."

Oh my god, that's my song. How could he know that? Alexis closed her eyes and pretended that Tyrese was up on that stage singing to her, although Gavin wasn't too far from it.

I think I can worry about Thomas later.

Once the song was over Gavin stepped off the stage and walked over to the table. She stood up and they hugged.

"You like?" Gavin asked.

"I loved," Alexis told him and she did. "I've never had anyone sing to me like that before."

"I'm glad I was the first."

Gavin pulled out her chair. "Finish your drink and then we're going next door."

"Next door?" The only thing she saw next door was Dave and Busters and that was a game room.

"Yes, next door."

"To Dave and Busters?"

She must have been frowning because he told her, "Don't knock it until you try it. Watch, you'll have fun, you're with me."

Alexis wasn't really into arcade games, but shit, she was willing it give it a try. Who knew, she just might have a good time.

After finishing their drinks and listening to the band play, Gavin stood up. "Are you ready?"

"Don't you have to pay?"

"It's on my tab."

Alexis smiled. "So, you have a tab here? You come here that often?"

"Nah, one of my boys owns the place."

Alexis thought of Shamel and his business and Thomas and his. It felt good to see black men doing their thing. Heck, she was starting to believe that anything was possible, especially with a black man becoming president.

"Well, good for him," she said while smiling.

"What's got you smiling?"

"It's just good to see black men succeeding."

Gavin knew where she was coming from because there was a time when he didn't think he'd make it out of the streets. He thought he would be a hustler for life but fortunately after a four-year bid in prison, he wanted more for himself. He had stashed his drug money with an old girlfriend he could trust, someone that wouldn't do him dirty. When he was released, he did the right thing, cut her off a nice chunk and opened his first detail shop. Initially, only the other hustlers were his clients but he hired this smart female, who told him to offer specials to businesses and their employees. Once he did that, it was on and business started booming so much so that he had to open another and another and another.

They were walking through the door of Dave and Busters and since this was her first time here, she asked Gavin if they could walk around first.

"It's your night; we can do whatever you want to do."

As they walked around Alexis found herself feeling like a kid. She noticed pool tables, video games, virtual reality stuff, skee-ball, basketball games, shuffleboard, and virtual golf ranges. Dave and Busters was definitely a family-friendly place. The children, teens, and adults all seemed to be having a good time playing games, laughing and just enjoying one another's company.

Eventually, she became overwhelmed because she didn't know where to start. "So, what do you want to try first?" she asked him.

"How about basketball?"

To basketball they went.

For over an hour, they played games. Come to find out, Alexis was more competitive than she realized. She even won a couple of small prizes.

Gavin watched her with amusement. It was obvious she was enjoying herself. Gavin asked her, "Do you want to get something to eat, grab a drink, or play pool? It's on you."

"Let's order something light and play a little pool."

As they were walking to the dining area, Alexis felt someone tap her on the shoulder.

She turned around and no one was there. "Mmm, I could have sworn I felt someone tap me on the shoulder."

"Maybe someone bumped into you and you thought it was a tap."

Alexis knew what a tap felt like. She turned

around and scanned the crowd, trying to see if there was someone she knew on the premises.

They found a table, sat down, called the waitress over and ordered appetizers and drinks. Alexis stuck with her Mojito, while Gavin ordered Hennessey.

Alexis just happened to glance at the television and on the screen was Thomas. Gavin must have been talking to her and she'd tuned him out because he touched her hand.

"Earth to Alexis."

She shook her head. "I apologize, I was watching the news."

Gavin turned around and glanced up at the television that was behind him. The commentator was talking about athletes and performers seeing underage girls and the kind of example they were setting.

"Why are you so into what they're saying?"

"Because one of the people they're talking about is a good friend of mine."

"Who? Thomas?"

Alexis was surprised to hear him say Thomas' name. "Yeah, how did you know?"

"I didn't, I was just guessing. Plus, he's from around here. As a matter-of-fact, he and I sponsored a few little league teams together. He's a decent guy."

Alexis didn't know what to say because all she was thinking was *this is a small ass world*.

"So, are you dating him?" Gavin wasn't one to beat around the bush. He wanted to know where he stood with her, if he even had a real chance.

Alexis didn't lie. "We've seen each other a few times."

Gavin knew what that meant. He knew because of the way her eyes looked and her body shifted when she said it.

"Are you two serious?"

Alexis looked him dead on then and told him, "If we were I wouldn't be here with you."

Gavin, relieved, raised his glass and said, "I'll drink to that."

The waitress came with their food and as they ate, they talked about themselves, how they grew up and where they saw themselves in the near future.

"I used to be holy and sanctified," Alexis told him when they got on the subject of religion.

"Get the hell out of here." Gavin just could not see it because when he thought of holy and sanctified, he thought of women in long dresses, no makeup, no jewelry, shouting in the aisles. "What happened, did you backslide?" he joked.

"I don't really know what happened. It's like all of a sudden I started living my life in a different way and started slipping away from the church."

"Do you not go at all now?"

"I haven't been. Sometimes I wonder if it'll make that much of a difference in my life if I did. Because honestly, when I was going, I wasn't that happy."

"Well, are you happy now?"

That was a question Alexis was really going

to have to think about. There were moments when she was content. She thought she was happy when she was with Khalil and now, well, she was just going through the motions.

Before she got a chance to respond, the waitress approached with another drink.

"I didn't order that," Alexis told her.

"I was told to deliver it to your table by the gentleman over. . . ." She turned to identify the person who sent the drink. "Where is he?"

Gavin turned to look in the direction she was looking in. He wanted to see who the hell was disrespecting him but no one was there.

"What did he look like?" Alexis asked.

"Tall, slim, brown skinned."

Alexis and Gavin waited on a better description and she gave them none.

"Is that it?" Alexis asked.

"Well, that's all I could remember."

"Well shit," Alexis said, "that's half the black men in here."

Gavin picked the drink up off the table and told her to take it back. Alexis didn't even stop him because she agreed.

Standing up, Alexis told him, "I'm ready to go."

"So soon?"

"I don't feel comfortable now."

Gavin told the waitress to bring the bill.

"Do you want to do anything else, go anywhere else?"

"No, I just want to go home."

The waitress returned, Gavin looked at the bill, pulled some cash out of his pocket and gave some to the waitress. "Keep the tip." He placed his hand on Alexis' arm. "What's going on?"

"I don't know Gavin. I hope I'm not being paranoid but I think someone is watching me, that I'm being followed."

They were heading toward the door. "What? Are you sure?"

"No, I'm not sure. It's just a feeling."

"Is there anyone that has something against you, that's angry with you?"

"Not enough to stalk me."

"Do you want me to stay with you tonight?"

"No, I'm going to call my girl Champagne and see if she'll stop by."

"Well, I'm going to follow you home."

When they were standing in front of his car, Alexis turned around and kissed him on the mouth gently. "Thanks for showing me a good time."

Gavin took her hand and told her, "If you need me I'm here for you, as your friend or as whatever you want me to be."

Damn, this young boy not only has all the right moves but he knows just what to say as well.

Alexis climbed into her car and drove off with Gavin following close behind.

Chapter 23

Know When to Go, Know When to Stop and Know When to Pause

Shamel was pacing the floor and his boys were watching him.

"Yo man, what's with all the pacing."

He looked at them. It was Big Tone, Ronnie, and True. He wondered how much he should tell them. Should he tell them he thought he was in love with Alexis? Should he tell them how far he was willing to go to get her?

Fuck it, they were his boys, if they said some wild shit and got out of hand, he'd just punch them in the fucking mouth.

"Yo, I think Alexis is the one. I'm considering making her my woman."

"Who? That chick you had Ronnie watching? The one who had that other ni—"

Shamel cut Big Tone off. "Yeah man, that's the one."

Big Tone, his main homie, who was sitting down, jumped up and said, "Oh, hell no, are you serious man? What happened to players for life? What happened to getting all the pussy you can?"

"Yeah man," True interrupted, "she must have put it on you."

Ronnie knew better than to open his mouth, so he just stood there. After all, Shamel paid his bills and he knew not to fuck with the man in charge.

"Ronnie, True, leave me and Big Tone alone."

True stood still, acting like he didn't want to move.

"Yo, I said step."

True turned and walked out of the room behind Ronnie.

Once they were out of the room, Big Tone asked, "What's up with your boy?" He was talking about True.

"He wants me to let him manage a club."

"So he's acting like a little bitch because of it?"

"Yeah, I guess so."

"You know you're going to have to handle that shit."

"Yeah, I know and I will, but that's not what I wanted to talk about."

"What you wanna talk about, this chick you got Ronnie following? What's up with that, man? Ain't no honey worth all the trouble."

Big Tone was Shamel's homeboy from childhood and he knew he could tell him anything. They went back to diapers.

"Yo dog, I guess I should have told you that I've been getting tired of this player shit. Ever since I spent the holidays with my family, I've been feeling like there's a void in my life. I want some little Shamels running around."

"Well, you can have that without getting serious with someone."

"I know but I don't want to do it that way."

Big Tone, who was once married and vowed never to entertain that shit ever again saw that his boy was serious and decided that he would not clown him but support his decision. "Man, if that's how you feel. You know me and my selfish ass. I felt that we were going to grow old banging pussy, smoking weed, and running these clubs."

"I'll still be doing that but I'll have my main girl at home waiting for me."

Big Tone laughed at this because although Shamel spoke of change, he didn't think he was really ready for commitment.

There was a knock on the door.

"Speak!" Shamel yelled.

"It's me Shamel."

"That's shorty?" Big Tone asked. Obviously he recognized the voice.

"Yeah," Shamel answered.

"I thought you weren't dealing with her anymore."

"I'm not."

"Come on Shamel, let me in!" the voice yelled through the door.

Big Tone looked at Shamel who gave him the nod yes.

Big Tone went to the door and opened it. "What's up Diamond?"

"Hey Tone, what's going up?" she responded while looking at Shamel the whole time.

"I guess I'll leave you two alone." He walked out and closed the door behind him.

"What should I call you? Diamond or Shay" Shamel asked.

"You can call me whatever you want."

"How about an underage liar?"

Shay stepped up to Shamel and wrapped her arms around his waist. "You mean to tell me, you honestly didn't know I was underage?"

He pushed her back. "Bitch, I ain't R. Kelly. You sucked my dick. I ain't never had sex with you."

Shay dropped her arms. "Why I gotta be all that? Why I gotta be a bitch?"

Shamel turned and walked away from her. He went and sat behind his desk. He knew she didn't really expect an answer. "Why are you working here if you're still in school, what's up with your home life?"

Shay dropped her eyes and told him, "I don't have a home life."

"What, are you telling me you're homeless?"

Shay didn't answer him.

"How come you haven't been to school?"

"What are you, my father?"

Shamel didn't even bother answering.

"What the hell I got to go to school for? I need to make a living. What, are you fucking Ms. Oliviá now? You don't want me anymore because of her old ass."

Shamel narrowed his eyes and told her, "Don't go there and who I'm fucking doesn't concern you."

Shay walked behind Shamel's desk and sat in front of him. She was wearing a jean mini-skirt with a yellow form-fitting T-shirt. She opened her legs and he wasn't shocked to see she didn't have any panties on.

"You mean to tell me you're going to give up this sweet, young pussy for hers?"

"Close your damn legs girl. I got business I need to take care of."

Shay didn't listen. She placed her hand on her pussy. "Look at it Shamel." She put her finger inside and pulled it out. "You know you want to."

He looked and his dick got hard immediately.

"What are you gonna do about it?" Shay was teasing him. "What are you gonna do about this tight young pussy?"

Shamel didn't say a word. He just stood up, unzipped his pants, pulled out his dick, pushed her back and shoved it in her pussy. Even knowing she was underage, he couldn't stop himself.

"Yeah, that's what I'm talking about. Fuck me Shamel."

Shamel placed his hand on her throat, "Shut up!" He continued to ram inside her pussy, making his dick go as deep as it possibly could. If he could have gone through her he would have. "Shit!" he called out as he pulled his dick out and came on her thighs.

"I knew you wanted this pussy."

Shamel pulled open the top drawer on his desk and pulled out a box of tissues. "Here, wipe off and let's talk."

Shay climbed off the desk and did as she was told.

Shamel fixed his clothes, looked at her and said, "I have something I need you to do for me."

"What am I going to get in return?" She wasn't doing shit for free, especially since he fired her ass.

"Don't worry about that. Just know that I'll take care of you."

"All right, what is it you want me to do?"

"It involves Alexis," he told her.

Shay rolled her eyes and said, "I should have known."

"I want you to go back to school."

"Back to school? For what?"

"Because you need your education."

Shay laughed out loud about that one. "You know damn well you don't give a damn about my education."

"I need you to do this so that no one's on my back about you. I don't want the police called and shit."

"Why would someone call the cops on me? I ain't nobody."

Shamel knew now was the time to throw on the charm. He touched her face and said, "That's where you're wrong. You mean more to me than all these hoes I got working up in here."

"Then how come I can't keep working here?"

"Because I want bigger and better things for you. I want you to work in my office, help me with my books and shit."

Shay may have been naïve when it came to

him, but she wasn't that naïve. "So basically, you want to keep fucking me and make good with Ms. Alexis so you can fuck her too."

Shamel was fed up with her asking questions, so he walked around her to the door, opened it and told her, "Get the fuck out and don't come back."

Shay didn't want to leave. She wanted Shamel any way she could have him and if that meant going back to school, she would but it would only be for a short while.

"All right, all right Shamel, I'll do it but remember you said you would take care of me."

He closed the door, "Come and give daddy a kiss."

Shay walked over to him slowly and wrapped her arms around him, "I love you Shamel. I'll do anything for you. You know that, right?"

Shamel could care less. He didn't want to hear those words from her, a high school student. He wanted to hear them from a grown-ass woman, a woman named Alexis.

Chapter 24

Why Be Afraid of the Unknown? You Won't Know If It's Your Cup of Tea Unless You Try It

Alexis waved to Gavin as she walked through her door. He followed her home just as he said he would. She didn't invite him in.

She pulled her cell phone out of her purse and sat down on the couch. She dialed Champagne's number.

"Hello?" It was Champagne. Alexis could hear people talking in the background.

"Hey, where are you?"

"At a get together."

Alexis was about to ask her, how could she be at a get together while Thomas was locked up, but then again, Thomas wasn't Champagne's man, Zyair was. *What am I so upset about? I don't go with Thomas, we're not exclusive. There's no reason for me to care so deeply.* Alexis tried to convince herself, but she knew she wasn't fooling anyone but herself because she found herself on more than a few occasions wondering what Thomas was doing, who he was with and if he was thinking about her.

"Why? What's up?" Champagne asked.

Alexis opened her mouth to speak but no words came out, instead she started crying.

"Are you crying?" Champagne asked once she heard a sniffle.

"No, no. I'm okay. It's just that. . . ."

"Just what sweetie, talk to me."

"I. . . ." She didn't know what she wanted. She didn't want to ask Champagne to leave where she was at having a good time and come sit with her miserable ass.

"Come where I'm at," Champagne said.

"Nah, I don't want to rain on your parade."

"Girl, come on. It'll take your mind off of whatever it's on and as you know there's nothing like girlfriends getting together. Plus I have someone I want you to meet."

Alexis looked around her empty house, then at her watch. It was still early and she didn't feel like being alone, so why not. Maybe the company of women was just what she needed.

"All right, where are you?"

After Champagne gave her the address, Alexis picked up her purse and opened her door. Before stepping out, she looked up and down the street to make sure there wasn't a car parked anywhere with someone sitting in it watching her. She was relieved to find that there wasn't.

*   *   *

Twenty minutes later, Alexis pulled up to the address Champagne gave her, parked and called Champagne on her cell phone. "I'm outside."

Less than ten seconds later Champagne was walking out of the door, waving her in.

"So, whose house is this?" Alexis asked.

"Sharon's."

"Who's Sharon?"

"The girl I was telling you about."

"What. . . ." Alexis didn't even have to finish her sentence because it hit her, it was "the girl". "The lesbian?" Alexis whispered.

"Shhhh. Come on in and meet her. She's having a get together."

Alexis followed her inside and prayed to herself that she wouldn't be uncomfortable or feel out of place. She'd never purposely hung around a group of gay women and wondered if anyone would try to come on to her.

When they entered the living room, Alexis felt welcomed immediately. Some of the women in attendance approached her with hugs and introduced themselves.

"I'm Sharon," one of the most attractive women there said. "Make yourself at home. Any friend of Champagne's is a friend of mine."

"Thank you." Alexis followed her into the living room where over twenty women were gathered drinking wine and having a heated conversation.

"Does Zyair know you're here?" Alexis whispered.

"I'm here as a friend not a lover and all he

needs to know is that I'm getting together with a group of women."

"She's very attractive." Alexis was talking about Sharon.

"Don't I know it."

"Shit, my vote went to Barack Obama," one of the women said. "Just because I'm a woman does not mean I had to go with Hillary. I'm black first."

Alexis looked at Champagne. "They're talking about last year's election?"

"Yeah, girl. That's because there's a republican in the house."

Alexis laughed and continued to listen.

"I know that's right, because the bottom line often comes down to race and not sex," another said.

"Not only that, she played dirty and he played fair. Remember how they were saying that the party was divided. That was some bullshit."

"Yeah and then there were people saying they wouldn't vote at all if Hillary wasn't running as his vice president."

"That was just plain ignorant."

"And now look, they're working together, making it happen."

"I'll drink to that."

Alexis just stood there and took it all in. She didn't even notice when Champagne walked off with Sharon.

"Hey, don't I know you from somewhere?" a voice whispered in Alexis' ear. She turned around to see who it was. It was a woman named Lana who helped her when she was out one night having a drink by herself.

Alexis knew she'd had one too many drinks but she didn't feel drunk, therefore she figured it was okay to drive home. Out of the bar she walked but the second she stepped out the door, she felt herself stumble.

"Uh oh, maybe I am a little tipsy," she said out loud. "This is not a good thing." She felt on her shoulder for her purse and realized it wasn't there. Just when panic was starting to set it, she heard someone yelling, "Ms., you left your purse."

Alexis turned around. "Oh my god, thank you. I was just about to panic."

"I tried to catch up with you before you walked out of the door."

Alexis couldn't believe her luck. "Damn, I can't believe you actually ran out here after me."

"There are still good people in this world."

"I see that."

"I'm Lana," she told Alexis as she handed her the purse.

"Alexis." Before she could get another word out of her mouth, she felt herself heave.

Lana took a step back. "Are you okay?""

Alexis shook her head and ran a couple of steps down the sidewalk. She stopped and threw up. Embarrassed out of her mind, she turned around to see Lana looking at her.

"Want me to get you some water or something?" Lana asked.

"You would really do that?"

"Sure." Lana turned around and started walking in the direction of the bar door but she stopped and looked at Alexis. *"Maybe you should come with me into the ladies room."*

Alexis followed and was basically taken care of. Lana helped her clean herself up and sat around and talked to her until she felt well enough to drive home.

"Oh, hey. How are you?"

"I'm good, how are you?"

Alexis wondered how long they were going to stand there and say hey, how are you? So she was honest and said, "Shit, I've had better days."

"Anything I can do about it?"

"Do you always help strangers?" Alexis asked.

"Well, you're not a stranger anymore. So, again, is there anything I can help you with?"

There really wasn't, so what could Alexis say other than "No thank you."

Alexis looked around the room and wondered if everyone was gay. Was she the only one in the room that slept with men?

"Who are you here with?" Alexis asked Lana.

"I'm a friend of Sharon's."

At the mention of Sharon, Alexis looked up for Champagne and noticed they were both gone. *I wonder where they went, are they making love?* After having that thought, she was surprised to find herself feeling a tinge of jealousy. What the hell?

"I'll be right back. I have to go to the bathroom." Alexis left her standing there and went to look for Champagne.

As she made her way to the back, supposedly in search of the bathroom, she peeked into a room that was empty. *For all I know they could be outside.* It was then she heard voices and if she wasn't mistaken, one of them was Champagne's.

The bathroom was next to the room where the voices were coming from. *I wonder if I can hear what they are saying if I go into the bathroom?* As it turned out she could. Not only could she hear what was being said but there was a door that connected to the other room.

Alexis made sure the bathroom door was locked and she cracked open the other door, hoping they wouldn't hear. If she got busted, she'd make up some kind of excuse. Whether it was believable or not, she'd deal with that when they time came.

"I can't see you in that capacity," Champagne was saying.

"Are we going to go through this again?" Sharon said. She stood in front of Champagne and pulled her to her so that their pelvises were touching.

"Go through what?" Champagne asked.

"Go through the whole I can't see you thing. You know you want to."

"I'm getting married," Champagne told her although she and Zyair still had not set a date. But there was no reason to tell Sharon that.

Alexis watched as Sharon kissed Champagne on the neck. *What the hell, am I becoming a voyeur? I wonder if Champagne is going to put up a fight?*

She didn't have to wonder because Champagne didn't. She closed her eyes and moaned instead.

"Come on, let me fuck you Champagne, let me do to you what your man does." Sharon then placed her hand on Champagne's pussy.

"You have company. You need to go entertain your company."

Alexis couldn't hear what Champagne said because there was a knock on the bathroom door. She had to quietly close the adjoining door.

After flushing the toilet and turning the water on in the sink, she said, "Just a minute." She looked in the mirror and found that her face was flushed. She took a deep breath, opened the door and walked out, letting the other person in.

When she entered the living room, Champagne was coming from the back and headed straight for her. She couldn't even look her in the eye.

Once she was up on her she said, "Let me follow you home, I need to talk."

Alexis looked at her friend who was obviously torn between her love for Zyair and her lust for this Sharon character and told her, "As do I."

They quickly said their good-byes to everyone and were on their way out the door when the female who assisted Alexis that night came up to them with a piece of paper in her hand.

She handed it Alexis, winked and told her, "Call me."

Alexis took it without saying a word.

When they arrived at Alexis' house, she was exhausted. It had been a long and draining day. It hit her the second they walked in. The last thing she felt like doing was having a conversation and it seemed like that was the last thing Champagne felt like doing as well.

"Girl, I'm tired. You mind if I stay in the guest room."

Thankfully, Alexis changed the sheets each time she slept in there with someone. "Where's Zyair?"

"I called him on my way here. He's at the courthouse. They finally got a judge to sign papers to have Thomas released."

"What the hell happened, Champagne?"

"I know what didn't happen and that's that Thomas was as surprised as anyone that those women were underage. He was surprised they were even there."

"You think he'll see me tomorrow?"

"I'm sure he will."

They were standing in the hall heading to

separate rooms when Champagne asked, "Oh, how was date with the young dude?"

Alexis smiled and told her, "It was really nice. I'll tell you about it in the morning."

"All right, love you."

"Love you too."

When Alexis walked in her room, she sat on her bed and thought about what she'd witnessed between Champagne and Sharon. She thought about how wet it made her and how fast her heart began to beat. She knew that she would have watched everything had something more gone down and if there wasn't a knock on the bathroom door.

Damn, was her curiosity getting the best of her? Would her openness and willingness to be this new sexual being allow her to sleep with a female? Was it something she could actually go through with?

Alexis fell asleep with these thoughts and perhaps that explains her having the dream she had, the dream about Lana entering her with a dildo.

"Come on, try it, you just might like it."

Alexis looked at her with the double-sided dildo in her hand. She wondered what she was going to do with that thing. So she threw up both her hands.

"Okay, you need to slow it down. I'm not ready

for that. Heck, I thought there was more romance to this whole lesbian thing. You're acting like a man that just wants a slam bam thank you ma'am sex session."

Lana smiled at her and said, "My bad. I just wanted to get it started before you changed your mind. In the past, it has been my experience that you first timers are less likely to stop once I penetrate you with the dildo, but I'm sorry, lie back."

Alexis lay back and Lana started to kiss her. In one smooth motion, they went from kissing to Lana pressing Alexis' breasts together and sucking on both nipples.

Lana started to go lower and kissed Alexis from her breast to her belly button. She was giving every nook and cranny of Alexis' body attention, whereas, some men couldn't care less.

Before Alexis could catch her breath from the tender kisses, she felt Lana's cold tongue run the length of her vagina.

She placed her whole mouth over Alexis' clitoris and started to lick and suck and lick and suck. Alexis' body started to react to every stroke of her tongue.

Before she knew it, Lana had placed a finger inside her vagina and was sucking on her clitoris and working her finger in and out. Just as Alexis started bucking her hips, Lana stopped and reached for a double-sided dildo. She gently rubbed it up and down the lips of her vagina until she finally slid it in.

Alexis felt like she was going to come immediately.

She heard Lana whisper, "Don't come yet.

Hold it. I want to come with you." Lana lay so that her pussy was facing Alexis' and she put the other end of the dildo inside herself.

They both started playing with their clitoris until they exploded at the same time.

When Alexis' woke up the next morning, her pussy was sticky and all she could do was smile, because she remembered every detail of the dream. Even though she smiled, she speculated on the meaning of the dream. What did it mean, if anything? Was the dream because of what Champagne was going through, was the dream because she was around a bunch of gay women or was she starting to get curious as well?

Chapter 25

Know Your Enemies as Well as You Know Your Friends. Know What Motivates Them to Despise You So

Zyair and Elliot Hart, Thomas' attorney, waited on Thomas to come from the back where the possessions he carried with him, when he was locked up were being held. It had been a long- ass night and a half for him and he couldn't wait to get home and take a hot-ass bath. Being in a cell was not something he wanted to experience ever again. It was cold, it was dark and there was a damp old smell to it that he knew was clinging to his body.

When he walked into the front of the county jail, he was surprised not to see any press. There sure was enough of it when he was getting arrested and when he was brought in but now that a brother was released, they were nowhere in sight.

Thank God his attorney had connections because they didn't have to appear in front of a

bunch of people. When they entered the court-
room, Thomas was surprised to find that it was
empty, except for the judge, a court clerk and
the bailiff. Judge Wilson was Spanish, female
and looked to be in her sixties. She was looking
at some papers when they walked in.

Elliot told him to take a seat behind the table
before the benches and walked up to the judge.
Judge Wilson looked up and smiled when he
approached her. It was obvious to Thomas that
Elliot and the judge had some kind of relationship and he hoped this meant something positive. After they exchanged a few words, the
judge asked him to come up and informed him
that no one came forward to pursue the matter
and that he could be on his way.

After thanking her, Elliot told Thomas he'd
wait for him in the hallway.

Zyair and Elliot appeared to be in deep conversation when Thomas saw them waiting.
Hopefully they were doing what he had been
doing all night and that's trying to figure out
who the hell was out to get his ass.

"I'm a free man!" he said by way of greeting.

Zyair was the first to stand up and give him a
brotherly hug. "What's up man? You okay? No
one bothered you in there, did they?"

Thomas shook his head and laughed. "Damn
man, you're acting like I was in prison and shit.
I was in a holding cell."

"You do know you're going to have to do damage control to keep your reputation, perhaps

put out a statement and give an interview," his attorney stated.

"Yeah, but that shouldn't be a problem. People know me and they know that underage shit wasn't my doing."

"I didn't think it was," his attorney said. Although one could never be sure what a person was or wasn't capable of. This was one case where he had no doubt because when the ladies arrived Thomas was nowhere to be found, and when they were questioned all they said was they were invited to the party. They claimed not to know the name of the person that called them.

"Sir," one of the officers said, "We need you to fill out some papers."

"Man, I'll meet you out front," Thomas told Zyair while he and Elliot went to sign release papers.

Once done and standing outside, Elliot told Thomas, "We'll talk later."

"I'll call you tomorrow." Thomas needed the day to think.

"Let's make it before then."

"Let's not." A bath, some rest and an errand were the only things on his mind.

All Elliot could do was agree. After all, he worked for Thomas not the other way around.

Once in the car, Zyair asked Thomas, "What the fuck is going on with you? Be honest with me man. Did you fuck with someone's wife or fuck someone over?"

"If I did, you would be the first to know. Not only that, but messing with another's man property, those days are long gone. You know I'm trying to make an honest man out of myself."

"Well, it's obvious someone is out to get you, first the car and now this."

"You think I don't know that? You think I didn't run down the list of people I know and have done business with?"

"What about that female who told Alexis she was pregnant by you? Shondell?"

"Nah, man. I don't think she has the kind of contacts for some shit like this, but you best believe I will either be stopping by her crib or giving her lying ass a call."

"Do you think that's wise?" Zyair asked. "I think right now your concern needs to be clearing your name."

Zyair was right, that should be his concern but he had another concern and that was Alexis. He'd thought about her all night. Was she that upset by what she was told that she chose not to come to the gathering? If she was that meant she cared for him more than he thought.

"Have you talked to Alexis? Does she know what went down?"

"Of course she does. Champagne stayed at her house last night. She said something about some dude following her."

* * *

Thomas didn't like what he was hearing at all. If he found out who this character was, he was going to get the beat down for real. Thomas knew what he had to do and that's call out the big dogs; the fellas from his past, perhaps even do some investigating. Damn, here he goes again investigating someone. He really didn't want to have to go there because Alexis was not happy with him about the first time. But at least she learned who Khalil really was.

The rest of the ride was silent except for the music playing in the background.

Thomas was thinking about Alexis and Zyair was thinking about Daneen, the girl he slept with when he thought it was over between him and Champagne. He ran into her a few days ago and found that he couldn't get her off his mind. He knew just thinking about her was trouble, but his mind didn't always do what he wanted it to. He was a good man, normally a faithful man who slipped that once and didn't plan on doing it again. It's just that something was going on with Champagne. She'd seemed distracted lately and he was feeling a little left to the side. They were going to have to talk about whatever it was and hopefully fix whatever it was. Then that way maybe, just maybe, his mind wouldn't wander.

Chapter 26

Before You Can Face Others, You Need to Face Yourself

Alexis was in her office with the door closed looking at the flowers Gavin had delivered to her.

That morning when she woke up, Champagne had already left. There was a note on the kitchen table. It said, "Hey girl, I didn't want to wake you up but I did want to let you know that Zyair picked up Thomas last night and I'll call you later."

Alexis looked at the clock and saw that she had hours to go. She needed to see Thomas and speak with him. She needed to hear his voice and know that he was okay.

No, she hadn't forgotten about Victoria's mother. At this point all she could do was hope that the pregnancy story was a bold-faced lie.

Alexis' schedule was packed for the day. She had a meeting with the school superintendent.

She also had to counsel a couple of students and get ready for a conference.

Normally, she tried to get out of going to the conference but because her life had become somewhat of a mess and her mind was confused about who she was and who she wanted to be, she figured the getaway this conference afforded her was just what she needed. Plus, it was in Tampa, Florida, which meant she could extend her stay and visit Miami.

Alexis picked the phone up off her desk and dialed Thomas' number. On the first ring, someone knocked on the door. She hung up because she didn't want a half conversation with him.

"Come in."

The person who walked in surprised the hell out of her. It was Shay.

Alexis stood up and went around her desk to greet her with a hug but when she put her arms out, Shay gave her a look that stopped her in her tracks. She quickly put her arms down.

"I'm glad to see you Shay."

"Are you?"

"I wouldn't say it if I wasn't."

Shay just stood there, not saying a word, just looking around.

"So?" Alexis asked, waiting to hear what she had to say.

"So?" Shay repeated.

Alexis could see where this was going and if it was going to go anywhere, it meant she was going to have to take the lead. Alexis sat down on the couch that was against the wall. She crossed her legs and thought maybe she should wait Shay out, let her have the first words.

Shay cleared her throat and tried to think of something to say. *I don't fucking want to be here. If it wasn't for Shamel's ass, I wouldn't be.*

Alexis looked at her watch. "I don't have all day Shay. You came to see me, so there must be something you want to say."

Placing her hands on her hips, Shay told her, "I ain't got shit to say. I heard you've been looking for me and wanted to know what you wanted."

Fed up with the attitude and not wanting to play who can be the biggest ass, Alexis patted the seat next to her. "Come sit next to me."

"I can stand," Shay told her.

"I have been looking for you. I've been worried about you."

"I can take care of myself," Shay told her as she tried to picture Shamel with her guidance counselor. Shay thought about what transpired in the office with Shamel, how he fucked her and basically told her to "step off." It was their first time having actual intercourse and she wanted it to be different. She'd gone down on him a few times over the past three months and she was trying to build it up to be more. She was hoping that he would become her sugar daddy and take care of her but after the way he treated her, she just didn't see that happening.

"How? By working at a strip club?"

Shay rolled her eyes. "I was doing just fine until you came in there. What were you doing in there anyway?" She wanted to see if she was going to tell her anything about Shamel, but Alexis wasn't falling for it. She was a grown-ass woman and she wasn't going to give a child information about her life.

"That's not important, what's important is why you've chosen to go the route you're going. Why are you stripping? You're smart, Shay. You used to be an honor student. What's going on with you?"

"You're asking a lot of personal questions."

"That's because I care for you. You're one of the few students that have unlimited potential. You're special Shay, too special to be showing your body to any Tom, Dick and Harry." Alexis didn't feel like she was being a hypocrite because she was an adult and was able to live her life and make responsible decisions without any repercussions she couldn't handle. Yes, she'd slept with three men in a month's time and yes, after some serious thought, she questioned her sanity but at this point it was what it was and she'd either keep on moving in that direction or make another choice. "You are a queen and you need to know that," she told Shay.

Shay looked at Alexis and saw the sincerity in her eyes.

"Please sit next to me."

For some reason Shay couldn't explain, she did just that.

"Talk to me. That's what I'm here for. Is something going on at home? Is there anything

I can do to help out?" Alexis knew she was going out on a limb but for very few students she would, and one of them was Shay. I went to the address in your files looking for you."

This threw Shay off. She didn't really know that Alexis was looking for her. "What!"

"I went looking for you."

"And what happened?" Shay wondered if her drug-addict mother answered the door. She was always fucked up. It could be by liquor or crack cocaine, whatever she could get her hands on. That's why Shay had to do what she had to do. That's why she stayed in motels with the money she made from stripping because most nights her moms had company and it was the kind of company she didn't want to be around because she was scared she might kill a motherfucker. Shay knew that she should share this information and that it was a burden she shouldn't have to carry herself but she didn't and she wasn't sure when she'd be ready to.

"A woman answered the door." Alexis watched Shay closely to see if she would get some kind of reaction. She wondered if it was her mother. "She was intoxicated and she told us—"

Shay grew alarmed. Who the hell did she take with her? "Us, who's us?"

"A male friend of mine," Alexis reassured her. "We were told you don't live there."

Shay crossed her arms. "That's because I don't."

Alexis leaned into Shay trying to create intimacy. "Was that your mother?"

When Shay didn't answer Alexis knew her answer.

"Where are you staying? Who are you living with?"

Fuck! Fuck! Fuck! Shay did not come here to be grilled.

"Damn, how come you can't mind your business?" Shay stood up to leave but Alexis grabbed her arm.

"You are my business. I want what's best for you." Alexis stood up. She took both of Shay's hands. "Do you remember when I first started counseling you and I asked you where did you see yourself after graduating? You proudly said college, and that you wanted to be a lawyer?"

Shay did remember but that was over a year ago. That was before her mother stopped caring, again. There was a time when she had it together but then she'd start getting high again and so the cycle went. Right now Shay didn't see college happening. She needed to survive.

"Do you remember how we mapped it all out for you?" Alexis let go of her hands and was surprised when Shay didn't move. She went to a file cabinet and searched for a file. Once she found it, she handed it to Shay. "Look inside Shay. Look at what you dreamed of no less than a year ago. That can still happen."

Shay didn't want to but she found herself opening the folder anyway and looking at the papers inside. She felt herself start to well up.

Alexis could see that she was having a small breakthrough. "Shay, all this is possible and so much more. You just need to let me help you."

I didn't come here for this. I didn't come here for this, Shay kept repeating to herself but Alexis' voice was overpowering hers.

"Look at you, you're smart, you're beautiful, you have more going for yourself than a lot of other students and you want to mess it up, you want to give up."

"I owe people money. I'm in debt. I have to help my moms," Shay told her.

"I'll help you get out of debt. We'll get you a part-time job." *What the hell am I getting myself into?* Alexis wondered but she couldn't stop. She felt like she needed to save this girl.

Shay couldn't stop the tears that were falling down her cheeks.

"What is it? Do you need somewhere to stay? Is that it?" Before she knew it, Alexis was saying, "You can stay with me until we figure something else out."

It was then Shay broke down. She sat down, placed her head in her hands and started crying. There was so much she wanted to say, so much pain inside her but it was hers and she didn't know how to share it. All she knew was that Ms. Oliviá believed in her more than she believed in herself. It was a first. No one else had ever done that. No one else had ever told her the world was within her reach. She wanted to believe it.

This stripping shit paid the bills and allowed

her to feed her mom but she wasn't responsible for her mother; she was responsible for herself. She did want out of the game. She just didn't know how she was going to escape it and here someone was offering her a hand.

I'm going to take it. I'm also going to tell her about me and Shamel.

Shay wiped her tears. She looked up at Alexis. "There's something I need to—"

Before Shay got a chance to finish her thoughts, Victoria came busting in the door.

"Ms. Alexis, I apologize. . . ." She stopped in her tracks when she saw Shay sitting there. "Oh, I'm sorry."

Shay stood up. "No, no that's okay. I'll come back."

Before Alexis could stop her, Shay was out the door.

Victoria looked at Alexis and asked, "Was Shay crying?"

Alexis didn't even bother to answer. She needed to go after Shay. "Why are you busting up in my office like that?"

"My bad. It's just that I wanted to apologize for my mother."

"Why are you apologizing? What your mother does has nothing to do with you." *With her lying ass, I hope.*

"I know. It's just that I got you all involved when you didn't really want to and well, I'm embarrassed."

Alexis had to ask. "Is your mom really pregnant?"

"I don't know. She said she is."

"Does she have anyone to help her out if she is?" What she was really asking was if Thomas had been around.

Victoria raised her eyebrows. "Why?"

Think fast. "Because I may be able to give her a number of someone that can help with doctor appointments and whatever else she may need help in."

Victoria thought this was strange. "My mother's not a child. She had me and she's taken good care of me."

"You're right, she did and she has." Alexis looked at her watch. "Listen, I have to go look for Shay."

"Is she okay?"

Of course, Alexis wasn't about to tell a student what was going on. "She's fine."

Five minutes later, Alexis was walking back into her office, alone. Shay was nowhere to be found.

Alexis had a few minutes before her meeting with the superintendent so she picked up the phone to call Thomas. She dialed the number and listened to it ring. She needed to find out what happened; if he knew who would set him up and to let him know that she believed in him and his innocence.

"Hello?" It was Thomas.

"Thomas."

"Alexis?"

"Yes, it's me."

"Can I see you tonight?" he asked her. "We have some things we need to talk about."

"That's just why I was calling. I'll be by around 8:00 pm."

After hanging up Alexis asked herself yet again, "What the hell am I getting myself into?"

Chapter 27

Sometimes the Best Thing to Do Is Give In, Especially If It Pleases the One You're With

Alexis was sitting in front on Thomas' house trying to figure out what she wanted to say. What right did she have to ask him if what Shondell said was true? What right did she have to ask about what transpired the night of the party?

However, she needed to know. She had to know because against her will and against her better judgment, her feelings had gotten involved. She was starting to care for him more than she wanted to admit even to herself.

She looked up at the door and glanced at the window. She saw Thomas looking out the window and she knew he was probably wondering why she was sitting in the car. Did she need a moment and what for? They caught one another's eye and she looked at the door, which he had just opened. He waved her over and she put up one finger as in "wait."

She didn't want to be rushed and she wanted to come in on her own time. After counting to ten, she got out of her car, closed her door and walked in the house.

"Thomas?" she called out.

Thomas came from the back. The second they saw one another, they wanted to run into each other's arms like they do on television, fall on the floor and make wild passionate love. They didn't because this was reality and there were some things they each wanted to say to the other.

Standing in front of one another, they eyed each other up and down, at first with neither saying a word.

"How are you?" Alexis asked.

"It's all good."

"Is it?"

Thomas took her hand. "Come on, let's go into the kitchen."

She didn't protest.

Once in the kitchen, Thomas poured them each a glass of wine.

"I didn't know you drank wine. I thought you were a cognac, Hennessey man."

"I'm that and more," he told her as he sat down on a stool and pulled out one for her.

"What's going on Alexis?"

"Shouldn't I be asking you that?"

"Zyair told me you came across Shondell."

Alexis didn't feel like beating around the bush. "Is she having your baby?"

"Would it matter to you if she was?"

Alexis placed her wine glass down and stood up.

"Where are you going?"

"I don't have time for games."

"Who's playing games? I just want to know if it would matter to you."

"I wouldn't be asking you if it didn't."

"Does this mean that you're feeling me on a deeper level?"

Alexis wasn't ready to admit it. "Is she?"

"The last time I slept with her was two or three months ago and it was that one night only."

"Did you wear a condom?"

"Of course. Do you really have to ask that question? You met her, she's crazy. That's why I stopped seeing her in the first place. Yes, we used to deal but it was just sex. Every now and then I'd help her and her daughter out. But when she started stalking and questioning me, I knew it was time to call it quits."

"How do you know she didn't poke a hole in the condom or something?" Alexis had heard of women doing this all the time, especially when the man involved was well-off. "Was it your condom or hers?"

"It doesn't matter," Thomas told her. "Just know that I'm going to get to the bottom of this."

Thomas didn't want to think about Shondell and the condom. That was the last thing he wanted to think about. What he wanted to think about was asking Alexis point blank to be his lady. After being arrested, getting his car destroyed and having his reputation put on the line, he knew that it was time to cut out all the bullshit and settle down. The one he wanted to settle down with was sitting right in front of him.

Ever since they hung up earlier, Thomas had been rehearsing his "I want to be serious speech." Well, not really rehearsing but going over in his head what he wanted to say.

"What are you going to do about her?"

"The only thing I can do; confront her."

Alexis stood up, "Let's go sit on the couch."

Good, this means she's staying and she's trying to get comfortable.

Once they were sitting next to one another, Alexis asked, "So what happened the other night?"

"You know what, I have no idea. What I do know is that someone is out to get me."

"Are you sure?"

"I'm not one to be paranoid or suspect shit for no reason. I know when something is up and right now something is up. I just need to find out what and who is causing this shit to happen."

Alexis leaned back on the couch and closed her eyes.

"Are you okay?" Thomas asked.

"I am. I've just had a long day, that's all."

Thomas moved closer to her and put his arms around her. He pulled her into him. "Alexis?"

"Yes?"

"You know I want to be with you, right?"

"Thomas, don't start this right now."

"Start what? I'm not starting anything. I'm stating a fact and that fact is that I want you to be my lady."

Alexis wasn't stunned. She knew that this was coming. She just didn't know that it would happen so soon.

She pulled away from him. "Thomas, how can you ask me that? You know I'm not ready to be in an exclusive relationship. You know my recent history. Hell, you played a part in me finding out about Khalil and how he played me out. You know it left me hurt and damaged."

"I do know these things, but what he did has nothing to do with me. I'm not him."

"How do you know that you are ready for a serious relationship? How long have you ever been faithful to one woman?"

Thomas didn't answer.

"Exactly. Thomas, right now is not the time to be playing with my emotions."

"Why do you think I'm playing with your emotions? I'm asking you some real shit right now. I'm asking you to be my lady."

"I can't say yes to that. Right now I just want to keep it light. That's all I can handle." She was saying those words but did she really mean them? Did she really want to keep it light? She wasn't even sure.

Thomas stood up in front of Alexis and started pacing. "You know what Alexis, you're right about me and you raised some very good questions. You're correct in saying I have never been faithful to one woman. Shit, I never tried.

How do I know that I am ready for a relationship? Well, I'm not ready for any relationship. I'm ready for a relationship with you. I know this because when I wake up in the morning I think about you and whether or not we're going to speak. And when I think about who I believe will make me a better man by just being in their presence, all I see is your beautiful face."

He stopped pacing, looked at her and noticed that he had her undivided attention. "I adore you Alexis and what I haven't done in the past is simply because I haven't run across another you."

"Thomas, I'm not ready to make you any promises."

Thomas sat back down and placed his finger gently on her lips. "Nor am I asking you to. I want the ball to be in your court. I am relinquishing control and placing my heart at your mercy."

Alexis was blown away by what Thomas just said to her. Shit, he'd blown himself away by being so deep.

If he's running game, he is doing a hell of a job. If it's just sex he's after, hell, he was going to get that anyway.

"Thomas?" She wanted to distract him from this line of conversation. He was being so serious with her. Didn't he know the fear of being hurt was on the forefront of her mind?

"Yes?"

"Make love to me."

Thomas stood up but Alexis pulled him back

down. "No, make love to me right here, right now."

Thomas looked her straight in the eyes as his hands touched her face. *Damn, I'm really in love with this woman.*

He moved his hands and pushed her back and started to kiss her. The longer they kissed, the deeper and more intense it became. Alexis had to pull away because there were so many feelings flowing through their lips.

She reached for his shirt and tried to pull it over his head but he told her he'd do it. He stood up and took off his shirt. She unbuttoned hers and unsnapped her bra. He pulled down his pants and she slid her skirt up.

"Oh, so it's like that."

"Yes, it's like that."

Thomas laughed as he bent down to pull her panties off, but not before rubbing her through the material causing her to moan.

"Do you want me to taste you?"

"No, I want you inside me."

Alexis reached out and touched his dick. She pulled it gently toward her. He knelt between her legs and let her guide him inside her pussy with her hands. They both closed their eyes until he settled inside her.

Slowly, he began to move inside Alexis as her pussy walls clinched around his dick.

"Whatever you're doing, keep doing it," he told her.

She started to work her vaginal walls even more, hoping he felt every squeeze. Thomas started pulling all the way out and going as deep inside her as he could. He'd pull out slowly again and go deeper. Once he was in as far as he could go, he started moving his body in a circular motion.

The rhythm he had going was causing her to shudder. Alexis was feeling a sensation that she hadn't felt before. It felt like she was going to urinate. She found herself contracting her muscles and trying to pull away but Thomas wasn't going to let that happen.

Please don't let me pee on this man, Alexis thought to herself as she tried to pull away again.

"Relax, let it happen," Thomas told her.

Please don't let Thomas be into golden showers. "I feel like I have to pee," she broke down and told him.

Thomas laughed as he continued grinding into her.

"Stop Thomas, it's not. . . ." She couldn't continue her thought process because suddenly she felt a tingling sensation that felt like pressure in her stomach that moved down to her vagina. Before she could stop, she found herself searching for his mouth with hers and as she felt her orgasm build up, she bit down on his bottom lip. Alexis arched her back, grabbed his ass and pushed him as deep into her as she could as she felt wetness coming from her vagina.

Exhausted from what just happened, she looked up at him but he had his eyes closed and was on the verge of his own orgasm. She started to slowly move with him until finally he collapsed on her.

After a brief second or two, he looked at her and she asked, "What was that?"

Of course, Alexis didn't expect an answer. She knew what it was. It was the first time she'd had a vaginal orgasm; an orgasm strictly from dick with no clitoral stimulation. Something that she'd only heard about and never thought she'd experience because according to Oprah over 75 percent of women didn't.

It was then that it started to hit her and she knew. She knew that Thomas just might be the one.

Chapter 28

When You Know It's Over, Don't Look Back

Shay was nervous as hell. She was going to tell Shamel that after working with him and being available to him for three months she was through with him; that she decided to live her life right and that she was worthy and could no longer be his play thing sexually or any other kind of way.

He really shouldn't have a problem with it. He can have any girl he wants. Shay tried to trick herself into believing this, but she knew Shamel. She'd been dealing with him for over a year and she knew that he would give her a hard time just because he could.

I have to try and better myself. Ms. Oliviá believes in me and truth be told, I believe in myself. She offered to help me in any way she could and the least I can do is take her up on that offer. If it doesn't work out, if I fail for some reason, at least I can say I tried.

Shay walked up to the club and stopped in front of the door. She had to go through with this.

It's his fault anyway. He's the one that sent me to her, talking about "Go back to school. I want you to work in my office." I can be a lawyer. Fuck working in an office.

No one was standing at the door because it was still early, so Shay opened the door and stepped in. After adjusting her eyes to the dim light, she glanced around and saw the usual suspects. The only person she didn't spot was Big Tone.

She didn't see Shamel so she asked the bartender, "Is Shamel here?"

He looked toward the back. Shamel was walking out of his office with someone that looked familiar. Once they were up one on another, she noticed that it was Karen, this girl from her biology class.

Karen looked up and saw Shay looking at her. She quickly looked away.

Shay watched as Shamel popped her on the ass and told her he will see her tonight.

He looked at Shay and told her. "Follow me."

She does. *Should I tell him that Karen's underage?*

Once in his office, Shamel closed the door. "Did you go to school today?"

"Yes." *Maybe what I need to do is warn her.*

"Did you see Alexis?"

"Yes." *Maybe I should tell Ms. Oliviá.*

Shamel can sense something was up. "Why

the fuck are you giving me one word answers? What's up?"

"I've decided not to deal with you anymore." *There, I've said it.*

Shamel thought this was the funniest shit he'd heard in a long time.

"What's so funny?"

"You're what's funny. What are you going to do if you're not with me? Go work in one of those hell-hole strip clubs where no one will look out for you? You need me Shay and you know it."

Shay looked at Shamel like he was crazy. "I don't need you. Ms. Oliviá said—"

Shamel got in Shay's face. "Said what? That you got potential and that you could do better than being a stripper? Hah, that's a laugh. That's what she gets paid to say."

"She's a good person Shamel. I don't know what you have planned to do with her or to her but I don't want to lie to her. . . . She told me that I don't have to dance anymore and that she would let me come live with her and help me pay you all the money that I owe you."

Shamel grabbed Shay by the neck. "You . . . You told her my name? You told her you owe me money?"

Shay put her hand over Shamel's and tried to pull it away. "No, I just told her that I owed somebody some money and I was dancing to pay back the debt."

Shamel took one step back. The look in his eyes frightened Shay. She turned to walk away but he grabbed her arm and held on tight.

"Let go of my arm Shamel. You're hurting me."

"First of all, you silly little young-ass hoe, I own your ass."

Shay tried to pull away but he was holding her too tight. "What the fuck is wrong with you Shamel? Are you crazy? Let me go!"

He didn't because something in him clicked. "I tell your dumb ass to do a simple task, go back to school, suck it up and act like a good girl. But no, you come back to me with this new life plan shit. I see you lack discipline, and it's my job as head of the family to see to it that discipline is enforced. You disobeyed me, and for that you must pay."

What the hell is he talking about? Whatever it was, Shay knew it was going to be brutal because of the look in his eyes. She'd seen him react physically to men in the club before. She'd seen him grab the women forcefully and she'd felt his hands around her throat and there was a look each time. The look he had now was it.

She started to scream but Shamel pulled her into him and placed one hand over her mouth and put his legs between hers in a way that she wasn't able to move.

He took off his thick leather belt with the other hand and raised it high. In doing so, Shay was almost able to escape but he grabbed her arm and started striking her over and over. He was hitting her everywhere, on her arms, her legs and her face.

"Stop! Please stop!" Some kind of way she got loose and tried to run toward the door but he grabbed her again and started smacking her in the face with an open palm.

Suddenly he heard someone trying to get in the office with a key.

The only person that had a key was Big Tone.

Before he had a chance to stop him from entering, Big Tone walked through the door and noticed Shay on the floor bleeding with a belt next to her and Shamel with his arm raised.

"What the. . . ."

Shamel dropped his arm and looked at Shay then Big Tone.

"What the fuck did you do?" Big Tone asked.

"Get her out of here," Shamel said after kicking her.

"Get her out of here? Just what am I supposed to do with her?"

"I don't know and I don't care."

Big Tone reached down to help Shay up. He looked at Shamel and told him, "You fucked up man, you fucked up big time."

Big Tone half carried her to the bathroom that was attached to the office and in a low voice told her, "You need to go to the hospital. I'm going to drop you off."

Shay could barely speak. She was in shock and in pain.

"Just don't say who did this to you because if you do, you know what'll happen."

Shay knew that was a warning and it was one she wasn't going to take lightly.

Chapter 29

Sometimes You Have To Get Involved. Don't Think Of It As a Chore, Think Of It As a Gift To The Other Person

Alexis was home sitting on her couch, relaxing and thinking about the conversation she and Thomas had. She was seriously considering giving this relationship thing a try again. That meant she was going to have to call Shamel who had left her several messages, and tell him they couldn't go out anymore. As for Gavin, well, she enjoyed the time they spent together and she could see them being friends.

She was also on the couch wondering if she should call the police and report that she thought she was being followed. She didn't know what to do because she hadn't seen anyone and she was just going off a hunch. Well, more than a hunch. When she arrived home from Thomas', there was a note attached to her door that said, "How's Thomas?" That shit scared the hell out of her. She tried to call him but the phone went right into voice mail. She didn't leave a message.

Alexis was supposed to be at work but she called out. She just didn't feel up to going and had some things she needed to think about.

She'd left a message with the secretary and with Maya, telling them if they saw Shay to have her call her cell phone and that it was very important.

"Are you sure you want us to give a student your cell number?" they both asked.

She was sure she told them.

Alexis picked up the remote to turn the television on when her cell phone rang. She'd left it on the kitchen table when she made breakfast. She stood up to get it but it stopped ringing. Before she had a chance to sit back down, it started ringing again. This time she made it into the kitchen. Not even bothering to look at the caller ID she answered, "Hello."

"Hey sexy." It was Gavin.

"Hey you."

"I'm coming by the school to drop something off for my sister. Do you mind if I come by your office?"

"I'm not there today. I called out."

"Really? Well, how about having lunch together?"

Alexis figured she'd say yes, because it would give her an opportunity to tell him about Thomas. "I'd like that. Where do you want to meet?"

"How about I come pick you up?"

She saw no harm in it. Plus, if someone was following her like she thought, they'd see a man coming to her door and maybe, just maybe they'd go away. That thought alone made Alexis go to the window and look out. "That's cool."

"What time?"

When she looked out, she saw a car drive by slower than usual. She quickly closed the curtains. "The sooner the better."

Gavin could hear panic in her voice. "Is everything okay?"

"I don't know, Gavin. I think I told you before that I think someone is following me."

"Yeah, I believe you did tell me that."

"Well, I think the person is on my street."

"What! Are you sure?"

"I don't know. I just might be paranoid. It's just that I looked out the window and I could have sworn this car was driving by real slow like."

"What kind of car was it?"

That was a question she didn't have an answer to. "It was black."

Gavin waited to hear more, but when she didn't say anything he asked, "That's all?"

"I don't know cars Gavin. The only thing I know about cars is how to drive them."

"I'm on my way over."

"You don't have to come right now. I'm in the house. I'll be all right."

Gavin wasn't hearing that shit. He was on his way anyway. "I'll see you shortly."

When they hung up the phone, Alexis looked

out the window again and this time there was no car riding by and everything on the block looked normal. She also tried to call Thomas again, but it went to voice mail. "Thomas, it's me, your . . . your. . . ." She wanted to say your woman but the words were stuck in her throat. "It's Alexis, call me."

She hung up and sat back down on the couch. While waiting she thought back to her childhood and her father, who she still had not called.

She thought about how he would tell her that *"You determine your path and you teach people how to treat you."*

Back then when he would drop those bits of wisdom, it went in and out. Now that she was older, she realized he knew just what he was talking about.

She was here, in this place, unmarried, with no kids and doing a job that she used to love but now tolerated because of the choices she made.

She was here in this place seeing three men, sleeping with them, even though she knew better.

She was here in this place unfulfilled by her decisions because of the choices she made.

That's right, the choices she made.

She knew it was now time to make new choices and the first one would be to commit to Thomas.

If she was honest with herself, she liked him all along, even when he was screwing a bunch of women. She just didn't take it anywhere because she knew better. She didn't want to set herself up for heartache.

Alexis shook her head because that's just what happened anyway. She ended up getting her heart broken by another man.

Please God let this be it for me. Let Thomas be the one. He sounded sincere in his words and I do want to take this chance with him.

Prior to meeting Khalil, Alexis was all into church. She attended every Sunday, went to Bible Study on Wednesdays and even attended prayer service. She was a Bible toting, scripture-quoting woman. *Maybe I need to go back to church. Maybe Thomas will come with me.* Although she tried to act like it was no big deal that she wasn't in the church anymore, she knew it was. Her being a female player wasn't really working for her the way she thought it would. She didn't feel complete. She didn't feel satisfied and she didn't feel she was being true to herself. She knew she was playing a role.

She thought about why she stopped attending church and what caused it. What happened? Khalil happened.

Initially he was going to church with her. Then one Sunday he said he wasn't going and asked her to stay home with him, which she did and then it happened another Sunday. The next thing she knew, she wasn't going at all. There was some guilt on her part but she was in love and she believed or wanted to believe that God understood.

I'm going to church this Sunday. I need to get back in the Word. God forgives all, He knows all and He sees all. I wish He didn't because I've been acting out of character. I've been acting like what I would have called a slut a short while ago. God, I know you hear my thoughts. Please show me the right way once again. I promise I'll come back to you.

The difference this time would be that she wouldn't go overboard preaching to everyone and trying to save everyone. There was a middle ground in religion and she was going to find it.

There was a knock on the door, she looked out the window and saw that it was Gavin. She opened the door.

"I told you it wasn't necessary to come."

They gave one another a hug as he stepped in. He went to kiss her on the lips and she turned her head. It didn't go unnoticed but Gavin figured he'll leave it alone for now. "What kind of man would I be if I didn't come running when you said you think someone is following you."

"I just might be paranoid."

"I always say if you think it, there's a possibility it might be going on and that applies to almost everything." He followed her into the living room. "I rode around your block a couple of times. Nothing stood out."

Alexis felt a little relieved. "No black car?"

Gavin smiled. "There were a lot of black cars but no one was sitting in any of them."

Alexis sat down and Gavin followed her lead.

"Gavin, I want to be honest with you about something."

Gavin did not like the sound of this, so he sat back and waited to see what she was about to say.

Before she could say a word, her cell phone rang. "Excuse me," she told him. She reached over to answer it, but first she looked at the caller ID. It was the school calling. "Hello?"

"Alexis?" Whoever it was sounded rushed or panicky.

"Hello?"

"Alexis, it's me. Maya. Shay is in the hospital."

"What did you just say?"

Because of the alarm in her voice, Gavin stood up.

"Shay is in the hospital. They just called here asking for you. Something about her being beat up and they found your card on her."

'I'm on my way there." Alexis hung up and stood. "I have to go."

"What's going on? Where are you going? Is everything all right?" Gavin was throwing questions at her.

"My student, Shay. Maya said she's in the hospital and they found my card on her."

"That was Maya?"

Alexis started looking around for her purse. "I have to go. Call me later."

"Let me drive you."

"I don't know how long I'm going to be there."

"It doesn't matter. I'm coming with you."

Alexis didn't feel like putting up a fight. "All right then, come on let's go."

While they were in the car, Alexis figured she'd let Gavin know where her mind was as far as a relationship was concerned.

"Gavin?"

"Yes. Thanks for being my friend." She threw the word friend in there hoping he would get the hint.

Of course he didn't because he told her, "Well, I'd like to eventually be more than a friend."

Alexis didn't say a word, so he thought he'd repeat himself. "I'd like to be more than a friend."

He knew he'd told her otherwise at one point. He also knew that she thought he was too young for her, but people were entitled to change their minds. He hoped to get her to change hers.

Alexis turned in the seat to face him. "That's just not possible right now." She could see from the look on his face that he was hurt.

"For real? You're serious?" Gavin asked her.

"Yes."

"Damn girl, you're breaking my heart."

"I'm sorry. It's just that . . . Well, you know I've been dating other people."

He kind of figured he wasn't the only man in her life.

She continued. "There is one in particular

that I'm thinking about seeing on a monogamous basis."

Gavin was disappointed but it's been his experience that he if stuck around long enough, the woman just might come around. "I understand and like I told you before I'm here for you as a friend."

Alexis wanted to reach over and hug him but in the car that wasn't possible so she kissed him on the cheek. "Thanks Gavin." She hoped that they would be friends for a long time because she genuinely liked him.

Finally they pulled up to West Point Hospital. As they were getting out of the car, Alexis said, "You know Gavin, this is probably all my fault. I asked her to change when she was not ready to change."

Gavin didn't understand how that could be Alexis' fault. "And? How is that your fault?"

"I think she got beat up because she was trying to start a new life."

They started walking toward the entrance.

"What are you talking about?" Gavin asked, still not getting it.

"My student Shay, the one I told you about that was stripping. She came by the office yesterday and we had a heart to heart. I convinced her to stop living the way she was living and I told her I would help her."

"And?"

"Maybe she went and told someone and they didn't want her out. Shit, I don't know."

"Damn, you really think someone would harm her because she wanted a better life?"

"Stranger things have happened."

"Damn, that's fucked up. Who would do some shit like that?"

"I wish I knew. Hopefully we'll find out."

Alexis and Gavin went to the front desk to find out what room Shay was in. After being given the information, they got on the elevator and pressed the appropriate button. Gavin hated hospitals. He'd been here a number of times because quite a few of his boys had been shot, stabbed or injured in some way due to the drug game. The smell of it, which reminded him of a wet mop mixed with cleaning supplies, made him sick to his stomach. The sounds of people crying and moaning depressed the hell out of him and the sight of people in uniforms reminded him of prison. This time it was no different. If it wasn't for Alexis he would not be here.

Alexis was nervous as hell. She didn't know what she was about to see. She looked over at Gavin. He told her, "I'll be in the hallway if you need me."

She was so glad she agreed to let him come along.

When they stepped off the elevator, they followed the signs until they found Shay's room. Alexis stepped inside, while Gavin waited by the door.

When Alexis pulled back the curtain she saw

that Shay's right arm was held in the air by supports. Her face was so swollen that she could barely see her eyes. There was a bruise on her cheek shaped like a handprint. As Alexis got closer to her, she noticed handprints around her neck.

Alexis rushed to the bed. "Oh my god baby! Who did this to you? Are you okay?" Alexis chastised herself for asking such a stupid question.

"I'm okay," Shay responded in a groggy voice. She was obviously drugged. She tugged on her hospital gown to pull it down.

Alexis took her hand.

"I need to know something," Shay said.

"What baby, what do you need to know?"

"Did you really mean it when you said that I can come live with you? I mean can I still come?"

Alexis couldn't believe that with all the pain Shay was probably enduring, all she cared about was if Alexis would still let her move in.

Alexis grabbed her left hand and looked her in the eyes. "I would like nothing more than for you to come stay with me."

Shay tried to smile. All she ever wanted was a place to call home and a semblance of a family.

Shay's moment was interrupted by the sound of Gavin's voice. "Alexis, can I come in?"

Alexis looked at Shay for permission. Shay nodded.

"Come in Gavin."

Shay immediately dropped Alexis's hand. "Gavin, did you say Gavin?"

"Yes."

Before she could say anything else, Gavin appeared and the look on Shay's face when she saw him caused Alexis to be alarmed. "Shay, what is it? What's wrong?"

It's obvious she recognized him. "You! You! Get out of here. Get out now!"

Gavin was looking at her like she'd lost her mind.

"What are you doing here? Get out, I don't want you here."

Alexis glanced from one to the other. "What the hell is going on?"

Gavin had no idea and he told her this. He then looked at Shay. "I don't know you sweetie. How do you know me?"

Shay was almost in hysterics. "You don't know your own flesh and blood. I'm Shay, Cassandra's daughter."

Gavin looked like he was about to fall out.

Alexis asked, "Who's Cassandra?"

"Cassandra is my sister," he told Alexis while staring at Shay. "And that means you're my niece. You're little Shameka?"

Gavin was in shock. Alexis was sitting on the edge of the bed with her mouth wide open. "Are you serious?"

Shay started to cry. "Yes, we're serious."

Gavin didn't know what to say. All he could do was stand there and stare at Shay, while he repeated, "I don't believe this. I can't believe you're little Shay."

Shay allowed the tears to fall down her cheeks. "What happened to you? You promised me that that you would always be there for me, but just like everyone else you weren't."

Alexis looked at Gavin. She too was waiting on an answer because he wasn't saying anything. He was just standing there staring. Alexis nudged him.

Gavin stepped closer to the bed. "I can't believe this. I am so sorry. You have no idea how sorry I am. I did tell you that and I meant it. But I got locked up for four years and when I got out I came looking for you and your mother."

"Obviously you didn't look hard enough."

Alexis didn't feel the need to interfere. Shay seemed to be handling this situation well enough.

"Yes," Gavin answered, "I have to admit I didn't look hard enough. I got so caught up in my own life that I neglected those I love. I know it's selfish and I swear to you I am so sorry. You have no idea how sorry I am."

Shay didn't say anything.

Gavin continued. "I should have been there for you. I will be there for you from this point on. You can come stay with me. I'll take care of you."

Gavin's apology was so sincere that Shay, Alexis and the nurse who was standing at the door were all crying.

Shay looked away and Gavin placed a finger

under her chin and turned her face toward him. "Please, just give me a chance."

Alexis interrupted. "Shay, I believe that your uncle means what he is saying. For the short time I have known him he has been a stand-up guy. I think you should think about forgiving him. There is nothing like family."

Shay was stubborn, but she wanted to be loved more than anything in the world.

She placed her left hand in her Uncle Gavin's. "I hated the thought of you for so long. I'm scared to trust you. I always believed that no matter what, you would come rescue me but you never came."

"I'm here now," Gavin told her. "Let me show you what it's like to be part of a family."

There was something nagging at Alexis and suddenly she realized what it was. "How come Maya never said anything?"

Shay looked at Alexis. "Who's that?"

"Ms. McMillan," Alexis told her.

Shay looked puzzled. "Why would she say anything?"

"She's my half sister," Gavin told them both. He then addressed Alexis. "We have the same father but not the same mother. My father was a rolling stone as they say. Shay's mother has the same father as well but as kids we didn't associate. There's just too many of us."

Alexis was blown away.

"Princess, please let me be there for you," Gavin said to Shay.

When he called her Princess, Shay melted.

That was the nickname he gave her before her mother started wilding out.

Without any assistance and what surely must have been painful, Shay sat up and held her arms out. Alexis got up off the bed and allowed them to hug one another.

"I'm going to leave you two alone for a little while. Shay, do you need anything?"

"Just some clothes, a toothbrush, a book or two—"

Alexis cut her off. "Hold up, hold up. I don't have my car. I came with your uncle."

When she said uncle, they both smiled. Gavin took his keys out of his pocket and handed them to Alexis. "Here, take my car and get what you need. I'm going to stay here a while." He looked at Shay. "If it's okay with you?"

Shay nodded.

"Are you sure Gavin?" She knew men didn't give up their cars that easily.

"I'm sure. I want some time alone with my niece."

"I'll be back sweetie," Alexis told Shay. "When I return, we need to talk about what you're going to tell the police."

"I'm not telling them anything."

Alexis didn't respond. She'd deal with it when she returned.

The second she was gone, Gavin asked, "Who did this to you? I promise that he will not hurt you again."

Shay, remembering that her uncle was always thought of as the bad seed or a thug, knew that his words were true. But she also knew Shamel and she knew his ass was crazy. "I don't want to start any trouble. Can't we just leave it be?"

Gavin shook his head. "I can't do that. Whoever did this to you needs their ass kicked."

Shay turned her head.

"Either you tell me or I will find out another way."

Shay wanted to tell but she was scared. She wanted Shamel to get his ass kicked but she didn't want Gavin to get hurt. Hell, she'd just gotten him back. He'd just reentered her life.

She turned back toward Gavin. "I don't want you to get hurt."

Gavin laughed at this. "Baby, I'm not the one that's going to get hurt. You best believe that."

Shay wanted to believe that. She didn't want her uncle hurt. Still, after what Shamel did to her, she did want him to pay. As a matter-of-fact, she wanted him to pay with his life. Although she felt this way, she found herself speaking in a low tone.

"I didn't hear you," Gavin told her.

She said the name again. This time Gavin had to put his ear near her mouth. She repeated the name in a low tone. "His name is Shamel, Shamel Walker."

Gavin knew he'd heard that name before. He tried to place it.

Shay continued. "He owns the strip club on Waters Street."

Oh yeah, I know that motherfucker, Gavin thought to himself. He'd run into him a couple

of times in the past, drug dealings, of course.
"I'll be right back," Gavin told her.

"Where are you going?"

"In the hall to make a phone call."

Shay wasn't stupid. She knew just what kind
of call he would be making. She just hoped he
knew what he was doing.

Chapter 30

Give Yourself Time and the Answers Will Come

Alexis was heading toward the parking lot. In her mind she was making a list of the items Shay needed when she noticed a note on Gavin's windshield. She looked around to see if she saw anyone hanging in the area. There was no one there. She looked back at the note and noticed her name on it. She took the note off the windshield and read it. It said, "Choose."

Alexis turned the paper over in her hands, expecting to see more and wondering what the hell that meant. Panic started setting in because someone was fucking with her emotions, playing on her fears and she had no idea who.

She opened the car door and was about to shut it when she heard someone calling her name.

"Alexis! Alexis, hold up!"

She looked in the direction of the voice and saw that it was Finn. He'd left a couple of messages earlier that week telling her whenever she was ready; he'd get her car fixed.

She waited until he was up on her. "Finn? Hey. I'm sorry but I don't have time to talk. I have some things I need to do."

"It won't take long. I just wanted to tell you I'm still waiting to hear from you."

At the rate things were going, she doubted she would have the opportunity to call him at all. She looked around the parking lot again.

He followed her gaze. "Are you okay?"

"Yeah, yeah. Listen, did you see anyone put something on this car?"

"Nah. I saw you walking so I hurried up and parked to catch up to you."

"Oh, okay. Listen I have to go."

"You still have my number right?"

She was sure she did. "Yes."

"Call me. Let's get that car fixed."

"I'll do that." Alexis closed her door, started the engine and left him standing there watching her, while she wondered who was at the hospital he knew.

It was then she heard her phone beep. There was a message. It must not have been able to connect while she was in the hospital. She reached over and pulled her cell out of her purse and pressed the button to connect to voice mail.

It was Shamel. "I'd like to see you tonight. I have something I want to ask you."

She hung up and told herself she'd call him either later if she got the chance or tomorrow.

While she had the phone in her hand, she tried to call Thomas. Again, there was no answer.

I will not panic. He's not with another woman. I won't think that. Shit, we haven't even gotten started yet. Shay, concentrate on Shay.

"Thomas, please call me. I need to see or talk to you." Damn, did she seem desperate already? She hoped not.

Chapter 31

Pick Your Battles Slowly: Don't Go Charging In

Thomas wasn't with another woman. He was wrapping up a meeting with his attorney. The charges had been dropped because there was no evidence that he ordered the girls to the house. Several people also came forward to say that he wasn't even around when they arrived.

Now, what he needed to find out was who the hell sent them and who the hell fucked up his car. He also needed to go and confront Shondell about this baby situation.

Please God, don't let this crazy woman be having my baby. That's the last thing I need right now especially since I believe Alexis and I are going to be together.

Thomas reached inside his glove compartment for his cell phone. It wasn't there. *Shit, where did I leave it?* He tried to retrace his steps in his mind.

Did he have it when he left the house? He believed so.

Did he have it at the attorney's office? He wasn't sure.

He did remember calling Zyair as he was walking out the door.

Thomas turned the car around and headed back to his attorney's. *It has to be there.* Good thing he was only a couple of blocks away because when he pulled up, the attorney was walking out of the building.

"What's up? You're back?"

"Yeah, I think I left my cell phone in your office."

"That's why I keep two, one on me and one in my car."

"Is your receptionist still there?"

"Yeah, just tell her to go in my office and look around."

"All right, thanks man."

"I'll put it on your bill."

A few minutes later Thomas was getting back in his car with his cell phone. He'd just heard Alexis' message and tried calling her back but his phone died.

"This is some bullshit!" he yelled out loud. *I'll call her after I leave Shondell's house.*

Thomas made the decision to just go straight to Shondell's house. He hoped she still lived in the same place. He would call her but he deleted the number out of his phone and erased it from his memory purposely. Also, the way he figured, if he confronted her face-to-face, he'd be able to read her. *If she is pregnant, why would she tell Alexis and not tell me? Does she know what Alexis means to me?*

Before he knew it, he was in front of Shondell's door about to knock when it opened.

It was Victoria.

"Mr. Thomas? What are you doing here?"

"I came to see your mother."

Victoria looked behind her and stepped out into the hallway. "I don't think that's a very good idea."

"I need to speak with her Victoria."

Victoria placed her hands on her hips. "About what? You broke up with her remember."

"Is your mother pregnant?"

Victoria grabbed his arm and pulled him away from the door. "Where'd you hear that?"

"It's not important. Is it true?"

"I think so."

"Did she tell you I'm the father?"

Victoria honestly didn't know who the father could be. She knew her mother slept around quite a bit but she also knew her mother was obsessed with Thomas. As she stood there she thought about how they could have a better life if the baby was his, so she told him, "Yes, she told me you were the father."

Thomas didn't know what to say. This shit could not be happening, not right now. "I need to speak to her."

"She's asleep right now. Can you come back another time?"

Thomas didn't want to come back another

time. He wanted to settle this now but then again, he knew he needed to calm down. Too much shit had been happening and right now he was operating off pure emotion. Plus, he needed to call around and find out how soon he could take a paternity test. It'd been over two, almost three months since their last encounter. From an experience with one of his clients, he knew there was such a thing as a prenatal paternity test which uses only the mother's blood and samples from the alleged father(s) to determine the paternity of the child as early as thirteen weeks into the pregnancy. No blood is taken from the alleged father(s). The only samples that could be taken from the alleged father(s) are a buccal swab from the cheek, hair or forensic samples from toothbrush, water bottle, chewing gum, etc. He wanted to get this taken care of as soon as possible.

"Tell your mother I'll be by in the next few days."

Victoria watched him walk away before going back inside the house.

His next stop was to the detective he'd hired to investigate who was fucking with him but first he needed to call Alexis again. He looked at his cell phone which he'd placed on the charger and saw there were a couple of bars on it.

He dialed her number and once again her voice mail came on. *Where is she? She left me a message saying she needed to speak with me then why isn't she answering her damn phone?*

* * *

Less than ten minutes later Thomas was sitting in Mike Jones' office. Mike came highly recommended by several of his clients. He was told if there was some dirt, if some shit was going down, about to go down or someone was out to get you, Mike Jones, was the man with the plan. Thomas hoped so because he didn't come cheap.

Thomas was sitting in front of him. "Please tell me that you found out something regarding all these so-called coincidences that are occurring in my life.

Mr. Jones leaned back in his seat. "I think you're going to be very happy with what I uncovered for you."

"Well spit it out." Thomas wanted this information so he could do what he had to do and if that meant fuck someone up, well, so be it. He was tired of this bullshit. Here he was, trying to live his life right and someone was trying to throw him all off track.

"Does the name Shamel Walker mean anything to you?"

Thomas repeated the name several times in his mind. "It rings a bell but I can't place it."

"He's the owner of several strip clubs and bars in the area."

Thomas looked at him and waited for more.

Mike pulled opened a folder that was on his desk. Inside were pictures.

Mike handed the pictures to Thomas. "Isn't that your lady friend?"

Thomas first thought was *there is no way he's*

talking about Alexis. How would he even know about me and Alexis? But then again, let his clients tell it, Mike Jones knows everything about a client before he takes them on.

Thomas took the pictures and there it was in color, pictures of Shamel and Alexis.

Thomas stared at the picture. It hit him all at once. *This is the motherfucker me and Alexis kept running into. Don't tell me she's seeing this asshole. I can't believe this shit.*

Thomas looked up at Mike. Just as he is about to say something Mike's phone rang.

He looked at the ID. "Excuse me," he told Thomas, "I have to take this."

Thomas didn't say a word. He watched as Mike listened to whoever was talking on the other end.

Whatever that person was saying caused Mike to look up at Thomas in alarm. He placed his hand over the mouthpiece. "This is my associate. According to him, Shamel is on Alexis' porch."

Thomas jumped up out of his seat and was out the door before Mike could stop him.

Chapter 32

Keep Your Cool and Never Let Them See You Sweat

When Alexis pulled up to her house she was surprised to see Shamel on her porch. She looked around and noticed a car in front of her house, a Lexus. She wondered if that was one of his cars.

What the hell is he doing here? Didn't I tell him once before I don't like drop-ins? Well, good this will save me a phone call. I'll let him know now.

As she got closer, she noticed that he looked frazzled, not as together as he normally looked. He was sweating, frowning, pacing and it looked like he was talking to himself. She also noticed a spot that looked like blood on the front of his shirt. This was cause for concern.

Why would he have blood on his shirt? What the hell happened? Is he hurt? Did he hurt some-one? "Shamel, what happened? Are you okay?" she asked as she approached him.

He didn't answer her. He just looked at her.

"Are you okay?" she asked again.

"Where the hell were you?" he asked in a tone that was low and almost menacing.

It threw Alexis off for a second. His tone frightened her but she told herself not to show it. "What's wrong with you? What are you doing on my porch like this?"

"I've been waiting on you."

Alexis didn't like how he sounded. His tone implied that she should be at his beck and call. "Waiting on me? Waiting on me for what?"

"We need to talk about us, our relationship."

What the hell is he talking about? We don't have a relationship. And why the hell is he looking at me like that; like he's about to snap? Alexis knew without a doubt that she was making the right decision in not seeing him anymore. With the way he was acting now, she just had to figure out a way to tell him.

Alexis tried to get past him. "Shamel, you're scaring me. I think it's best if you leave." He didn't move an inch. *Okay, now why isn't he leaving?*

"I ain't going nowhere until you talk to me," he told her.

He has lost all his mind.

Shamel looked at the car in the driveway. "Whose car are you driving?"

"A friend's."

"What friend? Another man's? Is that where you were? With someone else?

Alexis tried to get past him again but he stood up and blocked her path.

"Answer me. Where the hell were you?"

Alexis decided to try another tactic. "Shamel,

why don't you call me later, we'll talk. I need to get back to the hospital. One of my students is in the hospital."

"Yeah, I know. I know about Diamond or Shay as you call her. I heard about her little incident."

How did he hear that? Was he behind it? With the way he was coming across at the moment she didn't know what to think. "Listen you need to move. I need to go in the house." Once again she tried to brush past him but he grabbed her arm so tight that she told him. "You're hurting me. Let go of my arm."

He ignored the request. "Who the fuck you think you're talking to? All the shit I've done for you to get you."

Alexis looked at him like he was crazy. *What the hell is he talking about? What has he done for me?* "What are you talking about?"

He didn't answer the question. He just told her, "Open the door Alexis."

"No." She took a quick look around and hoped that someone saw what was going on and that they would come to her rescue because at this point that's just what she felt like she needed.

"Open the goddamn door!" He gave her a look that told her if she didn't he wouldn't think twice about hurting her.

"Please don't hurt me, Shamel. Talk to me. Tell me what's wrong. What's going on? Why are you acting like this?"

"I won't hurt you, I promise. I just want to talk."

Alexis felt like she had no choice but to do what he said. She moved past him and unlocked the door. "I'm expecting company soon," she lied.

"I thought you said you had to get back to the hospital."

She didn't answer, there was no need to.

She tried to walk through the door and close it on him but he pushed it open and stepped inside. Within the blink of an eye, he had a gun pulled out on her.

Initially she thought her eyes were deceiving her. It only took a second for her to realize this was real. Water formed in the corner of her eyes from the fear she was feeling. She put her hands up as though she could protect herself from a bullet. *Please God, you promised you would protect your children from harm. Well, I need your help now.*

Alexis looked up at Shamel and in a calm tone asked, "What are you doing? I thought you said you wouldn't hurt me."

She watched as he scanned the room while still holding the gun in his hand. "I'm not. I just want your cooperation."

"My cooperation? I thought you said you just wanted to talk." *Why is he doing this?*

"I do want to talk," he told her, "I want to talk about how I'm tired of you trying to play me."

Alexis glanced around the room to see if there was something, anything she could grab ahold of so she could fight back. "Play you? Why do you think I'm trying to play you?"

He pushed her on the couch and stood over her. "I'm not stupid Alexis. Don't you know I could have any woman I want? Don't you know that?"

She nodded her head. "I do know that Shamel and you could have had me." *Why did I say could have, why didn't I say, he can?* Alexis wished she could backtrack.

It was as if he didn't even hear her. "But I want you! You're the one I want!" He bent down and tried to kiss her but she turned her head.

She didn't know what to say about any of this. She figured the best thing she could do was keep her mouth shut.

"Nah, but you want to fuck around. You want to mess with that nigga Thomas. I tried to show you who he was, a pedophile, but that's not enough for you. Oh hell no, this shit will not happen to me again."

What does he mean, he tried to show me who Thomas was? Was he the one who set him up?

Shamel turned his back to her for a second. *This is my chance.* She tried to get off the couch but he turned back around too quickly.

He pushed her back down. "Where do you think you're going? You think you can get away from me like that? You think it's going to be that easy?" Still holding the gun in one hand, he started taking off his belt with the other hand. "You can't fool me. This shit happened to me before. Every time I love a bitch, she ups and leaves. I'm about to teach your ass a lesson. You think I beat Shay's ass; it's your turn."

When she heard this, her initial reaction was shock. *So, he's the one that did that to her.* She almost expected it. Then she started to scream.

Champagne had just pulled up and turned her engine off. She heard Alexis screaming. She jumped out of the car and ran to the door and knocked.

"Alexis! Alexis! What's going on in there?"

Inside, Alexis could hear Champagne calling for her. She looked up wide-eyed at Shamel.

He put one finger to his mouth and placed the gun on Alexis' temple to stop her from calling out.

I can't believe this is happening to me. I can't believe I didn't know any better. I'm smarter than that, Alexis thought. *Please let her call someone. Please don't let her just leave.*

Champagne continued to call out and tried to look through the curtains. She couldn't see anything, but she was sure she heard screams. She was positive of it. She looked at the car in the driveway and at the car in front of the house. She wondered who the cars belonged to.

Inside the house, Alexis was staring at the door as Shamel stared at her.

Champagne ran back to her car and pulled out her cell phone and tried to call Zyair. He didn't answer. *Where the hell is he?*

Champagne reached into her glove box and pulled out the gun she just picked up from the gun shop. She was actually stopping by to see if

Alexis wanted to go to the shooting range with her later. It was a new hobby Sharon introduced to her. She had no idea whether or not the gun would come in handy. She hoped it wouldn't come down to that. But if it did, so be it. She looked at the gun and sighed. *The Lord works in mysterious ways,* she thought as she put the bullets in the chamber.

Just as she was getting out of the car with the gun in hand Thomas pulled up.

Thomas shook his head to get the image out of his mind that he thought he was seeing. The image of Shamel and Alexis.

He shut the engine off and climbed out of his car. Immediately he noticed an unfamiliar car in Alexis' driveway and the gun in Champagne's hand. He knew some shit was about to go down, so he opened his glove compartment and pulled out his own gun.

Champagne ran up to him. "I heard Alexis in there screaming."

She didn't need to tell him anything else. He motioned for Champagne to go to the back of the house.

She nodded her understanding. As she ran toward the back of the house she glanced down the street at a car that was parked. For some reason it felt funny to her; a little off.

Down the street in the black car that was parked, an individual was watching with anticipation.

The second Thomas stepped on the porch, Gavin pulled up with one of his boys. Both of them got out of the car. Gavin was packing too. He and Thomas looked at one another. As they did, they heard Alexis scream.

"I'm here to help," Gavin told Thomas as he stood next to him.

Thomas instructed the man Gavin was with to take the back. He then turned his attention back to Gavin.

They gave each other the nod. Thomas put up one finger, two fingers, then kicked the door in. They rushed in, only to find Shamel with his pants open and the gun pointed at Alexis.

Her shirt was torn and tears were running down her face. When she saw them, she thought about getting up but the gun stopped her.

When Shamel heard them rush in, he didn't bother turning around. All he said was, "If you don't stay back, I'll kill her. I swear I will."

"Come on man, you need to let her go," Thomas told him.

"Why? So you can have her?"

"That's not what this is about. This is about me and you and you know it."

Shamel started laughing. "You really think that don't you?"

Champagne and Gavin's boy were standing back where Shamel couldn't see them. When they had arrived at the back door, Champagne recalled that Alexis kept a key inside the flower pot for emergencies.

They crept in silently while trying their hardest not to be seen or heard. However, Gavin spotted them out of the corner of his eye. He tried to let her know he was aware of their position.

Champagne backed up some when she heard someone else walk in the door.

"Shamel!" Big Tone had walked in the house. "What the fuck are you doing?"

Shamel had no idea what Big Tone was doing there. "How did you know I was here?"

"I always know where your ass is."

Shamel didn't like the sound of that. What the fuck was Tone doing keeping tabs on him? "What?"

Big Tone shook his head. "Man, I've been keeping tabs on you ever since you started talking about this girl. I knew this shit was going to happen again. This shit has got to stop and it needs to stop right now."

Everyone was watching this exchange and took note of the word "again."

"What matters right now is all these motherfuckers got a gun on you. You need to think about what you're doing."

"This shit ain't your business. It has nothing to do with you."

"It has everything to do with me, because if you fuck up, the business is fucked up and then I'm fucked. What you need to do is put the gun down."

Gavin, tired of the back and forth, stepped up with his gun pointed at Shamel. "Enough of this talking shit."

Shamel pressed the gun to Alexis' head. "All

y'all motherfuckers need to get the fuck out of here or I'm going to shoot this bitch on the count of three."

Alexis could feel herself start to shake. She felt like she was having an outer body experience. It was as though she was a spectator watching this happen to someone else. She was in shock. Had her Lord let her down? Was He not going to come to her rescue? Was this her punishment for sleeping with three men? Is this how she was going to die, right here, right now in her home without even experiencing real love, without having children, without being married? Was this really it?

"All right, we're going to back up," Thomas told him.

"I ain't going no fucking where motherfucker. Shay is my niece, motherfucker." Gavin was ready for whatever.

"Gavin, please," Alexis begged. "Please back off."

Shamel started to count. "One."

Gavin looked at her, then at Thomas. It was almost as if they had a secret code. In the meantime Champagne and Gavin's boy were creeping up behind Shamel.

"Two."

"Please everyone. Calm down," Alexis begged.

Shamel shoved her in the face with the gun. "Shut up! Shut the fuck up!"

Big Tone yelled, "Shamel, behind you!"

Before Shamel could respond or say "three", Alexis pushed his arm away and rapid gunfire was heard.

TO BE CONTINUED

COMING SOON

Sister Girl 3

And here's a Teaser from

STILL FAKING IT

Chapter 1

QUASSMIRAH/CARESS

My life is finally almost where I thought I want it to be. Am I happy about it? No! Am I with the man I thought I so desperately wanted? Yes. Is it working out? No! Do I have any regrets? Yes, a whole lot of them, but you know what, it is what it is and I'm going to have to deal with it. For now.

That is, until I find another way, a better way, a way that's going to take me where I should be and where I should have been a long time ago. Rich and famous.

Yes, people notice me now but not to the extent that I want them to. I want to hear people screaming my name. Caress! Caress!

Some of you may already know that my actual birth name is Quassmirah Caress Layton. Why am I going by my middle name? Well, according to the man in my life, Wesley, who is also my producer, it's more appealing to the masses. When they hear the name, Caress, they'll think sexy and sensual.

Have you ever wanted something so bad that you were willing to do just about anything to get it? That you would risk everything short of your life to achieve it?

Well, I do. I want success. What does success mean to me besides money and fame? Well, it means being able to purchase what you want when you want it. It means being able to book a first-class flight and feeling like that's where you belong. It means not having to stand in lines at clubs and traveling anytime to anyplace when I feel like it. It means living in the house of my dreams and getting massages and pampered once, twice, maybe three times a week and again it means money and fame.

Sex? Will I have it to achieve this? Yes. Betrayal? Am I capable of it? Yes. Backstabbing? Lying and starting unnecessary drama. I'll do that too. Not that I look to do these things but if they fall in my lap, so be it. I do want to change my ways. I don't want to be this person. I really don't and I won't be when I get where I want to be in life. So, I say all this to let you know I do the things I do for a reason not just because. So please don't judge me because you can never say what you wouldn't do.